NO POPES IN HEAVEN

by Hal Malchow

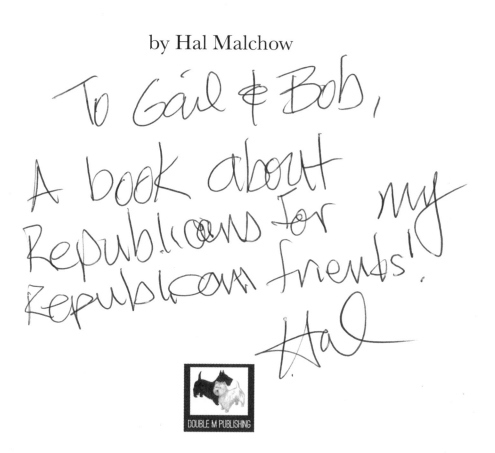

To Gail & Bob,

A book about
Republicans for my
Republican friends!

Hal

DOUBLE M PUBLISHING

Library of Congress Control Number: 2018945146

ISBN 978-0-692-12098-9 (regular edition)

ISBN 978-0-692-12099-6 (Ebook)

Printed in the USA

First Edition, June 2018

To Anne Mahoney

ACKNOWLEDGEMENTS

I would like to acknowledge Susan Shallcross for her direction, advice and beautiful editing skills in making No Popes in Heaven a better book.

I would also like to acknowledge the following persons who read the book in advance and offered many helpful comments and observations that reshaped the manuscript.

Mimi Dawson

Les Francis

Al Garrard

Wilson Golden

Scottie Greene

Rick Malchow

Carrie Rutenberg

Grace Terpstra

Jennifer Topple

Prologue

The consequences of tragedy are impossible to know.

For some, the pain can linger a lifetime and its power withers the will. But for others it can twist something deep inside, igniting an unreasonable drive, a powerful resolve unknown to the ordinary among us. There is no better evidence of this effect than the fact that a quarter of all American presidents lost a parent before turning eighteen.

For Colleen Keegan, who just three days earlier was named chief executive officer of Miradol, the third largest pharmaceutical company in the world, the consequences of tragedy had fueled her rise.

Her dad died when she was only seven. But her mom, the only child of a mother who drank too much and married four times, was no more than an aspiring adult. She was erratic, impulsive — prone to outbursts and long episodes of sometimes hysterical anxiety. Colleen, the oldest of four children, learned quickly the benefits of self-reliance, thinking for herself and an unbending will.

Her mother, however, left her a second inheritance. Keegan suffered attacks of anxiety, mostly hidden in bathroom stalls, behind locked office doors or in taxis that ferried her home. Her secret condition was carefully guarded, known to a tiny few. Anxiety was her nemesis, her opponent, though, on most days, she tamed its effects.

Her selection to lead Miradol shocked the industry. She was no scientist, no Harvard MBA and no man. She had studied archeology at Oberlin and after graduation had headed for Pakistan to dig at a site near the Bolan Pass. But archeology was no profession for a woman without patience. After a year of restlessly sifting pottery shards, she returned home, earned an MBA and took a job as assistant product manager at Miradol.

Over her twenty-five-year career, she spotted opportunities others overlooked. She championed a drug for attention deficit disorder and hyperactivity that outsold Viagra. She had no patience for dogma or tradition. In pursuit of her goals she was single minded, ruthless and willing to break the rules. She was a tough, clear-headed leader who was unafraid to rattle the status quo. At Miradol, a company rocked in the past six months by two failed drug trials and falling stock prices, the status quo had to go.

Reeling financially, stung by a torrent of negative publicity, the Miradol Board of Directors passed over three obvious candidates and selected the tall, red-headed woman from management's second level. Known in the office, but not in her presence, as "Big Red," Colleen Keegan became the company's new face and its agent for change.

Her challenge was formidable. A dark cloud of pessimism had sapped morale. No new blockbuster drugs were ready for trials. There was but one hope, a miracle really, that was working its way through the labs.

Miradol researchers had its sights on a condition that had plagued humankind since the dawn of time. The market that awaited might be the largest noncompetitive market in the history of the commercial world. Tomorrow she would meet with her top staff to move this product forward.

She looked out the window, and just above the Golden Gate the sun peeked between the clouds and the light danced and sparkled against the stone-gray sky. A tiny light made large by the darkness behind. She wondered if it might be an omen.

. . .

Keegan checked her makeup in her private bathroom before entering the conference room just off her office. Although she would have denied it to anyone, her looks were important to her and she pinched her cheeks in a futile effort to bring color to the wan look that three crowded days of meetings and decisions had produced. She smoothed back her vivid auburn ponytail and took a little satisfaction that her green eyes were still bright and sharp and her forehead, even at fifty-one, was virtually unlined.

She took a deep breath and entered the room. Around the large oval conference table sat the key leaders of Miradol, vice presidents all, leading research, regulations, finance, marketing, and legal. Keegan cleared her throat and the room fell silent. Despite the enormity of the subject before them, she made no flowery introductory speech. Just business. "Devon," she said, nodding to the tall, studious-looking man to her left. "I think you are first."

Devon Foley, chief scientist at Miradol, stood quickly, then nervously shuffled his notes before clicking the remote in his hand. A white screen on the far end of the room sprang to life: "Clinical Trials on AFZ 4."

The confidence in his tone belied his nervous manner when he began, "I think you know the background here. Six years ago, we looked at experiments in which the blood of a young mouse was combined with the blood of an old mouse. The young mouse got old. The old mouse began partying after midnight." He smiled without looking up. There was soft laughter throughout the room.

"Our lab spent six months analyzing how the composition of blood changes with age. We identified several differences that we thought might affect aging. The most important ones involved messaging that turned on or turned off genes inside the cells. This research identified a number of proteins that signal our genes, positively in the young and negatively in the old. Two years ago, we began trials with rats, looking at the effects of several protein combinations."

He advanced a slide. "There are a number of ways we measure aging at the cellular level. The first is inflammation. In youth, inflammation is narrowly targeted and for positive purposes. But as we age it loses discrimination and turns on the body itself. It especially targets joints, arteries, and brain cells. Its occurrence is correlated with many cancers."

He advanced through several slides, including a particularly unpleasant one of metastasizing cancer cells. "Then there is the thymus. Who knows what the thymus is?" Foley asked with a smile.

The executives shook their heads, their eyebrows knitted in their seriousness. Keegan smiled slyly and waited. Henry Quinn, the regulatory VP, finally raised his hand. "T cells. Provosten is conducting trials."

"Right!" Foley said, excitedly, pointing at Quinn and advancing to another slide. "The thymus is the primary organ of the immune system. It is where T cells mature. Over the human life span the thymus reduces in size—often to ten percent of its original youthful size."

The Miradol team exchanged nervous glances as the mostly older crowd wondered just how much they had left.

"A third measurement is apoptosis. I won't even ask who knows this word. It means cell suicide. Again, in youth it's a positive response. A cancerous cell, for example, will self-destruct to protect the body. But later in life healthy cells take up the practice. You can also measure aging by the growth of new neurons in the brain or the activity of stem cells." Foley was hitting his flow now. "Finally, you have the famous telomeres." He clicked to the next slide and a strand of DNA appeared, the spiraling helix. He clicked again and the end glowed pink.

"That piece which caps the helix is the telomere, and inside your body here is what is happening. Each time your cell divides, each strand of DNA splits and reconstitutes into a new strand. But each time that happens your telomere gets shorter."

He clicked again. A piece of the telomere disappeared. "The body can regrow the telomere. There is an enzyme, telomerase, which can make the darned thing just like new. The body has plenty of telomerase. But it does not use it. Why?"

Silence. There was a glint in Keegan's eyes. She knew.

Foley leaned forward into the table with an easy smile. "Because your genes want you to die. When it comes to death there is the Telomere Principle. The shorter your telomeres, the shorter your life," he said matter-of-factly, throwing up his hands.

"You made that up!" Keegan responded with a laugh.

"Well, it is true," Foley said, a little defensively.

"No, the principle. There is no Telomere Principle."

"Oh, I made *that* up," Foley admitted.

"Well, henceforth, we shall refer to it as the Foley Principle," Keegan responded, still smiling. "Please continue."

"Okay, so here is where we stand. Our genes are working against us. They tell the thymus to get smaller. They tell everything else to get larger. They watch while our chromosomes unwind and do nothing about it even though they could. And the stem cells? Your genes are sending memos that say, 'After all this time you deserve a vacation.'" He shook his head ruefully. "Your genes are not on your side. And they win every time because in the end, we all die. We can't beat our genes. We will never win. But the question is: Can we trick these genes and cheat them out of a few more years of healthy life? Can we send the signals that repair the telomeres, stop the unnecessary suicide, grow back that little old thymus, and shrink inflammation? The body can do all that. We just need to break the code. That is what I believe we have done." He paused for effect. Around the room his colleagues looked on with rapturous attention.

"After testing a number of combinations the winner is a drug called AFZ 4. It's a combination of four chemical signals found naturally in human blood. Two of them restore proteins found only in younger blood. Two of them suppress proteins found only in older blood. All have been synthesized in our labs. We are excited about this drug and we put it to the test."

Foley clicked again. The screen showed a rat in a coffin. "Here we see a late example of Rattus Norvegicus, or the common lab rat. Its life expectancy is approximately two years. We used AFZ 4 only on rats a year and a half old. We observed mortality among the rats receiving AFZ 4 and morality in the control group. What was the result?"

Click. The screen showed a bar chart comparing the life span of rats in the treatment and control groups. At the end of each bar was a dead rat.

"AFZ 4 extended the life span of these rats by thirty-eight percent."

Excitement surged through the room as the Miradol team began whispering enthusiastically among themselves. Keegan smiled.

Foley went on to list key measurements by the six aging indexes: Inflammation, down twenty-seven percent. Thymus, four percent growth. Apoptosis, down thirty-one percent. Telomeres, twenty-nine percent growth. New neuron growth, twenty-eight percent. Stem cell activity, up eighteen percent.

"These are outstanding numbers," he noted. "Keep in mind that life span extension is easier in simpler creatures than in the more complex. If we were dealing with worms or fruit flies these numbers might be higher." He clicked to a new slide.

"Now, the primates. We conducted trials on the Japanese macaque monkeys. Most macaques live twenty years but the Japanese version lives only six. We began tests in their fifth year. Some of these macaques are still living but so far we have extended their lives twenty-three percent.

"So, let me first provide the measurements on the macaques—treatment versus control." Foley ran through the numbers—each one higher than in the rat trial. "These numbers are higher perhaps because our treatment is based upon human blood components and the macaque is more closely related than the common lab rat," he added with a smile, winking at the legal counsel. "At least in most cases."

"How do you think that translates to humans?" Keegan asked.

"We have no human trials."

"Give me an estimate," she pushed.

"If I had to give an estimate it might be fifteen percent."

Keegan leaned back in her chair, her chin rising in contemplation. "So, if the average life span for humans is seventy-eight years, those taking AFZ 4 might expect to live to ninety?"

"Actually, it would probably be higher. Remember that seventy-eight is an overall average life span that includes early deaths by accidents and disease. The life expectancy for someone who has already reached fifty years is higher. If we can expect a fifteen percent extension, which is speculative, then the number will be closer to ninety-five. But who knows? It might not work so well on humans at all."

Colleen Keegan leaned forward, eyes narrowed. "The medication is based upon human blood."

"It is."

"It might work better."

"It might."

"So, okay, let's assume, just hypothetically," Keegan continued, her voice hardly containing her anticipation, "that we have a winner. Let's talk about how to get this approved." She looked at her corporate legal counsel. "We have the patents, right?"

"We do," Bob Egan responded slowly, knowing that the patents were important but it was FDA approval that was the big obstacle. There were plenty of patents for drugs that never worked and were never approved.

She turned to Henry Quinn, the regulatory VP. "Okay, Henry, how do we get this to the market?"

Quinn was a small man with closely cropped gray hair. His speech was insistent, even irregular, as if his words were struggling to catch up with a faster mind. Thirty years earlier, Miradol plucked him out of Stanford Law School and he never left.

"Colleagues," Quinn began, "we have some issues to address. Since this is all based upon synthesized proteins found in human blood, safety issues should not be large. The big problem with the FDA will be how we define effectiveness. You delay aging, you extend life. But we can't go that route. Measuring life spans takes many years. Even if all they wanted was a ten-year trial, the cost would be astronomical."

Keegan looked at him impatiently. "How much?"

"It might cost a half-billion dollars. First, we need to go to the FDA and have the pre-IND meeting." "IND" stood for Investigational New Drug application. It was a lengthy document describing in detail the drug and the clinical trials the drugmaker proposed. If the IND was approved, stage one trials, which were mostly about safety, could begin. Stage two were smaller trials testing effectiveness. Stage three trials were larger. If stage three were successful, the FDA approved your drug.

"We have to describe our drug," Quinn continued, "what it does and how we plan to run the tests. And I don't think we can make it about aging."

Keegan pursed her lips, contemplating the obstacle. "Okay, let me summarize," she began. "We can't test this drug for aging because the trial will take too long. So, it has to fix something else. Then we start the trials. Stage one, two, and three. What is that? Five years?"

"At least," Foley responded. "It could take seven or eight. And that does not include the IND."

"We can do the IND in a month," Keegan said, dismissively waving off a valid concern. The IND was a mountain of paper, sometimes a hundred thousand pages long. Her regulatory and science veeps exchanged nervous glances.

"We need some strategy here," Keegan continued, pressing toward decisions. "It's not just about the cost of the trials. If we have a drug that delays aging, the market is beyond description. Every week we lose might cost us hundreds of millions of dollars."

"We can find something," Quinn responded. "Aging causes a whole host of diseases. Cancer, heart disease, Alzheimer's—we know the list. It shouldn't be hard to find something among that long list of untreated conditions, something that preys on older people and is driven by age. So, if we have something that slows aging, it has to fix something else."

"We need to find one, and fast," Keegan commanded. "Devon, are you on it?"

"Yes, ma'am."

"So, what all this means," Keegan continued, "is that we are going to have to sell AFZ 4 off label."

Off-label sales are sales for a purpose not approved by the FDA. Many drugs are sold "off label." In fact, more than twenty percent of all prescriptions are written for a purpose not approved by the FDA. There are rules about promoting off-label sales. Those rules specifically exclude advertising.

Keegan rose from her chair and slowly surveyed her leadership team. They all shifted uncomfortably in their seats and studiously avoided her direct eye contact.

"Okay, if you don't understand the stakes here, allow me to explain. There are almost eight billion people on this planet and every one of them is afraid to die. Well, maybe not EVERY one, but the ones who aren't are either crazy or depressed and we already have drugs for both.

"There have been products with universal markets—the automobile, the telephone, the television, the smartphone. But no other company has ever had a universal market with protection against all competition.

"We are the number three pharmaceutical company in the world, and do you know what I think about being number three? Number three sucks. Number two sucks.

"Getting to number one is a cruel, grueling journey. But we played it smart. We spent $400 million on a bet against a terrible and immutable and incurable condition central to the human existence. We bet against aging. By all evidence we have seen today, it looks like we are going to win." She paused to let that sink in. "So find the decoy. Find the untreated condition that AFZ 4 can address. Find the unaddressed condition that will get this drug to the market as soon as we possibly can."

Keegan leaned over the table, placing her hands firmly in a combative stance, palms down, leaning in, staring down her team. "I don't care what it costs. The market is unprecedented. People will beg for this drug. We won't be able to count the money. Now get out of here and get to work."

And when her team scrambled from the meeting room, not a one of them wishing to appear unhurried, Big Red eased back into her chair, folded her hands together, and for a few minutes counted the money, so much money her mind could barely imagine the sum.

CHAPTER
One

Six years after that fateful meeting at Miradol, as the drug giant navigated its drug AFZ 4 to market, another meeting, seemingly unrelated, was taking place. In the nation's capital, two Republican members of Congress, one from the conservative Freedom Caucus, the other a moderate, both in states of advanced exasperation, were trying to decide who would become the next speaker of the House.

"Goddammit, Earl, we have to find someone."

Congressman Augustus Rhodes was not one to swear in frustration, but the conversation was going nowhere. Earl Ackerman chaired the Freedom Caucus, a band of Tea Party loyalists who were a powerful force in the Republican Congress. The Republicans controlled the House, winning it back in the midterm elections after a disastrous presidential campaign. Counting heads, Republicans had a majority but their margin was just five votes. Inside the Republican caucus, these 222 members had strong disagreements. Rhodes pushed back his chair and removed his glasses to rub his eyes. He reflected on how they had gotten to this desperate place.

Picking a speaker was usually an easy matter. If you won the House, the minority leader got promoted to speaker. There was a line of succession. The whip moved up and became majority leader. Then a bunch of wannabes scrambled to be whip. Not this time.

Jess Philips, the House minority leader, would have been the obvious choice. But he had lost a late primary and was no longer around. The fact that he had been opposed at all was a source of anger inside the caucus. He was no liberal. Give him a bill and he would sniff the paper just to see if it *smelled* liberal. But he was also the leader. His job was to stop Democratic legislation, and to do that he needed votes.

There were always some Democrats you could get. Their caucus was full of liberals who had to prove to their voters that they were nothing of the kind by voting for guns, lower taxes, and making membership in Planned Parenthood something close to a crime. But winning required a majority. A Republican minority leader needed his own votes and then some more. It took deal-making and coalition-building. And unfortunately for Jess Philips, these exercises required compromise.

The high priests of low taxes, a well-armed citizenry, and mandatory church attendance had a different view. *Compromise*, despite Merriam-Webster's view, was a four-letter word.

Big-funding PACs like the Club for Growth hardly cared about legislation at all. We had too many damned laws already. Congress was about winning elections, and the reason Republicans were losing was they were just too unprincipled in their message and their conduct. At least that was their view.

They looked at Jess Philips with disdain. Instead of reading from the liturgy, he was cavorting with sinners.

So they did something about it.

They found a farmer and ran him against the top leader in the whole Republican caucus. Their guy wasn't much of a candidate. He spent the whole campaign talking about "freedom unabridged and uncompromised." Banality won't win an election but it won't lose one either. Their dumbass farmer hardly mattered at all. What mattered was $2 million in negative ads telling Republican primary voters that Jess Philips had sold out to Democrats— and liberal ones at that.

On Election Day, with barely fifteen percent of the voters showing up at the polls, Jess Philips lost. But he did not just lose. He was trounced.

The Philips fiasco left Republicans with two problems. First, they had no frontrunner for speaker, and with just five votes above a majority they needed a good one. The second problem was a bigger one. The conservatives had just toppled the leader. If you can topple the leader, you can topple anyone. The Freedom Caucus was small and noisy, but they were feared across the House.

The election for speaker began with a wide-open race. Five candidates declared and they all had support. After a series of votes, three dropped out, leaving the caucus with only two choices: one, Will Baker, a champion of the Freedom Caucus, and the other, Liz Pinter, a "pragmatist" who actually spoke to Democrats on the other side, an act for which she refused to apologize.

The Freedom Caucus believed it was their turn. Earl Ackerman and his Freedom Caucus weren't about to settle for any half-ass, hand-wringing, foot-shuffling conservative. The president of the United States, Mario Marino, was a Democrat. He no longer had his majority in the House. He held the Senate by two votes. He had had his way for two years. Now, it was time to settle some accounts.

But the Freedom Caucus and their campaign against abortion, environmental regulation, and actually taxing the rich made a lot of members nervous. Theirs was not a great message, especially if you had been treated shabbily in redistricting and needed a few moderate votes to win.

So, the battle lines were drawn. Civility was abandoned. As the campaign proceeded, bitterness grew. By the time the final vote had arrived, most members were at least thankful to see this contest brought to an end. The ballots were counted. The result was announced.

A tie vote.

· · ·

The day after the vote, Republicans convened Congress with an adjournment. They adjourned because the first order of business was to elect a speaker of the House and they had no speaker to elect. The media, which never liked them anyway, ridiculed their failure. They needed a speaker and fast.

The revote was scheduled for the next day. Suddenly, the lowest and most ordinary members, those who barely deserved a nod of recognition from a regional whip in an empty hallway, possessed real power. One decision, by one member, might actually select the second most powerful pubic official in America.

Over the next twenty-four hours, representatives who might be open to change were lavished with offers of prized committee assignments.

"Bill, I know you've always wanted to serve on the Ways and Means Committee."

"Rita Takeshita, I need you on Energy and Commerce!"

Chairmanships? Several were promised. Some more than once. After all, if you get to be speaker you can always give them something else.

Some members had pet legislation, small causes for which they had labored for years without the slightest success. Suddenly, those prospects improved.

"Of course, we can end the regulation of pickup trucks under the Commercial Motor Vehicle Act. I have found that issue deeply troubling for quite some time."

"Exempting sage grouses from the Endangered Species Act? I think we can find a solution."

Of course, a speaker has money, his own and his party's. Money was dropping like rain in a category four hurricane.

"Don't you worry at all, Cynthia, I can make some calls. If I end up getting this job, I think raising you $200,000 is a perfectly reasonable expectation."

These entreaties, intense and urgent, continued through the wee hours of the morning.

Did the prospect of power, influence, and legislative success actually change a single vote?

Of course, it did. By the time of the revote the next day, thirty members had changed their votes. Both candidates, proud of the votes they had converted, were certain of success.

Once again, the ballots were collected. Once again, the votes were counted. Of the thirty members who switched sides, half switched to Pinter and half to Baker.

The vote remained a tie.

Members rose, one after another, to level charges of misconduct. Earl Ackerman, chair of the Freedom Caucus, promised a walkout if Pinter was elected. A bluff, probably. But coming from a guy like Ackerman you never really knew. Just as all hope for resolution appeared beyond reach, from the back of the room, Representative Embry Jones, congressman from Iowa, rose to speak.

Jones had served in the House for thirty-two years and the House was, to him, a beloved institution. To him, the House was no collection of egocentric assholes grubbing for their own gain. To him, the House was history, democracy, a sacred temple of the American way. Illusion or not, in his mind, the great unfolding tragedy was not the inability to choose a speaker. It was the diminishment of the Congress itself.

"Colleagues," he began in a slow, soft voice. The members uncharacteristically fell silent. "We must all remember the truths we share: that smaller government is the best government, that free enterprise enriches one and all, and that we are engaged in a great and honorable contest to protect the traditional values which we all—every one of us in this room—honor."

A few Ackerman loyalists looked suspiciously around the room.

"But if we are to serve these values, we must be truthful," Embry Jones continued, his tone still quiet but earnest. "We have reached an impasse, and the election of either candidate will so deeply divide this caucus that we risk losing any opportunity for success."

A murmur spread throughout the room but Embry did not pause. "I propose a new solution. We need a speaker who can work for both sides. If we're going to find that person, we need both sides at the table. I suggest that we send Earl Ackerman and Augustus Rhodes to a room. They each represent one wing of this party. Their job is to find a speaker they can both support. When they can agree on a candidate, then I promise that candidate will have my vote. I am certain that many in this room will do the same."

Members looked around the room, measuring the response of their colleagues. They were the majority party in the US House of Representative, unable to even convene the Congress. They were the butt of jokes across America. They needed a fix and they needed it fast. Several members nodded slowly and a murmur of assent grew in the room. Considering their predicament, Jones' solution sounded pretty damned good.

CHAPTER

Two

So, there they sat, coffee cups littering the table in a seldom-used caucus room in the Rayburn House Office Building. Augustus Rhodes represented not exactly what you would call the "moderates" but conservatives who still believed that compromise was no grounds for excommunication. And Earl Ackerman represented truth and the purity of belief. They had discussed candidates for three hours and not one single name had garnered the two votes necessary to win.

Augustus Rhodes ran his fingers through his hair and looked Ackerman in the eye. "Earl, we've been through almost every name in the caucus. Every name you offer is nothing I can sell. And every name I offer won't work for your caucus. What the hell are we going to do?"

Earl Ackerman climbed back on his high horse. "Look, Gus, it's our turn. Don't expect me to back down. If we get another vote, I know we can win."

"Maybe, but, Earl, what if you can't? What if we go another week without a damned speaker? We will be ruined. Earl, I've got an idea. Take this piece of paper and write down three names that are acceptable to you but that you think I might support. Forget the usual suspects. Think outside the box. Three members who are capable of doing this job that you could live with and you think I might, just might, live with as well. Don't give me any of your fire breathers. Give me three choices in the middle. I will do the same." He took a page from his legal pad, tore it in half, and gave Ackerman his piece.

Ackerman smiled. "How about…?"

Rhodes smiled. "Don't even say it."

After five minutes' thought and slow penmanship, they traded lists. There was one name on both lists. Joe Hazeldine.

They both looked up in disbelief. They had both included Hazeldine knowing that he would never appear on the other's list. And for good reason. Hazeldine was about the last person you could ever imagine with the gavel in his hand.

A speaker needed diplomacy. Hazeldine was a straight shooter with a vocabulary a lot closer to a sailor than some state department smoothy. A speaker needed a good television appearance. Hazeldine was overweight and by three in the afternoon he had a five o'clock shadow that would have made Dick Nixon blush. He bought his clothes off the discount rack, and for all he knew Armani was a diner that baked second-rate pizza.

But Joe Hazeldine had one plus and it was a big one. These days success was less about issues and more about screwing the Democrats. As to that noble undertaking, Hazeldine was the champ.

As chair of the House Oversight and Government Reform Committee, Hazeldine led a series of investigations that had embarrassed and even humiliated those Democrats in the Marion Administration. A former trial lawyer, his preparation was meticulous; his examination of Administration witnesses was legendary. He was the pit bull from Fort Wayne, Indiana.

Another thing about Hazeldine: he was a hard worker. He had no kids—well, one but she had passed away long ago. He was estranged from his wife. Congress was his life. As hit-man-in-chief for the House Republicans, he had admirers in both factions of the caucus.

Rhodes and Ackerman just looked at each other, not sure how they had arrived at this unlikely choice.

"I guess this is the best we can do," Ackerman stated, shaking his head. "I hope he can clean up his language."

"Do you think he can do the job?" Rhodes asked, still dubious of the wisdom of this course of action.

"He'll be tough on the members."

"True, but does that work anymore?"

"Well, what does work? The question is—will he do it?"

Rhodes smiled. "He's going to have to."

"I wouldn't be so sure but we're about to find out."

. . .

Late that evening Joe Hazeldine was at his desk reading a report on possible Democratic corruption—the only kind he cared about. It seemed Democratic donors in New Mexico were getting an unfair share of the federal housing dollars. "Unfair" in Hazeldine's mind was any contract at all, but he would need more for a hearing. Something was fishy and the US attorney, a Democrat, was looking the other way.

He reached for his pen to start writing what would be a long list of questions. He didn't look up until the phone rang at half past midnight.

"Joe, this is Earl Ackerman and Gus Rhodes."

"I am sorry, guys, but if you're calling to ask my advice about this speaker job, I don't have a thing to say. I don't know why anyone would want it. It's the worst job in America."

"Joe, this is Gus. We are not calling to ask your advice. We are calling to offer you the job. We want you to be speaker of the House."

"What?" Joe thought at first he hadn't heard Gus Rhodes correctly. It took him a full minute to digest what was actually taking place and he did not like it at all.

A speaker spent his days kissing asses when ass-kicking would be far more appropriate. A speaker groveled for money from people who wanted bad things and usually got them. A speaker measured his words when a little profanity could convey a lot more meaning with a lot fewer syllables. Joe Hazeldine was no speaker.

"Excuse me, but you guys can't be serious."

"Joe, we're dead serious," Ackerman responded. "We're in a jam and you know it. We can't even form the government. The caucus sent us to find the one person both sides of the Republican caucus could possibly follow. There weren't many options. We decided that person is you."

"Well, we are in a helluva shape if you ask me."

"Joe," Rhodes answered. "We are in a helluva shape. That is why you have to take this job. You can do it. I know you can."

Hazeldine thought for a long time. He had done nothing to prepare for this role. He could not understand why he would be their choice. But he cared about the country. The House was his life. What could he say?

"Well, gentlemen, I guess we are going to find out."

. . .

The next morning, Joe Hazeldine sat at his desk thinking about the strange turn of events. As he did every morning, he looked at a picture that stood on the desk. It was a photo of a three-year-old girl. His daughter, Amelia, was so beautiful in the photo, with her impossibly deep dimples and blond ringlets and laughing, always laughing, blue eyes. The photo had been taken a year before she died, before the disease had ravaged her looks and taken the glow from her dimpled cheeks—had taken everything other than her laughing blue eyes.

She had a rare disease that strikes fewer than ten thousand children every year. She had been on medication, Pheleptenol, that kept the disease at bay and she had fought hard. But the cost of that prescription was $80,000 per year. Then the disaster struck.

He was working as a young attorney for an insurance defense law firm fighting personal injury lawsuits. The year before, the Indiana legislature had passed "tort reform" legislation making it more difficult for attorneys to bring "frivolous lawsuits" on behalf of their injured clients. He supported the legislation. It was ridiculous what some of those lawyers did, threatening and intimidating insurance companies to get money they did not deserve at all.

But the victors did not celebrate long. Fewer lawsuits meant less business for his firm. Eight months after passage, the managing partner called him to his office and told him that they were cutting staff. His job was gone. Losing his job meant losing his health insurance. Without insurance, there was no way to pay for the drugs that kept his daughter alive. Six months later his daughter was gone.

His daughter had a nickname, "Babushka," which was taken from a Russian fairy tale. Babushka was a princess who learned a strange magic based upon finding a heart-shaped pattern among the stars. She used the magic to change her appearance and, while disguised as a hunched-backed old woman, she made a great journey to rescue her brother, who had been kidnapped by an evil king. But the magic did not last forever. On her return to the castle she took on the features of the princess again and, recognized immediately, she fell to the sword of an enemy soldier. The kingdom celebrated her as a great hero and believed forever thereafter that her spirit remained in the kingdom, guarding it from harm.

Amelia had asked Joe to read her this story again and again. He had once playfully called her Babushka. She never let him use the name Amelia again. On her last day of life, seeing her father distraught with grief, it was she who comforted him, telling Joe that she was like Babushka and that she would remain with him to guard him against all enemies.

Remembering this moment, Joe wiped his eyes, faced her photograph, and spoke. "Babushka, my princess, I have some news. I have been handed a big job. I'm going to be speaker of the United States House of Representatives." He talked to her every day, and often his words felt empty and unheard. But other times he convinced himself he felt her presence in the room. Today was one such day, so he continued, "I want to make you proud but it will be a battle. I'm counting on you to guard me from harm."

As he looked at her photo, he smiled sheepishly to himself. It was their secret. The words of a daughter comforting a father whose grief was beyond her own. Tonight, he could feel her looking back at him, listening. And on hearing his words her smile filled the room.

He turned and walked to his window. The sky was clear and for once he could see the stars. He saw it immediately. Eight stars perfectly aligned in the shape of a heart.

CHAPTER
Three

"Sam, I do believe this is the prettiest snow I've seen since we've been in Washington."

Pearl Kelley was right because today, in early December, the snowstorm was a sight to behold. The flakes were outsized, so large that instead of tumbling toward the ground, they seemed to challenge the idea of gravity, swirling softly in a pendular motion, back and forth, back and forth, until finally kissing the earth. The air was so thick with snow that it muted all sound, and even though it was late morning and the roads were crowded with cars, the city was hushed. This city of loud voices and boisterous horns was transformed into something else entirely—a silent movie, sensuous and white.

Pearl Kelley's comment was indeed a compliment because Pearl and her husband, Sam, had arrived here thirty-six years earlier, when Sam was first elected to Congress. He was bored with his insurance job, so when America entered the Vietnam War he volunteered right away. There he was awarded the Silver Star after jumping from a plane right into a nest of Viet Cong fighters. He lost an arm, but he wasn't the one retreating. No way. In the hands of his handlers, his story grew. Vietnam produced few heroes, but in his rural Tennessee district he became "single-armed Sam," whose courage taught those commies a lesson they would never forget. He won big and never had a race since.

Being a war hero is a good way to start, but it won't hold a job for thirty-six years. Sam had other advantages. One was his district. His district ran along the southern border of Tennessee. If you wanted to run for Congress in Sam's district, you had to buy TV ads in five different media markets—Chattanooga, Knoxville, Nashville, Jackson, and, just for good measure, Huntsville, Alabama, as well. Who could afford TV spots in all those places? Worse, every time you bought an ad, at least seventy percent of the audience lived somewhere else and could not vote for you at all.

Running against Sam was not just expensive. He was a Republican, and for a Democrat there were few votes to be had. Oh, some of those Middle Tennessee voters were still thanking Roosevelt for TVA, the New Deal program that brought cheap electricity and jobs to parts of Tennessee. But gratitude had its limits. Middle Tennessee was becoming more Republican every year. The rest of the district was so Republican that Democrats had to enter their towns under the cover of darkness and were often advised to leave before dawn.

So, Sam had maybe the safest district in the fifty United States of America.

But something happened the previous year that put Sam in a bad spot. They took a census and that meant redistricting. Sam was not really all that interested in state politics. In fact, he really wasn't that interested in campaign politics at all. He cared about policy and health care and his precious subcommittee. While the legislature redrew the districts, Sam paid no attention. When they announced the map, Sam Kelley, thirty-six-year veteran of Congress, Tennessee's longest serving public official, had been screwed.

Instead of clinging to those lines separating Tennessee from Alabama and Mississippi, the new district snaked north into the city of Nashville. Nashville was full of liberals. Worse, he lost every county that bordered Mississippi, counties where voters might not read or spell so good but sure as hell knew how to find the word "Republican" on the ballot. Instead, he got voters who could read both party names and might even think about which one to support. Worst of all, sixty percent of the district was new.

Sam did not hold town hall meetings or spend much time on all that constituent stuff. Even his old district did not know him so well. These new voters knew nothing at all. If they knew anything it was usually that Sam was seventy-eight years old, had been in Washington for thirty-six long years, and they couldn't think of one damned thing he'd done for them in all that time.

If all that was not bad enough, now Sam had an actual opponent, the first serious rival since "single-armed Sam" had waltzed into Congress decades ago. His name was Sidney Lund.

Lund was not much to look at. He had a nerdy appearance and always looked like he'd forgotten to wash his hair. His teeth were crooked and a little yellow, and he did not put his sentences together with any sense of style. At first glance, he might strike you as a surefire loser, but things were different these days and Sidney Lund had one serious qualification.

Money.

Lund made his money in an odd way. He invented a tiny microchip that could be imbedded in almost any small device. Your eyeglasses. Your keys. Your wallet. Anything you could lose. He did something brilliant. He gave his chip to manufacturers for free. Then he sold a cell phone app that let you find the item you lost. Phinder.com.

The timing was perfect. As the population grew older, people's memories grew shorter and they got tired of crawling on all fours looking under the sofa for those glasses that sometimes were sitting right on their own noses. People needed help and marketers were eager to provide it. If you sold keys, you labeled them as "phindable." Eyeglasses were "phindable." If someone stole your wallet, Lund's cell phone program told you where your wallet was, told you who lived there, and practically posted a picture of the thief on the post office wall.

What was Sidney Lund worth? About a half-billion dollars by most estimates. He could run his campaign on the interest and still fly first class to Acapulco, on short notice, any weekend he wanted.

So at this moment, Sam Kelley was not thinking about the snowstorm his wife thought was so pretty. All he could think about was the life he hated, the life he had miraculously escaped all these years—the campaign life plodding through county fairs and courthouses, shaking hands, answering questions, and making speeches—all those things that inevitably got in the way of good public service. And why on earth did they have to have this campaign meeting so darned early—two years before Election Day?

"Now, Sam," Pearl weighed in. "I know it is going to be hard but you listen to these consultants. They know how to get you re-elected. It is what they do."

Sam's sleeve, the empty one, began to twitch.

CHAPTER
Four

The meeting room at the National Republican Congressional Committee, better known as the NRCC, was not impressive. There was a fake wooden table surrounded by plastic and aluminum chairs, all of which had seen better days. There was a screen on the wall, and the pollster Sarah Whiteridge was hooking up her PowerPoint. She turned to greet her new client.

"Sam, so great to see you again!"

Sam and Sarah had met once after the party committee told him he needed a pollster and she was the one to hire. Now she was running the show.

It was a small meeting. There was Sarah, Sam, Pearl, and Sally Benjamin from the NRCC. The NRCC's sole purpose was to help Republicans get elected to Congress. It raised money—hundreds of millions of dollars. It had a bureaucracy of advisors, like Sally Benjamin, who told campaigns what to do and how to execute the "modern campaign." They had "microtargeters," computer nerds who used big data to figure out which voters were voting their way, which ones weren't, which ones were still up for grabs, and which voters believed Elvis was still alive and might write in his name on election day. Another group ran control group experiments to measure whether any of these tactics worked at all. It was tough work. After all, how do you get a voter to stand in line on a cold election day to vote for a candidate owned by interests whose main skill was screwing people out of their money?

But these tawdry questions did little to diminish the stature of the NRCC. When the NRCC spoke, candidates listened. If they dropped you from the target list, you were toast. It was a signal to donors that the race was lost. If they withheld their money, a candidate would be short on ads.

Of course, none of this applied to Sam. He was a thirty-six-year incumbent. He took their phone calls and thanked them for their help but did not have to take their advice. And he did not think much of the advice he was getting.

Then there was Michael Barbier, who had been hired to produce the campaign's TV ads. Barbier used to be a leading media consultant, but he got tired of politics and started making movies—well, actually documentaries that everyone praised but no one watched. Sam's closest friend in Congress lived in LA and knew Barbier, who was a little down and out because his Hollywood work was not making much money. Sam's buddy said he could get Barbier to do Sam's campaign. Sam liked that. This guy made documentaries, so he wasn't one of those untrustworthy political hacks. And when the NRCC tried to tell him who to hire to do his media, he responded with a casual air, "Michael Barbier is coming back from Hollywood to do my campaign." No one at the NRCC was impressed.

There was one more person who had not yet arrived. Sam's niece, Ann Bell, who was never referred to as "Ann" or "Ms. Bell" but in the fine southern custom of the double name "Ann Bell." Sam had hired her to run his campaign. She had a junior position in a small marketing firm in Nashville. A campaign was about marketing, so Sam had brought her on board. She had no campaign experience and was barely old enough to have cast two votes. The chair of the NRCC was apoplectic. And now Ann Bell, already the subject of controversy, was late to her very first meeting.

Not in attendance were the consultants Sam had failed to hire. First was the campaign research firm that dug up dirt on your opponent. Essential! And the direct mail firm. A lot of people don't watch TV, at least not those broadcast channels with all the commercials. A serious candidate needed mail as well. Despite the urgings of Sally Benjamin, Sam had postponed hiring these specialties, suspecting that they were more interested in his money than votes.

Sam stood and briefly welcomed the small group to his campaign. He was a square-shouldered man, a little more than six feet tall with a forward lean and eyes that seemed always to be focused somewhere else. When you had his attention, he had an easy smile. He still had most of his hair, although every bit of it was white and carelessly combed. His empty sleeve was rolled up almost to his shoulder and sometimes twitched, signaling excitement or a change in mood.

When Sam sat down, Sarah Whiteridge, the pollster, glanced about the room and rose to speak. She was tall and thin with the posture of an unsharpened pencil. Her hair, every strand in place, was cut in a perfect line, rounded slightly at the bottom, one and three quarters inches north of the shoulder. Her business suit was perfectly pressed and her manner nothing if not proper. In her late forties, she did not advise the senators, the governors, or the presidential candidates of our world. She was second tier. Her world was Congress, but at the NRCC she was a star.

She picked up a clicker and aimed it toward the screen. The first slide appeared: "A Survey of Likely Voters in the Fourth District of Tennessee."

"Sam, there is a lot of news in this poll and not all of it is good. Let me start with what the voters know about you and their current opinions."

Click: "Name Recognition."

"I'll begin with the voters who know you best, the voters who were part of your old district—before redistricting. Among likely voters, only sixty-two percent are able to offer any opinion about you at all. Of those who have an opinion only eight percent are very unfavorable, thirty-nine percent are somewhat unfavorable, forty-nine percent are somewhat favorable, and only four percent are very favorable. What about the new part of the district? Among your new voters only thirty-two percent have any opinion at all."

Whiteridge adjusted her glasses and peered at Sam, her expression serious and stern. "These are not good numbers," she admonished. "The good news is no one knows Lund at all."

Click: "Generic Partisan Horse Race."

"Not only do you lack a strong personal base of support, the district is also no longer an easy Republican seat. We asked voters, generally, would they prefer to be represented in Congress by a Republican or Democrat."

Click.

The slide showed the stark reality: 36% Republican, 34% Democratic, 25% No Difference, and a rambunctious 5% stating "Neither!"

"So, both parties are even. From that standpoint the race is wide open."

Click: "Current Candidate Standings." Republican Sam Kelley 42%, Democrat Sidney Lund 31%, Undecided 27%.

"It is a common rule of politics that any incumbent who enters a campaign with less than fifty percent of the vote is in trouble," Whiteridge continued, her gaze resting for a moment on each member of the campaign team.

Sam looked across the team as well, waiting for someone to argue. No one spoke up.

"Not only are you below fifty percent but only thirty percent are strongly supporting your candidacy." Click. A third of his voters, colored yellow, were labeled as "weak."

"So let's summarize—"

The door opened and in stepped a woman, almost a girl, surely not yet twenty-five, slightly overweight and blinking nervously as she took in the room.

"Hi, I'm Ann Bell. Sorry to be late. I guess I still don't know my way around Washington."

Whiteridge and Benjamin exchanged smirks.

"Have a seat," Whiteridge offered, nodding coolly. "I was just explaining to your uncle that after thirty-six years he finally has a race."

"Oh, my gosh," Ann Bell replied and grabbed an empty seat.

"So," Whiteridge continued, "we have a wide-open race. What happens when the two candidates make their case?" Click.

A slide entitled "Leading attacks on Kelley" appeared.

This is the part in every poll where you sling the mud and measure how well it sticks.

"As you can see, our opponent has a lot of ammunition," Whiteridge said, looking hard at Sam as she tried to gauge his understanding of the situation. The slide listed possible attacks on Kelley; underneath each attack was the percentage of voters who were "much less likely" to vote for Kelley after hearing the statement.

> "Sam Kelley is seventy-eight years old and no longer has the energy or new ideas to serve us in Congress."
> MUCH LESS LIKELY 47%

> "Sam Kelley has served in Congress for thirty-six years. We need new blood and new ideas in Washington."
> MUCH LESS LIKELY 45%

> "A chairman of the committee that controls the Food and Drug administration, Sam Kelley could have done something about high prescription drug prices. Thanks to his inaction, high drug prices are bankrupting Tennessee families."
> MUCH LESS LIKELY 52%

> "Sam Kelley has not held a town hall meeting to talk to voters in the last twenty years. He does not care about your problems and is out of touch with average Tennessee voters."
> MUCH LESS LIKELY 39%

"Wait a minute," Sam interrupted. "These things aren't true."

Sally Benjamin's hand shot to cover her mouth, not wanting to be caught laughing at a member of Congress.

"Sam, I know they aren't true," Whiteridge responded with an exaggerated patience. "At least in some respects. But these are the statements you will see in TV ads run by Mr. Lund. We measure what we expect to see."

Sam blinked, absorbing this surprising response.

Click: "Positive Arguments for Sidney Lund."

The list was strong:

> "A businessman who will bring ideas to grow our economy."

> "A strong leader who won't be part of the Washington establishment."

"An innovator who built a billion-dollar business from the ground up."

Each argument earned a strong score. No home runs. That almost never happened. After all, who really believed this stuff anyway? But there was no denying that, as candidates go, Lund had a good case and his case was strongest where Kelley was weak.

Whiteridge turned to face her candidate. "The final question is: 'How do we attack Lund?' To win, we need to disqualify him as a candidate."

Sam bristled. "I don't like that kind of campaign."

"Like it or not, negative campaigning is what wins elections these days." Whiteridge had her rules. If you broke them and lost, it wouldn't be her fault.

Sam stared back, silent.

Pearl spoke up. "Now, Sam, you have not been running campaigns. Ms. Whiteridge has experience. Just hear her out."

Sam shifted uncomfortably in his seat. His empty shirt sleeve began to twitch.

Michael Barbier, the media consultant who had been silent thus far, interjected, "Hold on, everybody. Let's get this right. Sam, this is your campaign and you get to run it the way you want. Understand?"

"Right," the congressman replied gruffly.

"But you can't close off options," Brazier continued. "No one has to decide anything today. But we need a research firm to find out who this guy Lund really is. What if he has done something terrible? Wouldn't the voters need to know?"

"It's possible," Sam replied without conviction.

"So, with your approval we will find a research firm and give you options. Is that okay?"

"Okay, but I am not committing to anything, just so everyone understands." Sam fidgeted in his chair. "All we are doing is looking."

"That's right," said Barbier, "we are only looking." He turned to Ann Bell. "Ann," he said, ignoring southern naming customs, "why don't you start work on finding a research firm this afternoon?"

Ann Bell looked up, surprised to hear her name. "Got it, but first a question. What exactly is a research firm?"

CHAPTER
Five

For the last six years the pharmaceutical giant Miradol had been working hard to bring its miracle drug to market. They found a condition, Recipothosis, characterized by skin rashes and weakening of the muscles in the upper arms and thighs that needed to be cured. There were theories about the cause but no one knew the answer.

It afflicted only fifty people in a million, or less than twenty thousand nationwide. It occurred mostly in old age and there was no FDA-approved drug that addressed its symptoms. The fact that so few people actually had this disease put it in a special category, rare or orphan diseases. Because these drugs have no market, developers got tax credits and other incentives to offset their research costs.

Because the number of sufferers was small, the trials were not large. They passed the stage one safety trial. Then they entered stages two and three, measuring the effectiveness of the drug. The trials were only moderately successful. Twenty percent of the treatment group showed improvement. Given that no other drug addressed Recipothosis at all, that would probably be enough. The FDA was conducting its review. Colleen Keegan was hoping for final approval within the next six months.

Now Keegan focused on marketing, and marketing was tricky business. They had come up with a new name for the drug. Someone suggested "Youthenel." Too obvious. What they ended up with was close. "Juventel." Maybe not that subtle, but better.

There were strict limits on marketing those sales. No TV ads. No social media. But Colleen Keegan knew the stakes. There was almost no limit to the amount of money this drug might make. In launching Juventel, they would cut no corners; they would spare no expense. She could not do TV ads but she wanted social media and she had an idea. She had called her vice president for Marketing, Casey Jacobs, to her office.

Tall and handsome with hair so closely cropped you wouldn't know the color in a bad light, Casey Jacobs still carried himself like the football star he had been in high school. He was just short of forty and from Texas, where he was a cum laude graduate in marketing at the university in Austin. He still spoke with just enough of an accent to let you know that California was not his home.

Pharmaceuticals are marketed on television, and Jacobs knew his TV. But social media was his first love. He had pioneered moving ads off the networks and onto the internet. He and Keegan had immediately formed a close working relationship from the moment she had taken the helm at Miradol. They were both change agents, willing to push the envelope to get to the next level.

"Casey, the big day is not far away," Keegan said excitedly.

"I hope so."

Colleen Keegan brought her fingertips together and paused for effect. "Casey, this is the most important project you or I will ever own. We need a huge launch. The biggest launch this industry has ever seen."

"Well, how do we do that? We can't buy TV ads and we can't pay for social media."

"I don't know what to do about the TV, but the social media. What if someone else paid for it?"

"I guess they could. But who?"

"I'll come back to that one. And what if the campaign came from six thousand miles away where no financial transaction could be tracked?"

"You're talking Russia?" Casey asked. He glanced out the window, avoiding eye contract. He was afraid of where this discussion was headed.

"Tell me about Russia."

"Well, as you seem to know, they have the biggest and most advanced social media operations in the world. They might have several hundred thousand people employed, mostly working for the government. Sinister. They are a tool of the state. They combat anti-government voices, meddle in foreign elections, and push Putin's viewpoint. These guys are good. They play the internet like a fine musical instrument."

"Would they work for us?" Keegan asked. "Do they do commercial products?"

"I guess anybody will work for anybody if there is enough money involved. Could they do products? They would probably need direction but I would say yes."

"So it could work?"

"Colleen, what are you suggesting?"

"Casey, you are the best in the business and, for that reason, I need your resignation."

"What?"

"I need you to leave Miradol, leave the country, and direct a social media campaign that cannot be tracked."

"This feels pretty messy to me."

"Casey, once you leave there will be no communication from me or this company. You'll be completely on your own. Miradol will have no say in this campaign."

"I don't know, Colleen. This doesn't feel good."

"It will feel good. It will feel very good. Just let me tell you how much money you are about to make."

CHAPTER

Six

Joe Hazeldine's new office was the finest in the entire Capitol Building; spacious, with a fireplace and two windows that looked out upon the long expanse of the National Mall. He could see the Washington Monument and, another mile beyond that, the Lincoln Memorial, a tiny white square. In this office, the walls were yellow and empty. Who had time to hang pictures? The speaker sat in a leather wingback chair, his leadership team assembled before him.

The party had chosen Joe Hazeldine as speaker, and the sound of the gavel had barely faded when the first crisis had landed in his lap. The budget.

The last Congress had passed a stopgap measure to keep the government running. They bought four precious months—the time it takes to avoid election controversy and pass on the task to the next Congress. The federal debt limit was $20.5 trillion. Borrowing had passed $20.3 trillion and economists estimated that by mid-February the limit would be reached.

The amount of debt was a catastrophe—a debt that would cripple the ability of future generations to pave their roads, staff their schools, put soldiers in combat, and pay for health care for the aging and infirm. But those consequences, while large, were nothing like the consequences of defaulting on the debt. With $20 trillion in debt the one thing you could not afford is higher interest rates.

A default would diminish the full faith and credit of the United States of America, alarming lenders who would, in turn, charge America higher interest rates for the loans they made. Bigger deficits would follow, leading to a downward spiral and an end that seemed beyond contemplation.

The president had a plan. The Democratic Senate had signed on. Now it was up to Joe Hazeldine to deliver the House.

Passing budgets was not what it used to be. Routine business such as passing a farm bill or transportation bill used to take a few months. Now they took years. Congress had not passed all of its annual appropriation bills in twenty years. Each year $300 billion in federal spending went out the door without proper approval at all.

There was a clear majority supporting the budget. If the budget got to the floor, some Republicans would join all Democrats in producing the majority needed to pass. But the Republican caucus had passed a rule. No proposal would go to the floor without approval by a majority of their party caucus. So to avoid default and pass a budget, the speaker had to muster the support of a majority of Republicans. With large numbers of Republicans eager to bring the government down to size, getting a majority was a daunting task.

"Welcome to the first meeting of our new Republican leadership team," Hazeldine said, looking around the room. There was his majority leader, Lindsey Barker. Barker was in her mid-forties with blond hair sculpted tight to her face and little eyes that seemed to be squinting even when they weren't. She was a nervous presence, and in meetings her legs crossed, her foot bobbing most of the time. Her hands, intertwined in her lap or on the table, barely moved. Stiff and precise with, above all, loyalties outside the room.

Barker was a member of the Freedom Caucus. He needed someone from the caucus on their team. She was the eyes of the leadership into their group. That was the theory. She was also the Freedom Caucus' eyes into the leadership. That was the practice.

The majority whip was Fred Baines from South Carolina, a moderate and good friend of Hazeldine. He was bald and small in stature, but his most noticeable trait was an energy that was hard to miss. He was straight-spoken, and Hazeldine could trust his word. To the meeting he had brought six deputy whips, each responsible for votes in a specific geographic region. Also present was Beau Jefferson, Hazeldine's chief of staff.

"Well, I guess we get to start with the easy stuff," Hazeldine began. Chuckles in the room. "Let me begin by sharing the details of my meeting with the president.

"The president and Senator Jameson, the Democratic majority leader, are of the opinion that they have the upper hand. They have offered us a deal, and if we don't take it the government shuts down. We get the blame. They also don't believe that we would let the nation default on the debt. In their opinion, they are holding all the cards. They are playing hardball and I don't think the sonofabitches are going to budge."

The speaker scanned the room for concern, but most bore blank expressions.

"We have two choices," Hazeldine continued. "We can call their bluff, shut it all down, and wait for them to move. Or we can pass something that resembles their plan but with some wins for us. If we do that we could at least trim some entitlements. Lindsey, if I put option two on the table, could it get any votes in your group? What would I need to include?"

"Our guys are pretty riled up," Lindsey answered. "They don't care about the shutdown. They want a fight."

Hazeldine grimaced. Not unexpected but not good. "So how many votes could we get on a budget that is close enough to get a deal?"

Baines spoke up. "I think we are twenty-five to thirty votes short. Heritage Action announced today that they are scoring this vote." That meant that Heritage Action Fund would use the vote in its scorecard, which rated the conservative fidelity of members of Congress.

Heritage Action scores were taken up by Tea Party activists, who shared them in meetings. Their votes included opposing new National Institutes of Health funding for research on disease cures and opposing the Democratic president's nomination for Librarian of Congress. Getting a bad score meant a lot of angry activists and, maybe, a primary.

Hazeldine was exasperated. "How can they score a vote on a plan that has not even been written? I am going to give their guy a call. So, Fred, do you have a list of people we can call?"

"I do."

"How many names?"

"Thirty-five."

"That's all?"

"You only need six out of seven to win."

CHAPTER
Seven

Sidney Lund had chosen to be the American dream. On this day, when he announced his dream of becoming the congressman from the Fourth Congressional District of Tennessee, he returned to the efficiency apartment where he had conceived his plan to create Phinder.com. He had not lived there long. His family was not poor. But the shabby building was the rags in his rags to riches tale.

John Steinbeck one said that in America "the poor see themselves not as an exploited proletariat, but as temporarily embarrassed millionaires." Sidney Lund was keeping hope alive. On the six o'clock news, WCSB gave this report:

> "Today, standing in front of the one-room efficiency apartment where his business dreams began, Nashville inventor and entrepreneur Sidney Lund did something no Tennessee citizen has done in almost forty years. He announced his candidacy to run against eighteen-term congressman Sam Kelley.

> "Lund brings an impressive resume to the task. Founder of Phinder.com, Lund made a fortune helping people find keys, cars, eyeglasses—all the items that once disappeared into the dust balls behind washing machines, under beds, and in our own back pockets.

> "But finding your house keys is a lot easier than finding a seat in Congress. Lund will have money and Democrats are excited to have any candidate at all. But political experts wonder, 'Who is he kidding?' Kelley may be getting old but this icon of volunteer state politics won't go down easy.

"My advice to Mr. Lund? Good luck! You're going to need it.

"This is Logan Ladner, commentator for WCSB-TV, Nashville."

CHAPTER
Eight

The speaker picked up the phone. Top of his call list was Aberdeen Francis, a Republican member from the Third Congressional District in Louisiana. Francis was in his second term, a good thing. These new members had to listen to the speaker. That's how they got on good committees. That's how they got bills on the calendar.

"Mr. Speaker, I wasn't expecting your call." A lie but a friendly one.

"Aberdeen, glad I could catch you. By the way, I noticed your work on the VA reforms. I want to help out. It's needed and you've helped make the case. Thank you."

"Thank you, Mr. Speaker. What can I do for you today?"

"Well, you know we've got this budget issue in front of us. It's about the god-damnedest way to start a new job I can imagine. But the stakes are pretty high here, for Republicans and for the country. If we default on our Treasury bonds there'll be hell to pay and Republicans will get blamed. I talked to the president. He knows he's got the upper hand and isn't budging on his plan."

"We are still a good ways from default, right? It's the shutdown we are talking about."

"We aren't that far. And if we don't want this hung around our necks, I think we need to pass something in the caucus that the president will take seriously. We can get something out of this deal. Not enough to please everybody—that's for sure—but some small entitlement cuts and maybe some other spending. I'm wrapping up the proposal now. Can I get your support?" The request hung a little too long in the air for Joe Hazeldine's liking.

"I don't know," Francis finally said. "I'm getting a lot of pushback from the other side."

"What are you hearing?"

"Don't back down," he admitted.

"We don't want to play chicken with the president. You know what he'll do? The Administration will step to the side and smile while we go over the cliff. It won't be their asses pasted on the ground below."

"Joe, you make a lot of sense but I am getting heat. The Tea Party nuts are all over me. Heritage is going to score the vote. Club for Growth called me. They did not threaten a primary but you could tell they were thinking about it."

"Look, you can vote against the proposal if you want," Hazeldine said, his tone as conciliatory as he was willing to go. "You can get your Heritage points and be a hero on the floor. I just need you to vote 'yes' in the caucus so I can bring it to the floor."

"Secret ballot?" Francis asked hopefully, seeing a way out.

"Absolutely."

"Okay."

"Aberdeen, I can't thank you enough. You are saving the Republican Party. You let me know what I can do for you."

"VA reform. You can help get it on the calendar."

One vote down. But the speaker's next three calls did not go so well. The conversations were pretty much the same.

SPEAKER: "It will be a secret ballot."

MEMBER: "They are going to ask me how I voted."

SPEAKER: "You can tell them anything you want."

MEMBER: "I am not going to lie."

SPEAKER: "We can't play chicken with the president."

MEMBER: "You want me to play chicken with the Club for Growth?"

SPEAKER: "If you get primaried I can help."

MEMBER: "What are you going to do? Seventy percent of Republican voters think our Congressional leadership has let them down."

Three days on the job and he had a string of rejections. The newbies, like Aberdeen Francis, needed the speaker. But the longer you hung around the less the speaker could do for you. You had your committees. The chair appointed subcommittee chairs. If you had legislation the speaker could help. He might even raise you some money. But as time went by you needed the speaker less and less.

Something else had happened too. In the past, Republicans ran against Democrats to keep their jobs. Not so much anymore. After the 2010 elections, when Republicans were swept into power in governorships and legislatures all across the country, they redrew the district lines. Most Republican members had safe districts—at least safe against any Democrat. Their exposure was now on the right. And on the right there were piles of money and thousands of Tea Party zealots waiting to punish any Republican who did not toe the line.

Hazeldine got his whip, Fred Baines, on the line. "What's the count?"

"Joe, it's pretty tough," Frank replied. "I only got three votes."

"How many calls?"

"Nine."

"I picked up Francis. How many do we need?"

Baines gave him the number.

"Jesus fucking Christ."

CHAPTER
Nine

Sam Kelley was preparing to make his very first fundraising calls. He had been given a list. He looked over the names—carefully typed with short descriptions of each potential donor—the phone numbers, and the amounts he would request. It was eight pages long.

And Sam was very nervous.

He looked up at Ann Bell. "This Carl Pierson. I can't call him. He's a good friend."

Ann Bell had expected as much. Making these calls would not be Sam Kelley's cup of tea.

"What about the next name?"

"Mary Aaronson. How can I call her? I don't even know her."

But before Ann Bell could point out that his logic might leave the campaign with no donors at all, her cell phone rang. It was Marshall Kelley, Sam's nephew.

Marshall was a young man struggling to find his way. He had been hanging around the headquarters not so much because he wanted to work but because he had no job and nothing else to do. He had made it to one semester of college but not to the workplace, unless you count short-term gigs as a liquor store cashier and telemarketing Viagra for the Canadian Pharmacy. He recently had a DUI.

"Ann Bell, I've got a job interview. Can I borrow the campaign car?"

Ann Bell was uneasy. "I have to ask Sam. I'll get back to you."

She turned and looked at her boss. "Marshall wants to use the campaign car. He says he's got a job interview."

Sam perked up. He had worried about Marshall.

"That's great news. Absolutely."

Ann Bell was not so sure. "Sam, aren't there rules about taking a campaign car for personal use?"

Sam paused. "I know you are right and we need to be careful. But look at Marshall. His life is a mess. He needs a job. We have to help him. Let him have it for a couple of hours. Tell him he needs to have the car back at the headquarters by six."

CHAPTER
Ten

Neon, in the shape of the Capitol dome, blinked three times, and into the camera marched a man, smartly dressed, swarthy, and small. But when he opened his mouth he unleashed the voice of a giant.

"Welcome to—" he bellowed before he stopped and tilted forward, his hand cupped behind his ear. The audience knew their cue.

"Washington–Believe It or Not!"

His eyes twinkled with a mischievous glow as he seated himself behind an anchor desk, circular and red. A new episode of America's top-rated political talk show had begun.

"That's right! Welcome to *Washington–Believe It or Not!* I'm Damon Rodriquez, your host of the show that brings you insight and commentary on this week in our nation's capital city. And what is our topic this week?"

The camera cut to three commentators seated smugly in a row at the opposite side of the stage.

"Joe Hazeldine!!!" the three commentators shouted in unison.

"That's right, America's newest power broker, House Speaker Joe Hazeldine, failed to get his budget through the Republican House caucus and sources tell us the vote was not even close.

"Our guests tonight are Robby Santino, former campaign manager for President Marino, Suzie Glint, former head of media at the National Republican

Congressional Committee, and Spud Stevens, founder of *Superspin*, a hot new political blog. Suzie, you are close to these Republicans. Here is my first question: Is Joe Hazeldine dead?"

"Not dead but in intensive care, that's for sure," Suzie responded, trying not to smirk.

"How did that happen?" Rodriquez asked, exaggerating his incredulity for effect.

"Well, I don't know, Joe. He's a little headstrong and he just misread the caucus. He wanted to keep the government open. The conservatives wanted a fight. He's the speaker and he just came up short on the votes."

"Short?" Robby, the Democrat, interrupted. "He couldn't have won if he had voted Arlington Cemetery."

"The Freedom Caucus spanked him," Spud exclaimed. "Ouch, ouch, ouch!"

Robby continued, "Listen, he was in a fix. Every time the Republicans shut down the government they lose, but they either have no memory or no self-control."

"Lemmings!" Spud added, a little too gleefully.

"But you know there was something more important here. Forget about the government. That's the side issue. He's the new speaker and he has to prove he's in control. Shut down or not, you can't afford to be on the losing side. You lose a fight like this one and you're toast."

"Blackened toast—unbuttered!" Spud added with a self-congratulatory smile.

"I think it was all pretty predictable," Suzie added with a sigh, looking like she had just been told about the passing of a not-so-favorite aunt. "The Republicans are so divided. Hazeldine was the best we could get. And it's already clear he is not up for the job."

The camera cut to Damon Rodriquez. "But what about the government? Are federal employees headed home?"

"Yes," Suzie said.

"Yes," Robby agreed, sadly.

"Yes!" Spud shouted.

"Next question," Rodriquez said. "How long will the shutdown continue?"

"Two weeks?" Robby suggested.

"Two years!" Spud responded.

Suzie chimed in, "These Tea Party folks are pretty serious. It could be a long time."

"And will there be a default?" Rodriquez leaned in expectantly.

The panelists exchanged nervous glances.

"Of course not," said Suzie without an ounce of conviction.

"Okay, panel, here is the last question. How many days does Joe Hazeldine have left?"

"I give him two weeks!" Bobby shouted, savoring the misery of an opponent.

"I give him two days!" Spud announced. "Who needs this guy anyway?"

"Don't be so sure," Suzie answered. "I just don't know who else we've got."

CHAPTER
Eleven

"Ann Bell, this call's for you. It's the police."

She grabbed the phone.

"This is Ann Bell, campaign manager for Sam Kelley. How can I help you?"

"Ms. Bell, this is Officer Stan Brown with the Nashville Police Department. A vehicle leased by your campaign has been in an accident."

"Oh my—is anyone hurt?"

"The driver of your car, Marshall Kelley, is fine, for the most part, but the other driver, Susan Weidman, has a broken leg."

"What happened?"

"Mr. Kelley swerved out of his lane. You should know. We put a breathalyzer on him. He is pretty drunk."

CHAPTER
Twelve

The room bubbled with tension. The vice presidents of Miradol—the significant ones at least—were all present. So was a small army of consultants for marketing, production, research, and, of course, government relations as well. It was a room full of thousand-dollar suits and ten-cent smiles.

There was good reason to be nervous. The FDA had taken an unusually long time to review Juventel and its decision was overdue. The agency had a lot of questions about chemistry and how Juventel actually attacked Recipothosis. They were good questions and Miradol had no good answers—at least none they could share. Aging advanced Recipothosis. Juventel attacked aging. But that was an argument they could not proffer.

Rumors flew around the company. Did the FDA know they had an off-label plan? No one was sure what to expect and Keegan had called this meeting, on short notice, at the end of the day. She cleared her throat and silenced the room.

"As you know," she began, "we have been waiting for FDA approval of Juventel. As you also know, it has taken a long time. There has never been a new product whose potential even remotely approaches the market for this drug. Juventel could surpass the sales of today's top five pharmaceuticals combined." She took a deep breath, her face grim, her eyes touched with despair. "I heard from FDA this morning and have an announcement to make."

It was all theater. Total theater.

POP!!!! A champagne cork sailed across the room.

The door flung open and a uniformed waiter entered the room pushing a silver cart holding more bottles than even this crowd could consume. The theme song from *Chariots of the Gods* echoed off the walls. The room exploded in a great cheer.

"Marketing? Are you ready?" Keegan shouted, throwing her hands in the air.

"Yes!" the entire team shouted back with more exuberance than they'd felt in years.

"Manufacturing? Are you ready?" The by-now-giddy CEO turned to another sector, crouching toward the group.

"Yes!"

"Well, enjoy this celebration because tomorrow we are going to transform this company, transform this industry, and transform the life span of humankind!" Keegan shouted as again she raised her champagne flute.

She paused. Silence fell.

"And also make more goddamned money than any of you ever imagined!" Her smile was broader than anyone in the room had ever seen it.

Another great cheer, a bigger cheer, filled the room.

They were ready. Colleen Keegan was about to change the world.

CHAPTER
Thirteen

The Sam Kelley Road Show pulled into Summertown, Tennessee, an unincorporated town of less than a thousand on Highway 20, about an hour south of Nashville. This evening Sam was scheduled to hold his first town hall meeting in at least twenty years. He was not big on this kind of constituent contact. He had talked with colleagues who did these meetings and the feedback was always bad. A lot of the questions were poorly informed. The people who showed up were almost always senior citizens with nothing else better to do. Mostly, they just liked to complain.

His staff had chosen Summertown to give Sam some practice. It was a strong Republican precinct. It was in the new part of the district, so this was his chance to introduce himself to people he had never met. His office had mailed three thousand postcards inviting voters to come to the Summertown Baptist Church and visit with Sam. The church was a new building with a tall steeple, at least for this tiny town, and gables that came to a sharp point. It could hold 150 people.

Sam was accompanied by his campaign manager, Ann Bell, and a district office staffer who would handle the follow-up tasks. When Sam arrived, only seventeen people were waiting. He noticed that one of them had a Tea Party announcement in his hand. Of the seventeen, all where elderly except for one young man who stood nervously in the back with a video camera.

Sam strode energetically to the front. He may have been seventy-eight but he still had spark in his step. "Greetings," he said with a smile. "It's a pleasure to be here in Summertown, introduce myself, and answer your questions."

Ann Bell had suggested that since he was new to these voters, he might begin by telling a little about himself. He rattled through a three-minute description of his life, but before he could finish an older women, heavy with white uncombed hair, raised her hand. She wore a dark frumpy sweater decorated with lint and a silver cross. "Congressman," she began, "that's all fine and good, but we came here with questions."

"Go right ahead." Sam smiled patiently and nodded.

"I am having a pretty serious problem. I got this prescription and it is all covered by Medicare and all but I have to drive twelve point five miles to get to a pharmacy and they still can't get it right. Who do I call to do something about it?"

"Well," Sam said after a pause, "I believe you have to talk to the pharmacy about that."

The woman glared back at Sam.

Ann Bell spoke up. "I bet if you called somebody in the regional office in charge of that pharmacy, they would get all this straightened out." She turned to the congressional staffer, who was clearly not happy to be spending her evening in Summertown, and said, "Beth, would you get the name of an executive who would be in charge of this local store? I bet they would want to put a stop to all this right away."

"Sure thing," Beth replied slowly as she made an overexaggerated effort to find her pad.

Sam looked at Ann Bell, impressed.

Two hands in the air. Sam called on the woman holding the Tea Party leaflet.

"Congressman, you're a Republican, right?"

"I am," Sam replied proudly.

"What is your position on shutting down the government to make them cut spending?"

"I am against it."

"Well, that don't sound so Republican to me."

Sam launched into a speech about budgets and interest rates and the difficulty of solving anything because of the small percentage of money that was not entitlements and that only thirty percent was discretionary and that of the discretionary spending a big part was the military and on and on and on. As he spoke, the woman who asked the question turned her head and looked out the window. After what seemed like ten minutes, Sam wrapped up. Two attendees had already left.

"Have I answered your question?" Sam asked hopefully.

"You sure have," she replied, a look of disgust on her face.

Then came a question about Social Security and problems getting a check. Beth added a call to the Social Security Administration to that unpleasant follow-up list.

Someone asked about dog seizures. Apparently, research labs were buying dogs from city pounds and using them for medical experiments. They paid money and bought only dogs that would have been euthanized anyway, but the People for the Ethical Treatment of Animals called these transactions "seizures."

"That is not in my committee," Sam answered as if it were the most logical response possible. The participants looked at one another in varying states of befuddlement.

One constituent asked if Sam was too old to be in Congress.

"I may be seventy-eight years old but I am proud of the things I still can do. I can't run anymore. My knees don't hold up and sometimes I have to walk slowly. But most days I walk at least two miles. My mind is still sharp. Every now and then I have a senior moment, but I can still make a speech on the floor of the House without notes. I chair a committee. I am part of the leadership of Congress and proud of it. There is no way a rookie can do more for you than me."

In the back of the room, the young man turned off his camera and exited the room.

CHAPTER
Fourteen

As Speaker Hazeldine entered his office, Beau Jefferson, his chief of staff, hurried to his side.

"Not a great weekend," Beau whispered in a playful tone. "Spud Stevens, on *Washington–Believe It or Not!*, says you have two days left. Better enjoy them while you can."

"I saw. How much vacation time have I accumulated?"

"Well, you've had this job five days. Maybe forty-five minutes. Joe, you shouldn't watch these shows. Let me do a Monday morning summary. Easier."

"Don't worry," the speaker answered. "I don't stay up at night worrying about Spud Stevens."

But the truth was that Joe Hazeldine was barely sleeping at all. He was mad. It wasn't Spud Stevens or any of those guys who made their living taking pot shots at guys like him. He was furious with Earl Ackerman. And he was angry at all those Tea Party mad hatters who thought their job was to stay pure and throw rocks at the people who cared about the legislation they were actually sent here to pass.

Most of all, though, he was mad at himself. He hated to lose. HATED it. Now he had not just lost. He had been humiliated and left as fodder for commentators who entertained the ignorant with opinions barely informed by knowledge or facts. Joe Hazeldine was, in fact, so pissed that he committed an act that was fast becoming a serious sin.

He picked up the phone and called a Democrat.

"Amos, this is Joe Hazeldine. Do you have a few minutes to bless me with your wisdom?"

Amos Tedford laughed out loud. Six years earlier, Tedford had stepped down as speaker of the House. His ten-year tenure was celebrated as one of the most successful in the history of the House. He had helped add prescription drug coverage to Medicare. He had helped enact, over the Republican president's veto threat, far-reaching environmental legislation. He was the master of divided government, almost always getting the best of the Administration in the never-ending debates about spending and budgets. In the world of House leadership, Amos Tedford was the gold standard to which every speaker aspired.

"Now Joe, if I give you advice, you aren't going to use it to undo all those good things I accomplished when I had your job, are you?"

Joe could feel Amos' smile at the other end of the line. "Amos, all I am trying to do is keep our government open. I have some caucus members with ideas that nobody talked about in your day."

"Indeed, you do. And watching all this makes me fear for our republic."

"Well, I need votes to end this shutdown and get us out of this mess. I have been on the phone, in their offices, and they nod and give me lots of sympathy but not any damned votes. Amos, right now I am a short-term failure and I have to do better. The country depends on it. You persuaded more votes than Sam Rayburn and Joe Cannon combined," he said, invoking the legendary congressmen so honored that the current House buildings were named after them. "Help me out. What worked for you?"

"What worked for me won't help you at all. You know how it is. You have people against you. You have people for you. In the middle, you have people who might have opinions but those opinions can be shifted with the right motivation. You give them a bridge with their name on it, a research center in their district, or a big grant to the local university. But those earmarks are gone. You can't bribe them anymore. In terms of actually getting things passed and serving the larger good, it's just about the damnedest shame that ever hit our democracy.

"Then there's money. I used to have all the money. They needed campaign money and they came to me on their knees. But now they passed laws that say a candidate can only take $5,000 and the party can't take much more and then the Supreme Court gets in the middle of all this and now you can set up a Super PAC that takes checks written by Exxon and Microsoft and God knows who else and suddenly the speaker's money looks like the Jerry's Kids coin box on the counter at the 7-Eleven."

"I know," Hazeldine sighed wearily. "Now they're a lot more afraid of the Club for Growth than they are of me."

"That's right. There are laws of politics just like there are laws of physics. If you want to get a majority you don't stand there on the far right, reciting the gospel, and expect the rest of creation to come running to confess their sins. You find the middle ground and you pull from both sides. It is the eternal method. But you damned Republicans have fucked this all up." Tedford added, "Pardon my French."

"It's okay, Amos. French is my first language."

"You drew all these districts where a Democrat doesn't stand a chance. So your guys don't have to worry about the moderates. Now they fear some Tea Party idiot and a million dollars of negative ads. You want someone's vote? Ask this question: What is the member's worst nightmare? It's not a Democrat anymore. It's those Tea Party crazies sending some kamikaze with a full tank of gas."

"Amos, tell me something I don't know."

"Look, there are three ways to get a vote. The first one is reason, to explain why they should do the right thing. Joe, you are learning that that method ranks a poor third. The second is love. You can get them a building with their name on it or a big grant to the university where they studied. But it is hard to give love these days. All you have left is fear, and it's getting pretty hard to muster."

"Those goddamned reformers have taken our power away," Amos Tedford continued, really on a roll now. "We used to have private meetings in these committees. The members could speak frankly, think outside the box, negotiate, and work out a deal—long before votes were ever taken. Now the whole damn press corps can attend. Have you ever met a politician who can stand in front of a camera without acting like an ass?"

"Not many," Hazeldine laughed, but Tedford was getting mad.

"And the junkets—those boondoggles or 'vacations of sin.' Those junkets were the only time Democrats and Republican ever got together in social situations, to talk, get to know each other, and actually let their guards down. They're gone. Now, no one talks at all.

"All these reformers don't understand a thing about government. They are so afraid we might do something bad that they took away our ability to do good. And who got the power we used to have? The predators. The Super PACs. The billion-dollar multinationals. The ideologues on the left and right. These groups don't give a goddamn about legislation that might help somebody. Just a bunch of greedy bastards who want money they don't deserve or, even worse, are on a jihad to punish the infidels."

"So, Amos, what are you telling me?" Joe interjected when Tedford took a breath.

"Being speaker is a whole lot harder these days and I don't envy your situation. You can't bribe them anymore because you've got nothing to give. Fear is all you've got and there's not much to be scared of anymore. My advice is to pull out all the stops. Threaten. Punish. Use what little power you have left. And when you have no power, bluff. We're in a mess. We need a different kind of speaker these days, and to succeed you need to be one tough, mean, courageous sonofabitch."

CHAPTER
Fifteen

Ann Bell had signed up for an education. She was back in Washington attending a four-day campaign management training conducted by the Leadership Institute, an organization that told Republican candidates and staff how campaigns ought to be run.

The first day had three topics—opposition research (that always comes first), developing a message, and cutting through the media clutter.

Under research, she learned all the amazing things that you could find out about a candidate—payment of taxes, real estate values, criminal records, marriages and divorces, traffic tickets, and, of course, every vote on every issue in every office any candidate had ever held. They reviewed a sample "opp research report" listing every sin and suspected sin the poor candidate had ever committed. It was 110 pages long.

Well, at least now she knew what a research firm did.

Research was complicated. Messaging was simple. "Find the sentence, the one sentence that summarizes why the voter should choose your candidate. Build all of your messaging around that sentence." She tried to think about Sam's sentence. "He has experience." Well, not really since no one is very happy with the experience in Washington these days.

"He has led the work to bring lifesaving drugs to the market." Since Americans pay five times what other countries pay for the same drugs, that might not be the right track.

"He is for free enterprise, small government, and low taxes." Maybe, but generic.

In "Cutting Through the Clutter" the political operatives posed the question another way. "What is the one thing you can say about your candidate that is different from all other candidates?"

Well, that one was easy for Ann Bell. Sam Kelley was honest, smart, and a really good human being. But how do you show that in a thirty-second ad?

The second day of the seminar was about targeting. What an eye-opener! The data geeks had gone wild. There was a list of all voters, and beside each name was a list of probabilities. The probability that the voter was a Democrat. The probability that the voter was a Republican. The probability that a voter was a conservative or a liberal. The probability that a voter believes in climate change. That probability that a voter thinks gay marriage is just fine or that transgenders need separate bathrooms. The probability that a voter will vote early. The probability that a voter will cast a ballot at all.

So if you want to persuade voters, you target probable independents who have a high probability of voting. If you want to turn out voters, you target people who are likely to be Republicans but are less likely to vote.

They were talking about issue targeting when she tentatively raised her hand. "If we want to target voters who care about Medicare, why don't we just target the older ones?" she asked. The instructor did not think much of Ann Bell's question, particularly because he made his money computing all these probabilities.

But all those numbers made her head hurt.

On the third day, they learned about the campaign plan. Each participant had to create "vote goals," how many votes they needed to win and where those votes were coming from: which counties, which ethnic groups, which genders, and on and on and on. Ann Bell wrote a budget, an early vote plan, an Election Day turnout plan, and a fundraising plan. She turned in her work and hoped they weren't giving grades. It was all so new and she really didn't feel confident she had any idea she knew what she was doing.

But today they were also talking science. Ann Bell liked science. Maybe this part would be fun.

The presenter was from a group called the Center for Strategic Initiatives. They measured things. If you wanted to know if your mailing actually got voters to the polls, you would mail some voters, not mail others, and after the election you could look at the turnout in each group. The voter list always showed whether or not you voted. If the voters in the group that got the mail turned out more than those in the group that didn't, your mailing probably worked. If they turned out a lot more, then your mailing definitely worked. Just like drug trials!

But when they explained what really worked, Ann Bell was shocked.

If you wanted to get Republican voters to the polls, she figured you sent them a mailing about free enterprise, lower taxes, and throwing lazy stiffs off welfare. Wrong! They showed an experiment. The classic Republican issue message increased turnout by 0.4 percentage points. Taking into account the cost of a mailing, that came to $95 per vote. Ouch!!

But if you sent voters a letter comparing how often they voted with how often their neighbors voted, that increased turnout by more than two percentage points. That cost per vote was less than $20.

She pointed out that her boss, Sam Kelley, would never send such a letter because whether or not someone voted was a private matter. Her instructor responded that it was indeed a public matter. You could look up anyone's voting record on the voter list. Besides, Sam did not have to send the mailing because the Republican Party would be sending it anyway.

The last day was about money. How to get big donations. How to get PAC money. How to do direct mail fundraising for small donors. The first thing she learned was that if the donors aren't complaining about how often you ask, then you are not asking enough. She learned that direct mail donors need "red meat"—heated conservative rhetoric and heavy use of the words "liberal" and "socialist" in describing your opponent. The instructors showed how to make successful phone calls to big donors so that the donor always felt like his contribution was the only thing standing between victory and defeat. "Make the donor the hero!" they chanted.

It was a lot of learn. She knew none of it. And the one thing that she'd learned for certain that final day was that what she really needed to know was how to get Sam to start making his fundraising calls.

CHAPTER
Sixteen

It was a blustery fall day in Washington, DC, and despite the weather Colleen Keegan was all smiles. She had hired a new lawyer.

Colleen Keegan hated lawyers. Just bring up the topic and she delivered her speech.

"I'm sick of these chickenshit lawyers who put themselves first. Give them a question and they think, *If I say 'yes' and it doesn't work out, then I get the blame. If I say 'no,' then I've got no exposure at all.* Where do you find a lawyer who will tell me what I can do?

"Nowhere!"

But she had, in fact, found that lawyer. His name was Jake Siskoff. Keegan's limo pulled up in front of the offices of Madigan, Stevens & Waggoner, where Siskoff worked. Siskoff had made his reputation working for Genovo, the largest pharmaceutical company in the world. He was a loyal guy and told Keegan repeatedly that he would never switch sides. "Never" lasted barely a week. Money talks. Siskoff was on Miradol's payroll now.

Unlike a lot of big-time Washington lawyers, Jake Siskoff had never tasted the silver spoon. He had never been spotted near an Ivy League school. His mom died when he was three. His dad was a bricklayer and a drunk who struggled to raise three kids in Reno, Nevada. The oldest, young Jake, worked part-time to support the family and helped raise his two sisters. He got his law degree at night school from the University of the Pacific in Sacramento. During the day he interned in the California legislature, where his talents caught the eye of a member of the Assembly named Flora Moscowitz. When Flora won her race for Congress, Jake was her first hire.

Washington was made for a someone like Jake Siskoff. He could read his friends and enemies alike. He knew knowledge lay not in what someone told you but in their silence, their unspoken purpose. He rose quickly to become chief of staff for House Speaker Amos Tedford. And when Madigan, Stevens & Waggoner offered him a fortune to join the firm, he told them that he did not like reading law books. They told him they did not care.

Keegan looked across the desk at Siskoff, hardly the image of a successful lobbyist. He was in his late fifties, with a full head of curly hair that was just beginning to gray. He was short with a thin frame, the kind of guy you would barely notice if you shared the back seat of a cab.

The meeting was about off-label marketing. The FDA had no authority to supervise or police prescriptions written by physicians. The doctors could do whatever they wanted and the practice was widespread. In fact, more than twenty percent of all physician prescriptions were written off label. Keegan planned to move that number higher—a lot higher.

To sell Juventel off label, she needed a strategy besides just social media. She needed the best damned marketing strategy that the industry had ever seen. But there were rules. Sometimes, those rules were loosely enforced but some people had actually gone to jail. That was why she was here on K Street in Washington, DC, to meet with the smartest lawyer in the business.

"Well, Colleen, you're looking well. And with Juventel in your pocket you ought to be. Congratulations are in order." Siskoff smiled his contagious smile, but Colleen Keegan did not respond. She was all business.

"Yes, this is a big one, but we have to get it right. You know why I am here. You're not one of those can't-do lawyers who say 'no' to protect themselves."

"They *are* a common breed." Siskoff touched his fingertips together as if to bless Keegan's belief.

"I'm not here to find out what I can't do. I am here to find out how to do what I want to do. We can sell five, ten times as much Juventel as any other drug that ever hit the market. But we can't wait for years of sales meetings where our reps spoon out their off-label pitches, ten docs at a time. Our market is every human being who is not in a hurry to die. I want to reach them fast."

"I understand all that," Siskoff responded. "And you know the obvious. You can pitch it to the doctors in person. You can get academic journals to publish your results. Are you measuring aging indexes, inflammation, thymus, telomere, and senescence for new customers right off the bat?"

"We don't need to. We ran all the measurements already in our Recipothosis trials. They are golden. They beat my expectations and I wasn't lowballing. Of course, we did not send that piece to the FDA."

"So you have that data already."

"Yes."

"Social media. We need to talk about that one."

"Forget it. We've figured that one out. I came here to talk about other vehicles."

Siskoff leaned back in his chair and his face glowed. He had waited for this moment. "So I have an idea," he said, "something completely new and innovative."

"I like that," she said, nodding.

"But first I want to confirm. You want a big launch, and a big launch is hard to do without TV ads. What if there was a way? Would you be willing to piss off the FDA?"

Keegan paused for a moment—a short moment. "Probably," she replied, slowly pronouncing each syllable.

"What else is in the pipeline? If they wanted to screw you, how much trouble could they make?"

"We've got three or four things coming up. Put them all together and they aren't ten percent of Juventel. Maybe not five."

"Then I have something for you to think about."

"Yes?" she cocked her head but could not hide the eagerness in her voice.

"The FDA operates under the Federal Food, Drug, and Cosmetic Act. That prohibits TV ads or any other advertising promoting off-label drug use. What would it be worth to be able to run those ads?"

"Billions. *A lot* of billions."

"I think there is a way to run those ads."

Colleen Keegan tilted her head to the side, her eyes squinting as she chewed her lip. For a moment, she looked hard at Siskoff, savoring the thought. "Well, Jake Siskoff," she finally said, "don't keep me in suspense."

"What if someone in Congress introduced a bill that amends the Federal Food, Drug, and Cosmetic Act to provide for the approved use of drugs addressing aging so long as the prescription has passed the stage one safety trials? It would skip stages two and three."

"That's ridiculous," she scoffed. "Congress would never do that. Sam Kelley— remember the guy who chairs the House subcommittee with oversight—would have a stroke! Give me a better idea."

"Wait a second, hear me out," Siskoff responded, his hands out in supplication. "You misunderstand the strategy. The strategy is not to pass the bill. You don't want that bill going anywhere. You want it to die a quiet and unnoticed death. But as long as there is active legislation before Congress, even if it does not have a single vote of support, you have a First Amendment right to promote that legislation." Siskoff paused for effect. "And that means you can run TV ads explaining how one pill a day can extend your life for five, ten, or twenty years."

Keegan blinked several times, speechless.

Siskoff, satisfied, continued. "You would have to mention the legislation but you can put it in the disclaimer at the bottom of the page, in fine type for a millisecond on the screen," Siskoff said excitedly before he realized he was getting carried away. "Well, maybe a little more than that. But there are no regs. No one has done this before. By the time they write the regs, you could put billions of dollars' worth of ads on the air. You could do direct marketing. You could do *anything*."

Keegan smiled broadly. "You are a fucking genius."

"Just trying to earn my keep," he said, leaning back.

"But the FDA will still be pissed. Really pissed."

"Sure, but they'll get over it—as long as the bill goes nowhere. Find the most incompetent member of the House. Raise him some money—not from your PAC or employees. You've got plenty of vendors. Then give him the bill. He gives it to the speaker; the speaker gives it to Kelley and it will die quicker than a crocodile chasing penguins across the South Pole."

"It's tempting."

"What's in the pipeline? You said ten percent?"

"Maybe five."

Siskoff looked at Keegan expectantly, his eyebrows raised. "In situations like this one there is a question you always have to ask. 'Who is fucking whom?' What is the price of FDA revenge? What is the profit on the table. The answer is in the math."

He was right, thought Keegan. But she needed to be careful. This was a big step. "You know, I just thought of something," Keegan offered. "Marvin Wellstone is leaving the FDA. If we do all this right after he leaves and before he's replaced…. Oh, the timing would be perfect. Okay, let me think about it."

Her words were cautious but her decision was already in her smile.

CHAPTER
Seventeen

"This is Mike Benjamin with KCLB talk radio. Billy Destin of Buckskin Joe, Colorado, you're on the air."

"Mike, I get up this morning and read about this new speaker we got. He's endorsed the president's budget. Here we are, in the middle of a government shutdown, with the Democrats' backs to the wall, and Joe Hazeldine is caving in already. Where did we get this guy?"

"I don't know, Billy, same place we got the rest of them if you ask me."

"Well, he's pretending it's *his* budget. Give me a break! What I hear is that it's so close to what the president wants. You'd need the entire staff of Price Waterhouse to explain the difference."

"You know the story, Billy. We elect these bozos to be Republicans. What do they do? They go off to Washington and sell us out!"

"Mike, when have we had a speaker who stood for honest Republican values— who had the backbone to punish those liberals who are taxing us to death, wrecking our economy, and sending transgender perverts into our bathrooms?! In my opinion, if the government shuts down and America defaults on its debt, it's the Democrats' fault. They're the ones running up big deficits and spending all that money."

"You nailed that one, Billy. In fact, I am so disgusted I'm gonna ask all our listeners out there all across these United States of America to send Mr. Joe Hazeldine a message. Go to our website at KCLB.com and click on the link that says "Send him a chicken." For six dollars and ninety-eight cents you can send Joe Hazeldine a yellow rubber chicken. Can you picture his face when he sees that chicken with his own name written right across the front?"

"Thanks, Mike. I am with you. I'm gonna to send him three!"

CHAPTER
Eighteen

Michael Brazier, media consultant to Sam Kelley, sat stiffly, leaning forward, his eyes glued to his laptop screen. Sidney Lund had just released his first ads. The first one opened with a dark shot of the US Capitol Building, ominous music, the voiceover deep and foreboding.

> "Government shutdowns. Name calling. Partisan disarray. Prescription drug prices spiraling out of control. Sam Kelley, thirty-six years in Congress and what has he done?"

Exorcist music fades out. New music, so upbeat, cheerful, and bright you expect at any moment to be looking up Mary Poppins' dress. While the sound lifts your spirits, the video shows Lund speaking to a meeting, energetic, enthusiastic but without his voice. The narrator does the talking.

> "Sidney Lund. An innovator, a visionary, a business success. With Congress failing Tennessee, we need a change. We've had enough of the Washington old guard that is holding us back. New ideas, new leadership. Sidney Lund is the change we need."

Brazier noted that Lund did not speak in the spot. That meant he was still clumsy in front of the camera. He pulled up the second spot.

More *Exorcist* music. Kelley's face on screen, a still picture frozen, distorted. He was too old to be a sex offender but that photo raised the thought.

> "Is Sam Kelley too old to be in Congress?"

Cut to grainy video. Sam Kelley appears to be standing in front of an altar in a church. Camera zooms into his face, close, uncomfortably close. Sam speaks.

"Sometimes, I have to walk slowly."

Cut to another shot. Clearly edited. "They have Sam on tape," Brazier thought miserably. "And they are slicing out the worst parts." Sam spoke again.

"Sometimes I have a senior moment."

Christ, another cut. "These voters are so ignorant, they won't even know the tape was doctored. Who could complain?" Brazier had done it himself. Sam continued:

"I am part of the House leadership and proud of it."

That was the worst. He picked up the phone and dialed Sam Kelley's cell phone. "Sam, we have a problem."

CHAPTER
Nineteen

Joe Hazeldine walked into this office to meet with his leadership team. He studiously ignored the growing pile of miniature yellow chickens with his name emblazoned across their chests.

"I think Mike Benjamin doesn't like you," chirped his receptionist.

"He will have to stand in line," said Joe with a smirk. "How many have we gotten?" he said, nodding at the chicken pile.

"Probably six thousand. So far."

Spread out on chairs and couches in the speaker's office, the leadership team looked cautiously at one another. The speaker was running late and there was an ominous silence in the room. There was nothing good about their current situation. The government shutdown had now lasted twenty-two days. Now default loomed. In five days, unless a deal was struck, the United States government, for the first time in history, would default on its debt.

The speaker had spent the better part of the week negotiating a deal. With default looming, the terms had improved. The deal would never be good enough for Earl Ackerman and his Tea Party crowd, but it gave Republicans more than the last deal.

Our course, the deal was not even done when Earl Ackerman rejected it. He was on TV telling Americans that the number one problem facing America was $20 trillion in national debt. "If default is the only way to get the president to do something about it, then we are ready for default," he bellowed before reading a list of budget cuts he demanded the president adopt.

Joe Hazeldine made a deal with the president, whether Ackerman had bothered to look at it or not. There was a meeting tonight. Hazeldine would put the terms in front of the caucus and ask for their vote. Not one person sitting in his office believed he had a chance to win.

Hazeldine entered the room, his chin up and a smile pasted on his face. Trailing behind was Frank Buntz, a Republican pollster famous for his success in strategically naming their proposals. It was his idea to stop talking about inheritance taxes and start talking about death taxes. He had placed poisonous names on other Democratic proposals as well.

"Why the glum faces?" the speaker asked in a chipper voice. "Let's figure out how to win this fight." He turned to Lindsey Barker, his majority leader and Tea Party rep. "Lindsey, do we have a single vote in your caucus?"

"Well," she stammered, "I am in a tough spot on this one. Is default a disaster? That may be the majority view, but to our caucus it is our chance for a showdown we've wanted for a long time. There are not many votes for you there. She looked down. "Mine included," she added.

"Fine," the speaker said curtly. He knew her answer before he asked. He just wanted to make her say it. "Fred," he said, calling on his whip, Fred Baines. "What is your count?"

"It's a little better than last time. I still think we are twenty votes short. Joe, I am not sure where we are going to find those votes. It is looking really bad."

"We will find them. Can you get me a list to call?"

"We've called everyone in play."

"Well, let's call them again," Joe answered with a sly smile. "Team, I brought Frank Buntz here this afternoon. He's been doing some polling on our issue."

"I don't think a new poll is going to get you anywhere," Barker interjected. "There are a hundred polls out there. Everybody knows we are taking a hit. It's just that a lot of people think it is worth it."

The speaker shot her a stern look and then nodded to his pollster as if she had never said a word. Buntz was not the shiny, polished presenter. He was a little rumpled. His face pudgy with soft brown eyes. He cleared his throat and began his report. "I know there are a lot of polls out there but sometimes the results can vary depending on how you ask the question. Sometimes by a lot."

Buntz walked through the basics. People blamed Republicans for the shutdown. They were irritated about it but not quite angry. Then he asked about a default. On that issue, the temperature went up, that was for sure. Sixty-seven percent called the event a "very serious failure of leadership." Independents and Democrats blamed the Republican House. But among Republicans, not so much. Republican voters, those who vote in primaries, blamed the president.

But Buntz had done more than ask about default. Buntz had used a common technique called a "split sample." Half the voters polled were asked the basic question. The other half got a question using different language. One half of the interviews asked about default. The other half asked how voters would feel if "America declared bankruptcy." The results shocked the room.

If you were talking about bankruptcy, even Republican voters labeled it a failure of leadership. Blame? On this issue of bankruptcy Republican voters were unforgiving—even for their own Republican House.

Lindsey Barker rose from her chair. "Joe, you aren't going to use that word, are you?"

A look of concern spread over the speaker's face and hooded his eyes. "Lindsey, there is no telling how the Democrats will describe what we do. We have to be prepared. You tell Earl we respect his position. We just have to know what's in store."

. . .

The next day, 221 members of Congress crowded into the largest caucus room available. The whole nation awaited their vote. Mainstream commentators explained in mind-numbing detail the consequences of default. But at Fox News, Ackerman and his supporters were heroes ready to slay the dragon of big government and crippling debt.

The doors to the caucus room closed. Joe Hazeldine gaveled the meeting to order. "Fellow Republicans," he began. "We are engaged in a great debate that will define our party in the eyes of our nation. We have our differences. We all know that. But I believe that the consequences of default and the blame we would carry are too great a risk. On the other hand, Earl Ackerman and the

Freedom Caucus see an opportunity for a showdown on the very issues that matter most to our caucus, our party, and the future of our nation. So I want to take a minute to congratulate the gentleman from Idaho, Mr. Ackerman, for his perseverance, his courage, and his adherence to the principles we all hold dear." Hazeldine's eyes searched the room until he found his colleague. He smiled. "Can we have a moment of applause for my esteemed colleague?"

A round of polite applause followed as confused expressions and nervous glances danced across the room. The members came expecting a war. What was Hazeldine doing?

"As you know, I have spent the week negotiating with the president. We have a deal that will avoid default and reopen the government. It is long. More than two hundred pages. It would be wrong for me to ask for any member's vote before you have time to review the document.

"There is progress in this deal. There are cuts in entitlements. There are tax increases, I know, but less than the spending cuts we achieved. If this deal is not what we want there is movement our way. And this progress will enable us to avoid default and the unknown calamities that may follow.

"So at the back of the room there are copies for every member of our caucus. Take a copy, read it, and when you return tomorrow to cast your vote, follow your conscience and do what is right for America."

Hazeldine then called for adjournment. The meeting had lasted just six minutes. In silence, the members watched as their speaker walked down the aisle and out of the room.

Lindsey Jenkins smiled. The speaker had caved.

Fred Baines had only one word for what he had witnessed. "Disaster. This is going to be a fucking disaster."

. . .

Outside the caucus room, a crowd of reporters waited. Many reporters had not yet arrived, expecting that the meeting would take hours. Quietly, Hazeldine had arranged for a platform and microphone to address the throng. From those present, questions erupted, so many and all at once so no particular inquiry could actually be heard. Hazeldine stood at the podium, his hands raised to silence the crowd.

"The House Republican caucus has adjourned until tomorrow to give our members time to review the details of the deal negotiated with the president," he said. "There will be questions. There will be discussion. But I know this caucus. They are patriots who will always put the American people first. We have taken a stand. We have permitted a shutdown of the government to send the president an important message—that runaway debt and runaway spending cannot continue.

"Tomorrow members of this caucus will cast what may be the most important vote of their political careers. And I have a message for all Americans. There is no way House Republicans will vote to put America in bankruptcy."

CHAPTER
Twenty

Winter Brooks hung up the phone. The Government Affairs office at Miradol had called, and they had a strange request.

Brooks occupied one of the common, and lucrative, professions in Washington, DC. She was a consultant. Her job? She sat in on conference calls. And in her own words, she earned her $10,000-per-month fee by saying something smart once a month—or at least most months. She was smart. Her advice was solid. But she also had connections. Her clients included the Congressional Black Caucus, the American Medical Association, AARP, the Democratic National Committee, Apple, and, of course, Miradol. She was a matchmaker in a town that thrived on unlikely unions. The more clients she had, the more she was in demand. Getting rich today made you richer tomorrow.

Not bad for a girl who grew up six blocks from a crumbling downtown in a black neighborhood in Jackson, Mississippi. And she was not headed back to Mississippi anytime soon.

Miradol needed a bill introduced in Congress. Usually, you wanted a leader, a committee chair, or someone with real juice who could get your bill through committee and, more importantly, on the calendar. Miradol had a different idea.

"We don't want this bill to pass," she had been told. "Find a congressman with no influence, no respect, no initiative, and who misses votes. The Republicans are in charge so make sure he's a Democrat. Throw him a fundraiser. We'll find the donors. Give him the bill but don't introduce it. Wait until we give the word. Then quietly drop the bill in the hopper and never mention it again."

So she needed a loser and she knew a lot of them. The question was which one. This was a payday for somebody. And if Miradol was asking nothing in return, she could collect the payback for herself. She only had to think for a minute on that. She had a project in Houston she was putting together. She needed a favor from the mayor. She picked up the phone and dialed.

"Office of Congressman Josiah Rush," answered an unfailingly perky young woman. However annoying Brooks found her tone, she knew not to be fooled. She probably had a graduate degree of some kind, as did most people answering phones on Capitol Hill.

Dr. Rush, as he was called, was no physician. He was pastor of the Jesus Is King Holiness Baptist Church in inner-city Houston. His degree, which he acquired for a fee of $39.99, was enshrined in the "Doctorate of Divinity" certificate, framed and prominently displayed on the wall of his church office. He sat on the lowest committee in Congress, Small Business. His owned no business himself but he did regularly shake down Democratic campaigns for his Election Day "Get Out the Vote" campaigns. These undertakings netted a handsome profit, so much so that they might not qualify as "small business" at all.

"Yes, this is Winter Brooks. I am an old friend of the congressman. Is he available to talk at the moment?"

"I am sorry but the congressman is in conference. Can I leave a message and tell him what your call is about?"

"Tell him I want to host a fundraiser for his campaign fund."

"One moment, please."

Within twenty seconds the congressman was on the line.

"Winter, so great to hear from you again."

It had been a while since someone offered to do a fundraiser for Dr. Rush. He had a district that was ninety-nine percent African American and its map looked like the pictures artists make by hurling cans of paint against the wall. All those scattered dots were where African Americans lived. In this case the artists were Republicans legislators who drew a district that would keep black voters in one place and out of the other districts their candidates would win.

Ensconced in this citadel of gerrymandered art, Dr. Rush had not seen an opponent in years.

"I've been thinking about doing some fundraising. So nice of you to call."

"Well, I've got a client who wants to help you out," Winter said casually. "I will work with them to put together an event."

"Who is the client?"

"Miradol."

There was a pause as Dr. Rush considered why the third largest pharmaceutical company in the world was suddenly interested in his campaign.

"As the Bible says, 'A generous person will prosper; whoever refreshes others will be refreshed.' Would you mind telling me what refreshment I am expected to provide?"

Winter Brooks smiled. Josiah Rush may not have been one of the stars in Congress but he had style. "Dr. Rush, this is going to be the easiest money you will ever make."

"How much?"

"We are hoping to do six figures."

"Hope sustains our spirit but nourishment is held in hand."

"Okay, Congressman, $150,000. Not hope. My guarantee."

"And how do I express my thanks?"

"I need you to call the mayor about a project in the Third Ward. I need you on record."

"Done."

"And I need you to drop a bill."

"What kind of bill?"

"It will give our seniors access to a drug that will let them live longer, healthier lives. No controversies. No work. Just drop in in the hopper when we give the word. Then forget about it."

"Bless you, my dear. For the Lord has rained down bread from the heavens and the righteous shall feast."

"Just make the call, Doctor. We are all righteous in our own ways." She paused before ending the call. "Dr. Rush, one more thing. This bill you are going to introduce. I will give you a copy. This is important. Don't put it in the hopper until I give the word and then don't mention it again, ever. If you do, my client will be very, very disappointed."

CHAPTER
Twenty-One

"Good evening, I'm Rolf Sabato with *ABC World News Tonight*.

"In a stunning announcement, House Speaker Joe Hazeldine told Americans that the budget stalemate is over." Cut to Hazeldine.

Hazeldine: "There is no way House Republicans will vote to put America in bankruptcy."

At the White House, press spokesperson Rita O'Malley issued a statement thanking Speaker Hazeldine and praising House Republicans. "The terrible calamity of bankruptcy has been avoided."

The news feed returned to Sabato briefly: "For more of the story, let's go to ABC White House correspondent Miller Greenwood, with tonight's report:"

"Twenty-three days into one of the longest government shutdowns in American history, the standoff appears to have ended. With money running out and bills to pay, Speaker Hazeldine promised that bankruptcy was not an option.

"There are reports that some in the Republican caucus are unhappy with Hazeldine's statement, made in advance of the actual vote. Leaders of the Freedom Caucus have declined to be interviewed. According to one House insider who declined to be named, there are still 'bankruptcy boys' in the caucus but they no longer have the votes to reject the deal worked out with the president."

Wrapping his report, Miller Greenwood added Hazeldine's spin. "Good news, Rolf. *Bankruptcy* is a pretty scary word."

"America bankrupt?" the anchor responded. "It is hard to imagine."

. . .

Earl Ackerman muted the sound on his TV and glared at the now-silent talk-ing heads. "Bankruptcy boys!" he steamed. Ackerman was a Christian and avoided the profane. But his turn would come. He would have his chance to settle this score.

CHAPTER
Twenty-Two

Ann Bell dialed into the weekly conference call for the Kelley re-election campaign and announced herself more confidently than she felt at the moment. "This is Ann Bell for the Kelley campaign. Who do we have on the call? Polling?"

"Here."

"Media?"

"Here."

"Research?"

"Here."

"Direct mail?"

"Here."

Ann Bell then introduced three new staffers from the campaign: the press secretary, the field director, and the fundraiser.

Sally Benjamin, the NRCC staffer, interrupted. "Before we get into the agenda, I want to talk about the tracker ad."

"What is a tracker ad?" Ann Bell asked, sighing inwardly at yet another unfamiliar term from the campaign world.

"I am talking about that ad they took from video at Sam's town hall," Sally replied, her impatience barely contained. "The video shot by the tracker."

"Oh, there was a young guy standing at the back with the camera," Ann Bell said vaguely.

"Yes, he is what is called a 'tracker,'" Benjamin explained, now with unhidden scorn. "He was hired by the Lund campaign to video Sam's speeches. He shot the town hall meeting and they turned it into that ad. Sam looked like he was in his last three days on earth."

"Oh, that one," Ann Bell responded, her voice barely audible, as the group began discussing strategies to block the tracker's camera or eject him from the room in the future. But tracking was hard to stop. Throwing out the tracker always made a scene.

When the discussion ran out of suggestions, Ann Bell began, "Well, we are especially happy to have Jessica Munoz of the research firm Opp Slayer, which I'm sure everyone will be glad to know is under contract and has a report ready to present on this call. Jessica, you're up."

"Cool name," opined Sarah Whiteridge, the campaign pollster.

"Thanks, everybody, and it is great to be part of the team. My report has two parts. First, we need to share what we have found on Sidney Lund. Then we will go over the Kelley record and where we may be vulnerable. Any questions?" When no one responded Munoz continued. "Good. First, Lund. We did an investigation of Mr. Lund and we have the same problem we have with most opponents who have never held public office. He has no votes in Congress, no actions as a public official. From a policy point of view, he has done nothing. As we all know, that gives him a big advantage because we have nothing to attack. He has made a few speeches and said almost nothing. He supports Social Security, Medicare, and a clean environment. Basic Democratic pabulum."

The researcher paused for comments. Hearing none, she went on. "On the personal side, we found the following. Three years ago, he paid a penalty for failing to file his taxes on time. He had a speeding ticket last year. His company holds a patent that is under dispute but unresolved. He once did an interview for the internet magazine *Orb*, where he was quoted as saying 'politics is for bozos' and admitted to smoking marijuana in college. Marijuana was not his only college recreation. He has a DUI from those days as well."

There were a couple of understated murmurs on the call, but by and large this was not earth-shattering stuff.

"How long ago was that?" the direct mail guy asked.

"Eighteen years." Munoz continued her report. "Here is the personal information. He owns a $5 million home in Briarwood. No mortgage. He pays his property taxes, hasn't had a date in three weeks, owns a dog—a pug named Appleton—and his company has a market capitalization of $746 million. The company, Pfinder.com, has had three sex discrimination lawsuits in the past two years, one of which settled on undisclosed terms. The other two are pending. We are chasing the information. All in all, we don't have much to work with. Obviously, we would like to go negative on this guy but there is not much there."

"We *have* to look harder," interjected Whiteridge, reiterating her rule that all campaigns are won with negative ads.

"We will," Jessica responded calmly. "We are just getting started. But let's move on to Sam Kelley because, obviously, we wanted to see where we might get hit. As you know, Lund was late filing taxes—once. Unfortunately, Sam has been late four times."

"Pearl does all the taxes," Ann Bell added, as if that would bar Lund from using that attack.

"Well, I might add," said Jessica, "that Pearl has three speeding tickets herself in the last two years. But look, we all know Sam," Jessica continued, her voice softer now. "He might get behind keeping up with administrative matters but his personal stuff is clean. Our problem is that Sam actually has a record." She pronounced the last word slowly as if it were some fatal disease. "Sam has a long list of votes we are certain to hear about. A few examples," she said, and everyone on the call could hear her flipping through her notes.

"He voted to put Social Security on the stock market and against cutting the cost of student loans. He supported reducing the rights of private citizens to sue big corporations, raised credit card interest rates, and, worst of all, has a long record of votes that have led to higher prescription drug prices. That list is just the start. Ann Bell, I know all these votes were complicated, but that is how Lund will characterize them in his ads." She paused to let that sink in. "Oh, and seventy percent of his money is from the prescription drug companies."

"That's because we haven't started raising money," Ann Bell responded, a little panic in her voice. "They send the money without being asked!"

"Well, let's sum it up. We have all seen this story before. An incumbent who is in the middle of all sorts of policy fights. A business guy with no record and nothing to criticize. The business guy goes negative. Spends lots of money. The incumbent is on the defensive with no counterattack in sight. Not a good situation."

"Keep digging," Sarah Whiteridge ordered.

"We sure as hell will."

Michael Barbier, the media consultant, changed the topic. "Ann Bell, we need to work on these town meetings. Let's make a list of possible questions he's likely to get hit with. Give him some practice. He can go on too long sometimes."

"That's true," she said, sharing Brazier's frustration.

"Let me come down for one of those meetings," Barbier continued. "He's going to be filmed. We have to be very careful."

CHAPTER
Twenty-Three

Jason Stockard was a fundraiser extraordinaire. His clients included Americans for a Pristine Earth, The Right to Choose Foundation, the Democratic Senatorial Campaign Committee, and Seniors United. On this night, however, he was not at his computer crafting a brilliant fundraising appeal. Jason Stockard sat in a hotel room in Houston, Texas, flipping through the channels. He was looking for the local news. One of his clients, The Heart Foundation of Greater Texas, was holding its annual fundraiser—the non-dinner. It was his idea and it was a big success.

Stockard sent an invitation to the non-dinner to large donors, the kind who attend a lot of fundraising events. The invitations said, "Finally, a fundraising event you do NOT have to attend." The invitation struck a chord with donors who were tired of these evenings full of dreary speeches and liquor you still had to pay extra for after coughing up $1,000 plus per plate. Their non-dinner invitation featured a long list of famous celebrities who WOULDN'T be attending.

Last year, Stockard's idea won a "Genius Award" at a cheesy ceremony of the Washington Society of Fundraising Professionals. Now he was in Houston for the second annual non-dinner, training the callers who would be wrangling donors. Their message? The donors did not have to attend but they added a faint suggestion that the permission would cost them some money.

Word was that a local news show was running a story on his event. Unfortunately, this was hotel TV and the channels were in no logical order. Click, click. His large frame spread across the bed, the remote pointed like a taser. He was overweight, and his thinning black hair clung closely to his scalp.

He fired the remote, again and again. *Dammit, who decided we needed 200 channels?*

The phone rang. A call from the office. Nothing big but when he turned back to the TV something caught his eye. A portly African American pastor with a thundering voice was telling his congregation they could live to be one hundred years old. Behind him stood a choir, resplendent in satin robes of orange and silver and at least two hundred strong.

"I am here to tell you," bellowed the pastor, "that our generation has been blessed by God. For millions of years, the fate of humankind has been the same. We rise from a single cell blessed by the Almighty. We grow into the full glory of adulthood. But in our later years, we weaken; our memories fade and we decline until the Lord Almighty summons us home.

"I am announcing today that there is a remedy, a prescription drug, that can extend our lives twenty, thirty, even fifty years. And I have introduced legislation in Congress to make that drug available to each and every person in this room, and to have this miracle covered by Medicare as well."

At this point the congregation shouted "Hallelujah!" And the choir lifted their voices to Heaven, singing, "I am fully saved today—all my guilt is washed away."

The camera returned to the pastor, whose name appeared on the screen. "The Right Reverend Dr. Josiah Rush."

"Holy shit," thought Stockard. He scribbled the name and called his Washington office.

CHAPTER
Twenty-Four

Casey Jacobs could feel the cold seeping into the skywalk. Outside, snowflakes pummeled the ground. He had just spent fifteen hours on an airplane, and, as he tried to clear his head, he remembered his wife's parting words: "February is no time to visit Moscow."

He checked his watch, blinking the sleep from in his eyes several times before he could focus and read that it was 10 a.m. Moscow was eleven hours ahead of West Coast time in the US, and his day was already flipped upside down. He retrieved his lone bag and searched the hordes of travelers for his driver. With some relief, he located a large, burly man who would not look out of place as an enforcer for the Russian mob. He held a sign that read "MISTER CASEY JACOBS."

Casey smiled wanly. His meeting was two hours away and he was already more than a little nervous. Modern Russia had mastered the dark side of the internet, and he held with the view that on some level, when you looked into the abyss, the abyss looks back into you. Social media had become a weapon of domestic control and international power. Want to tell the world Vladimir Putin is a corrupt and unscrupulous snake? Thousands of paid trolls move into action. They reply to your posts with testimonials about the wondrous accomplishment of Russia's beloved leader. They question your motives and level personal accusations your way.

That is the simple stuff. These trolls owned sites. News sites. Social sites. Topical sites. Many trolls owned a mini-publishing empire. Most of the content on these sites was legitimate. But they posted fake stories as well. A fake story was often picked up by legitimate reporters, lazy journalists who did not check their facts or sources. When that happens the click farm goes to work.

A click farm is a room or a floor or a building full of clickers. Once the fake story is on a legitimate site, these "clickers" search for the story and click. The clicks drive the story up the Google ranking. Soon a story saying that Juventel gives you ten years of extra life is near the top of the lists for "longer life," "delay aging," "aging science," and other terms. Suddenly, millions of internet users are encountering—and sharing—the story.

Then there are private Facebook groups. A troll might open a group that offers access by invitation only. He sets up a fake LinkedIn page so people check his credentials. He went to Harvard and works for a top hospital. Then he invites biologists, physicians, professors, and other professionals to the group. Again, most content is legitimate. But when a manufactured story hits a reputable news site, it hits the group.

The techniques are many. The scale is enormous. The Kremlin itself employs tens of thousands of these trolls in warehouses and office buildings in suburban Moscow and St. Petersburg. They are manned by smart, educated employees, fluent in many languages. Other authoritarian regimes use social media as well.

In China, the Womao, or government-employed trolls, have been estimated to number as many as one hundred thousand. They perform what is referred to as "public opinion guidance management." By one estimate they produce almost a half billion fake social media posts per year. But the Womao has proven difficult to control. They often criticize government officials. These trolls have become a powerful, and feared, force in government and across Chinese society.

For Miradol's current purposes, however, overseas social media was perfect. The pharmaceutical company had paid Casey Jacobs a huge severance bonus. He then took the money to Russia. The Russian transaction was secret. No SEC filings. No public reporting of any kind. You pay the Russians for the service. The service is delivered five thousand miles away. Trolls, bots, private blog networks…who knows where they are from? No one sees the service at all. The public sees the posts. They see the fake news. They never see the thousands of crowded cubicles that produce them.

Colleen Keegan held in her hands the opportunity of a lifetime. She was not above bending the rules to seize her chance.

His driver dropped Casey at his hotel and waited out front while he checked in, showered, and changed. An hour later, Casey arrived at a nondescript, four-story office building located in a suburb twenty-five minutes from central Moscow. A troll factory.

The driver parked and keyed Casey into the building and then into to a modest-sized office on the fourth floor. There were locked doors and a visible security presence throughout the facility. On the fourth floor, Casey was met by Yuri Kuznetsov, the president of a company whose name, loosely translated, was "World Chatter."

"Mr. Jacobs, so nice to meet you," Yuri Kuznetsov said in English, with a heavy Russian accent. His handshake was crushingly firm and Casey could not help but think that he would not be out of place as a Bond villain.

He forced himself to smile and returned the handshake as firmly as he could, determined not to wince. "Call me Casey. A pleasure to meet you as well."

"I have been briefed on your project. Very interesting. Perhaps I can acquire some of these pills for myself."

Casey wasn't sure if that was a joke or not considering the fact that Yuri looked to be about twenty-eight, so he just smiled and said, "I am sure that can be arranged. But first I want to understand who I am dealing with. Is this company an arm of the Russian government?"

Kuznetsov smiled. "We were but not so much anymore. This facility was a government facility but we have, how do you say, spun off? There is a commercial market for this work. We no longer work for the government."

"But who owns this business?"

"I am not at liberty to say." Kuznetsov smiled again but it didn't quite reach his eyes.

"I think I need to know," Casey said over the lump in his throat.

"We are privately owned. That is all I can say."

Casey stared hard at Kuznetsov for a moment, weighing his options. He decided he wasn't going to win this round. "Okay, so I read your proposal. Very interesting. Why don't you walk me through how all this works?"

"We have at this facility almost a thousand employees—'trolls,' I think you call them. They spend their twelve-hour days on the internet impersonating American and foreign citizens, providing testimonials for your product, promoting manufactured news, and countering those who criticize it. Do you have political targets?"

"No. All we want to do is tell people that Juventel is making them younger and they need to talk to their doctor to get it."

Kuznetsov gave Casey a quizzical look but continued. "We also use bots—automatic programs that patrol the internet for any Twitter mention of Juventel. The bot reads "Juventel" and it has an automatic answer. One bot says, 'I used Juventel and feel twenty years younger.' Another says, 'I started Juventel five months ago and my arthritis is almost gone.' Another might say, 'My mother has memory problems. We started her on Juventel. Now she recognizes her family again.'"

Jacobs cringed. "I need to approve the bot messages. We want clean, accurate information. Understand?"

"Are you sure you have no targets?" Kuznetsov was incredulous.

"No, I don't think we want to go after anyone. We just want to sell the drugs."

"That is easy enough. Although some of my employees will be disappointed. Some of them like the dirty stuff." He shrugged. "Much more creative."

"I want it clean," Casey said emphatically. "We want to launch in thirty days. I want to stay and watch the training. We want to get this right. What kind of supervision do you use?"

"We give them the big picture. We train them on the product. Then we let them go."

"Is that enough?"

"You can't control everyone. Sometimes they have a little fun. Trust me, it is enough. If one or two get out of line the internet is a huge place. Who will notice at all?"

Casey felt a slight wave of nausea brewing in the pit of his stomach but continued. "One more question."

"Yes?"

"What other American companies are you helping?"

"Our client list is absolutely secret. No one can know."

"That is the answer I wanted to hear. So what are my purchase options?"

"To put five hundred employees on the internet for the next three months will cost you $4 million. To put a thousand to work will cost $7 million. Which do you want?"

"That is not enough. $12 million. Give me all that $12 million will buy."

CHAPTER
Twenty-Five

"Mirabelle, you will not believe what I just learned," Jason Stockard, fundraiser extraordinaire, said, his tone not one bit immodest.

"It better be good," she answered, desperate for good news these days. Mirabelle Jenkins wore a haggard look on her still young face. Despite being less than forty years old, she was the president of Seniors United for a Guaranteed Retirement, the largest senior citizen organization in the world. At least until this year. In the past twelve months, its membership had collapsed.

What caused all those members to leave? There was a surprising answer. Success.

You see, if you live in Washington and are advocating to solve a problem—to clean up toxic waste, save unborn babies, or give same-sex betrothed couples the right to buy a wedding cake from the baker of their choice—you can make a lot of money.

First, you rent lists of donors who gave to similar causes. Then you send them letters and tell them that their $50 contribution is all that is necessary to erase this problem and restore justice to all humankind. Then, magically, return envelopes filled with checks arrive at your post office box. You count the money, build your membership list, and make a damned good living working for solutions to the problem you raised. But there is one mistake you cannot make.

You can't actually solve the problem.

For professional fundraisers, who also make good money writing these letters, there is a saying. "Nothing fails like success."

When the Supreme Court was considering overturning *Roe v. Wade*, money flowed so fast to Planned Parenthood that they barely had time to count it all. When, in 1992, the Court reaffirmed *Roe v. Wade*, their donors breathed a sigh of relief and Planned Parenthood's income fell by half.

Unfortunately, the Seniors United for Guaranteed Retirement had made the mistake of solving their problem. Baby boomers had finally become seniors and there were a LOT of them. Through a cleverly orchestrated campaign, Seniors United and other related groups had passed a new law that provided automatic tax increases in the event Social Security funds ran low.

Republicans hated it. They were never so fond of Social Security anyway, but tax increases ranked right down there with soliciting children or murdering your own dog. But for the Democrats it was political gold. Sure, young people would be screwed. But they didn't vote anyway. If you were seventy-five years old, you were eighty-five percent likely to vote on Election Day. If you were twenty-five you had a better chance of showing up in traffic court than arriving at the polls.

So, of course, the bill passed. Social Security was safe. Those seniors didn't need Seniors United anymore. Now, Mirabelle Jenkins was cutting staff, flying coach, and dodging the calls from her landlord, who wondered when the hell he was getting paid. If she did not find a new problem, she would be applying for food stamps and drinking $10 wine.

As a result, Mirabelle was not disappointed to receive a call from Jason Stockard, her small donor fundraising consultant. Hopefully he would provide her with some way to put out this five-alarm fire.

"Get this," Stockard began. "I have been doing some research—serious research. There is a bill in Congress and it's about aging. It seems that one of the pharmas has a drug that they believe can delay aging. They put a bill in the hopper to allow seniors to take any drug addressing aging as long as it passes the FDA safety trial—even before FDA approval."

"Who is behind all this?" Mirabelle asked, thinking to herself how improbable this all sounded.

"Well, I'm not entirely sure. It was introduced by Josiah Rush. He's just a do-nothing congressman, a preacher from Houston. Not on Energy and Commerce where the bill would have to move. Not a player. Not at all. So I called a few of my doctor friends to find out what's new. Miradol has a drug that is approved for some rare skin disease but their sales reps are talking about aging."

"Is it any good?" Mirabelle asked. Miradol was an established brand. Maybe this was real.

"According to the doctors, the numbers they are sharing are amazing. I'm meeting with a rep tomorrow. I don't know why no one has heard about this. You would think they would be marketing like crazy. Anyway, I want to test a letter that says there is a new drug that can help you live ten more years but Congress is standing in the way. You know the drill. Sign our petition, renew your membership, and, of course, send money."

Mirabelle took a deep breath. It was risky, but what choice did she have? "I like it. But first one thing. Make sure this drug is real."

CHAPTER
Twenty-Six

"I am not taking any calls," Colleen Keegan barked into her phone. She was meeting with the agency that was making the Juventel ads.

"I think you are taking this one," her assistant answered. "It's Marvin Wellstone at FDA."

Keegan froze. Wellstone was the commissioner of the Food and Drug Administration. They could not know already. The bill had not been introduced. She cleared the room.

"Marvin, how are you?" she said, even more cheerfully than she had intended. "Got any good hikes planned?" Wellstone was a trekker. Long hikes into the wilderness.

"Colleen, I am not calling about how I spend my leisure time. You know good and goddamned well what I am calling about."

They knew. Lying gets you nowhere. Come clean and get it behind you.

"Well, Marvin, I can imagine you are a little upset."

"Sixty years of tradition, Colleen—not to mention the law. Congress does not make decisions for the FDA."

"Well, here's the thing. What we are doing with research today has outpaced the old rules. We have a drug that delays aging. It is extraordinary. But who can afford trials that go on for ten or fifteen years? If it's safe, people should be able to try it now." She knew she was not convincing. She just had to hold the line.

"Colleen, that line is just bullshit and you know it. But what is even worse is that your legislation covers Juventel under Medicare. You have no proof it works. Yet here you are asking the goddamned government to pay for every pill. It is the greediest, most despicable action I have witnessed as FDA commissioner."

Keegan froze. The legislation they wrote had nothing to do with Medicare. Someone had changed the bill. She decided to go for the full truth. "Marvin, you need to know why we did this. Because we have legislation in Congress, we can run TV ads. It is our First Amendment right. I don't actually want to change the law. I just want to be able to run ads for a life-changing drug."

Silence. After absorbing the implications of Keegan's message, Wellstone responded slowly, carefully choosing his words, "You introduced the legislation so you can run TV ads to promote off-label sales? And you are telling me that you don't support the bill."

"Absolutely not. I will issue a statement tomorrow. We don't want it. Believe me."

"Legislation to get cover for TV ads," he said calmly, but there was barely controlled fury in his tone. "This is a sleazy town, Colleen, but you are setting an entirely new standard."

Keegan had expected this conversation but not so soon. If only she could have bought more time.

"Colleen, we have had a strong partnership with Miradol for years, but frankly I don't trust a thing you are telling me. We are going to fight this. The FDA would not have requested fifteen-year trials. We could have worked with you. We have had a good process, a process that has served this country for sixty years. Issue any statement you want but you have crossed the wrong guy. Don't expect any favors from me."

"Marvin—" He had hung up.

CHAPTER
Twenty-Seven

"Welcome to *Washington–Believe It or Not!*. I'm Damon Rodriquez, your host of the show that brings you insight and commentary on this week in our nation's capital city."

A picture of a smiling Joe Hazeldine filled the screen.

"Heeeeeee's back! Is politics an art form? If so, Joe Hazeldine may be the Leonardo da Vinci of our age.

"In one short week, he negotiated a budget deal with the president that gave Republicans key concessions and, surprisingly, won overwhelming approval of his House caucus. His actions rescued the ship of state from the treacherous shoals of bankruptcy. Boy oh boy, do we have a story to discuss tonight!

"Our guests are Fred Simon, former chief of staff at the Democratic National Committee; Suzie Glint, former head of Media Relations at the National Republican Congressional Committee; Nathan Jasper, a national Tea Party activist; and Spud Stevens, founder of *Superspin*, a hot new political blog.

"First question, Fred, it looks to me like the president got swindled," Rodriquez said gleefully.

"Now hold on, Damon, it was a fair deal, and frankly I thought the budget had no chance of passing that caucus," Fred Simon replied. "This was a big setback for the Freedom Caucus."

"Don't underestimate this victory," Glint chimed in. "Joe Hazeldine has skills—mad skills as my teenage son might say. No one expected it really. When you win one like this one it puts members on notice. People in this caucus are going to be afraid to cross him."

"Tea Party?" Spud weighed in. "Hazeldine crashed the party, dumped the tea, broke the china, and tossed them in the sea. Akerman got crushed. Crrrrrunnnnnch!"

"Wait a second," cautioned Nathan Jasper. "Don't read too much into one fight. I think our guys in the Tea Party got caught napping. Who expected this? One thing you have to admit, this Hazeldine guy is really good."

"A huge talent!" Glint added.

"Impressive!" Simon added.

"Just completely [BLEEP] amazing!" Spud chimed. "Sorry, guys, I was so excited I forgot we were on live TV."

CHAPTER
Twenty-Eight

Colleen Keegan had a hole in her schedule. Thirty minutes. No meetings. No phone calls. When you run a multibillion-dollar company these moments are rare. She leaned back in her chair, kicked off her high heels, and put her feet on her desk.

She had a couple of unanticipated problems. First, that damned preacher turned congressman had rewritten their bill to provide Medicare coverage for Juventel. Then, instead of waiting to introduce, he took the bill right to the hopper. No wonder Wellstone was pissed. The likely good news was that that provision meant the bill had no chance of passage, so who cared? Right?

Having sufficiently placated herself with that thought for the moment, she closed her eyes and indulged in what was her very favorite activity of late. She counted.

She counted the customers for Juventel. The market was forty-five million Americans and that was only people sixty-five and older. If you counted everyone fifty-five and older the number was sixty million. Those were baby boomers. Half of them were still working. There were SO many of them. The rabbit in the snake. That rabbit was pure gold. Oh my God!

Of course, not all of them would buy Juventel. She did not understand why not, but it would be good to be conservative. So she counted only half—though it could be higher. The initial cost for a month's supply of Juventel was $200. So low. Really, what would people actually pay to keep the Grim Reaper at bay? $200 was nothing. And what did just $200 mean? $6 billion. Six billion fucking dollars. And that was just for one MONTH.

Over the course of the year that would be $72 billion in revenues. Seventy-two billion dollars. Genovo had the highest revenues of all the pharmas. $57 billion last year. Miradol was going to beat them with one product. And that did not count foreign sales. Foreign sales would be HUGE.

"Genovo, I laugh at you," she thought with an evil smile.

And once everyone was buying it, then she would raise the price. $300, $400, $500 a month. Who knew the limit? She just knew it was HIGH.

She took a deep breath and composed herself. "Poise," she told herself. She was shaking with excitement and that was not good. Running a company required a clear head. They were launching. One smart minute might be worth $100 million—or MORE!

The phone rang. Annoyed, she snapped, "Stephanie, I thought I told you 'no phone calls.'"

"It's Ken."

Ken Pfister was chairman of the Miradol Board of Directors. She had succeeded him as CEO. He was a prince of a guy. Smart, level-headed, and he let her do her job. THAT was proving very smart.

"Ken, what can I do for you on this beautiful day?"

"Colleen, we need to talk," he said, his tone more serious than usual. "I hear that Casey Jacobs has left us."

"That's true, but it is not a bad thing."

"How can it not be a bad thing? We are launching Juventel and Casey is first-rate. You know that."

"You are absolutely correct."

Pfister waited for more but Keegan was silent. He continued, "There is another thing, Colleen. His severance. Why in God's name is he getting a $25 million severance check? He is just a marketing director!"

Keegan pursed her lips. How could she explain? "Ken, I know it looks bad but you have to trust me on this one. I have not asked many favors but I am asking one now. It may not look great but I know what I am doing. Frankly, you need to leave this issue alone for now."

"Look, is this a payoff of some kind? Sexual harassment or…something? Does legal know?"

"Oh, good God, Ken, no. Really, it's okay. It's legal. I promise. Really. There is another issue, though."

He sighed audibly. "What is that?"

"I got a call from Marvin Wellstone. FDA is pissed."

Pfister waited silently, a tactic of his that led many to slaughter when they rushed to fill the uncomfortable void.

Colleen continued, "We figured out how to put up TV ads for Juventel."

"How can you do that for an off-label drug? It's illegal."

"Not if the ads are protected by the First Amendment. Someone has introduced a bill to permit the purchase of drugs for aging as long as they pass the stage one safety tests. As long as there is legislation, we can talk about our product in the ads. We have to mention the legislation but we won't be loud."

"Jesus. Colleen, I can't believe we are really doing this."

"Ken, do you know the numbers? This drug could do $60 billion a year, easy."

"Colleen, I am chairman of the Board and I don't like it one bit. What do I tell the rest of the Board?"

"Tell them we are about to become the number one pharma in the world."

"And what do I tell them about Casey getting a $25 million bonus?"

"Tell them it is a personnel matter, that you and I talked and that the matter is over."

"Twenty-five million?"

"Yes. Twenty-five million. Ken, you need to trust me. I am making sure we can launch this product using every possible tool. If you want to know more I can tell you, but I suggest we end this conversation right here."

"Colleen, I have a fiduciary duty—"

"Ken, you might ask your shareholders about your fiduciary duty. Your fiduciary duty is to make them money. We can make Miradol money at a level no one ever imagined. That is what is in front of us. If we do, who the hell is going to care that our marketing director got overpaid? We can pay him any goddamned amount we want. As I said, it's completely legal. So what if the FDA has its feathers ruffled? They can't withdraw approval—not for exercising our constitutional rights."

"Colleen, I just don't know—"

Keegan cut him off. She was tired of his pussyfooting. "Am I being aggressive? I sure as hell am. You pay me to be aggressive. But trust me, Ken, I am not doing anything stupid."

CHAPTER
Twenty-Nine

Numbers.

A page of numbers was spread out on the table. Mirabelle Jenkins, president of Seniors United, and Jason Stockard, her fundraising genius, leaned over the table, their eyes wide open.

The first number was six. Six percent. Six percent of the members of Seniors United had responded to an email that asked for money to help convince Congress to free Juventel and extend their lives by at least twenty percent.

Of course, six percent does not sound like much. That means that ninety-four percent of everyone who got this email ignored it, deleted it, dismissed it, scorned it, or even unsubscribed. Six percent may look like nothing. But in fundraising six percent is pure gold. Seniors United still had three hundred thousand members. Six percent was eighteen thousand donations. The average gift was $25. That meant $450,000. In two days.

Mirabelle had already paid her rent.

Mirabelle could do a lot more than pay rent. Emails to former members, those who let their memberships lapse after Seniors United rescued Social Security from all future financial collapse, brought in a two percent response rate, almost $200,000 more. Fundraising was statistics. Mirabelle and Jason knew what these numbers meant—it meant Seniors United was back on the gravy train and they weren't riding caboose.

Email was one way to ask for money. It was quick and cost nothing. But, surprisingly, the breadwinner was still mail. Despite widespread rumors that the post office was shutting its doors, in the world of fundraising snail mail was still king. Mail response rates? Two or three times what an email might produce. With mail, with email, and with an issue explosive in power and reach, Seniors United would grow once more.

"Grow" was not an adequate word. These numbers foretold the future. Within a year, Seniors United would have more members than ever. Annual income? It might grow to fifteen, twenty, even thirty million—every single year.

Mirabelle could not only pay the landlord. She would be leasing new offices and hiring new staff. Instead of watching all she knew wither away, her star would soar again. She would be the queen of those blue-haired, walker-pushing, crackling-voiced seniors who would now look at the world in a new light because Seniors United was offering them an extended lease on life.

"What is the rollout?" she asked Jason, wanting to know how many pieces of mail they would be sending next month. There was a deliciousness to her question that made her glow.

"Five million to start," he answered.

"And how many after that, assuming it all works?"

"I think twenty-five million would work just fine."

CHAPTER
Thirty

Colleen Keegan checked her schedule. Jake Siskoff was in San Francisco, in a cab on his way to a meeting with her to discuss legal strategy. But Colleen Keegan needed more than advice.

She had a condition. Anxiety. And from time to time she even suffered full-blown panic attacks. Her heart would race. Her hands would shake. She would lose focus, become dizzy, and lose all perspective. It was a paralyzing experience. She had strategies to conceal her condition. She would sometimes disappear into a restroom or take an early ride home. She even took a medication, manufactured by a rival pharma.

But at this particular moment, Keegan had reason to panic. Their legislation was introduced while Wellstone was still at FDA. He was so mad there were even rumors that he would stay on for another year just to fight the legislation and make sure that no Miradol product ever got past his desk again.

In addition, instead of a well-kept secret with an ulterior motive, the bill had become a national sensation. Some crazy seniors' group was promoting it with millions of pieces of mail. Voters were calling Congress. Lots of them. The talk shows were buzzing. News coverage had made Juventel HOT. What looked like a brilliant maneuver had spun completely out of control.

Then there was Ken Pfister and the issue of Casey's "bonus." Pfister wasn't reading between the lines. Colleen was fighting hard to milk every single dollar out of this unbelievable opportunity. Pfister, that small-minded asshole, he was worried about a marketing director getting overpaid.

She could not think clearly. The room started to spin. She ran straight to the restroom.

. . .

In the taxi, Siskoff was listening to NPR. They were doing a story about the big pro-life march on Washington. They interviewed some pro-life leader and she rattled off her tired spiel about babies and murder. *This woman isn't news,* Siskoff thought. *Probably NPR trying to show balance. Give me a break.*

All of a sudden, the reporter asked about the Juventel bill. "The Juventel bill?" Siskoff thought to himself, *What does that have to do with anything?*

"You are right to life. Does that include supporting the Juventel bill that gives people the drugs they need to live longer?" the reporter asked the activist.

"Well, we don't have an official position but, if you ask me, everyone has a right to life."

Siskoff smiled. They had a quiet strategy that launched a national sensation. Maybe that was not so bad.

. . .

Colleen Keegan had returned to her office. As she settled into her chair Siskoff was ushered in by her assistant.

"Jake, Marvin Wellstone called. He was pissed," Keegan said, without introduction. "I've got Board issues too."

"I know," he replied. "We were going to wait until he left. How did this thing come up so soon?"

"I have no idea, but we've got problems. Big ones," she said, standing again and starting to pace.

"Colleen, sit down. Let's think this through. Slowly."

Keegan took a seat on the office couch. Her hands were shaking. Siskoff took the chair facing her directly and reached out to steady her hands.

"Okay," Siskoff began. "You can't put the toothpaste back in the tube. This is all out in the open. The FDA is furious and Wellstone wants to put Miradol in its place."

"Right."

"The FDA will never forgive you—no matter what you do. Do you understand?"

Keegan gulped. "Yes."

"So that battle is lost. Move on."

"What about my Board?"

"Well, that's another issue. Tell me about it."

"Pfister was already mad about the big bonus I gave to Casey to fund social media in Russia, which, of course, he doesn't know about. Now the FDA stuff has made him ballistic. I think he's after my job." She paused, clamping her hand over her mouth. "This conversation is privileged, right?"

"Absolutely. Colleen, the Board won't like the bonus. They really care about what goes on with the FDA. But what is the ultimate prize here? What do they want most of all?"

"Stock prices. And profits."

"Buy some time. Tell Pfister you can't make the meeting. So how are sales?" Siskoff continued, trying to get her to focus on the positive. "All this commotion in the press. All these calls to Congress. If you're not selling drugs you ought to be fired." He smiled.

Keegan smiled too. "I get reports at the end of the week. There's a lag. Those doctors are cautious. They don't like to prescribe off-label until everyone else is doing it."

Siskoff looked at Keegan with calm and determined eyes. "Get that report. Revise your earnings estimates. Give the Board a big stock price and they won't care if you ran over Wellstone's dog."

Colleen nodded, but she still looked pasty, with a thin sheen of sweat covering her upper lip.

"Colleen, let's talk about this legislation."

"Okay," she said, almost unwillingly.

"You can't say you are sorry or that it was all a mistake or some preacher congressman couldn't keep his mouth shut."

"Okay," Keegan admitted, nodding tightly.

"So why not pass the damned law?"

"You can't be serious."

"If you stand around shuffling your feet, making excuses, you are a sitting duck. You can't fix the FDA problem. Don't worry about the Board. You've got a million angry seniors clamoring for your drug and the legislation to make Medicare pay for it. None of this has gone as planned but we ignited a firestorm."

He reached and poured her a glass of water. She gulped the entire glass as he spoke. "You know what happens if this bill passes. Juventel will be legal and you will have all the marketing rights of an FDA-approved drug. It also means Medicare will pay for the drug. Every senior in America will use it and Uncle Sam will foot the bill.

"Politics is about openings, opportunities that open and close. We started this fire. You can watch it burn or you can pour on some gasoline. Colleen, push the throttle. Wellstone is just one goddamned bureaucrat. If you push the throttle, do you think Congress will care about his opinion?

"If you put up $10 billion in sales will the Board care about how much you paid Casey Jacobs? If you put up $20 billion in sales, do you think they will be crying about Wellstone? They will throw you a goddamned party, fill up your bathtub with champagne, and ask you if you want caviar for breakfast in the morning. That's what they'll do."

Keegan knew he was right.

"Jake, we can't call this the Juventel bill."

"I agree. We can't make it about your profits. We need a new name." He searched his mind for ideas. He remembered that NPR interview. The right to life guy. "I've got it," he said, snapping his fingers.

"What? What is the name?"

"The Life Bill. It extends people's lives. Let's just call it the 'Life Bill.'"

CHAPTER
Thirty-One

Sam Kelley answered the call reluctantly. There were fewer and fewer people he wanted to talk to these days. His media consultant, Michael Brazier, was on the line. "Well, Michael, my friend, how are you doing?" Sam said.

"I'm doing fine and I've been doing some thinking as well. Sam, what do you know about this Life Bill? We need an issue and I am thinking that this legislation is just what we need. It's in your subcommittee, right?"

"It is," Sam replied. "But I am not supporting it.

"You can't let the Congress get in the middle of these decisions. I have spent my whole career working with the FDA to create a process that balances safety against the need to bring good drugs to the market. It's a system that works."

Brazier had not expected this quick rejection.

"Sam, we need something positive, something hopeful in our campaign. We need an issue. I have a gut feeling about this. I have a feeling that this Juventel issue is going to be big."

"Maybe so, but I can't support it."

"If we don't get some issues, something to take attention away from your age, drug prices, and all your unpopular votes, we could lose the election."

"If I have to support that Juventel bill then I will just have to lose," Sam replied, digging in his heels.

"Think about it. Just give it some thought."

CHAPTER
Thirty-Two

Colleen Keegan was again considering her situation, as well as her future. The FDA was after her head. Her Board? She had gotten a call from Pfister that very morning talking about a specially called meeting the following week. She asked about the agenda. He said she ought to know.

There was a knock at the door. Colleen Keegan looked up from her desk with some trepidation. The door cracked open and her assistant leaned into the opening. "Sorry to interrupt but there is some news I think you will want to hear."

Keegan only nodded.

In walked the new Marketing director, Walter Schmidt. With him was the VP of Finance and a woman she did not know, probably from Accounting.

"Colleen, we have numbers. On Juventel," said Schmidt.

"I know this is about Juventel," she snapped. "Otherwise, why would all of you be in my office right now?" She looked hopefully at her colleagues and then she knew the news. It was written all over their faces.

"We sold $300 million in Juventel last week," Walter Schmidt said, unable to keep the excitement out of his voice.

For a moment Colleen was speechless. She understood exactly what $300 million meant. $300 million a week was $15 billion a year. $15 billion put Miradol number one in the world. They had not even started the ads. Those numbers would grow and in a big way. Relief flooded through her agitated system like a drug.

She decided not to tell Pfister just yet. She would walk into that Board meeting next week, throw down this report, and take him by surprise. After these numbers, Pfister's complaints would look like so much chickenshit.

She leaned back in her chair and smiled. Pfister's agenda needed one amendment.

Colleen Keegan was going to ask for a raise.

CHAPTER
Thirty-Three

"Here is Logan Ladner with tonight's WCSB Nashville news commentary."

"Thank you, Dan. I am standing here in front of the headquarters of the Sam Kelley for Congress re-election campaign. What is happening in this building can be described in one word. Panic.

"Kelley, long considered a shoo-in for his nineteenth term, received some startling news today. A district poll conducted by the *Nashville Tennessean* showed that his Democratic opponent and billionaire entrepreneur Sidney Lund has pulled even with the congressman among Fourth District voters.

"The news sent shockwaves through Tennessee political circles. Some of us had astutely predicted that this race would tighten. But a tie? With a year to go?

"Lund has been up with a huge TV buy suggesting that Kelley is too old to remain in Congress. And at age seventy-eight, the congressman is no spring chicken.

"Kelley, long a creature of Washington, has made himself scarce in Tennessee. For neglected voters, tired of failed Washington leadership, Election Day just may be payback time.

"Personally, I am not betting the other way."

CHAPTER
Thirty-Four

In Topeka, Kansas, Willard and Geraldine Cummings, a couple married for fifty-two years, were sitting on the sofa in their modest bungalow watching television. Their favorite show was on the screen. General Hospital. And this episode, in which Sonny seeks revenge and viewers learn about dark secrets from Julian's past, was particularly exciting. It hardly mattered that they loved General Hospital. They watched Days of Our Lives, The Big Chew, and, even though Ellen was gay, they even thought The Ellen DeGeneres Show was good.

At Word Worldwide, the advertising agency for Miradol, they knew about the Cummingses. They were retired seniors, just past seventy-five years of age. They had not saved much for retirement but it hardly mattered. Interest rates were so low that even with a nest egg they could barely afford the gas and hotel room needed to visit the state fair. So the Cummings of the world stayed home and watched TV—a lot of TV.

Word Worldwide knew the numbers. Viewers in the Cummingses' own special demographic averaged seventy hours of TV every week. Most of them didn't own a DVR so they did not record the shows or skip the commercials. They didn't subscribe to Netflix or Hulu or buy shows on Amazon. The world of television had changed. At Word Worldwide they held long meetings to decide how in the world they could put just one TV ad in front of twenty-five-year-olds with a college degree. But in their campaign to sell Juventel, Word Worldwide had exactly the target they coveted.

Willard and Geraldine Cummings were sitting ducks.

A woman, a young-looking seventy, appeared on the screen.

"I look back on my life and think about all the good times I've had. None of us can recapture our youth. But modern science has found a way to help each of us live longer, healthier lives. Juventel is a prescription drug that has been proven to slow aging. But Congress is making this drug harder to buy even though it has been proven safe in FDA trials. Ask your doctor about Juventel. And call Congress to tell them that YOU have the right to live a longer and healthier life."

Geraldine and Willard looked at each other.

"Should we try it?" Geraldine asked.

"I don't know," said Willard, the more cautious of the two. "They didn't tell us the side effects."

"Well, that seems like good news to me. They have to tell you that stuff. It's the law."

"I think I got a mailing about this. Is it covered by Medicare?"

Geraldine looked at Willard impatiently.

"Well, I am going to find out," he said as he headed for the stack of mail on the kitchen counter.

. . .

In millions of homes, on millions of sofas, viewing billions of soap opera episodes, Geraldine and Willard's conversation played out across America. Miradol had spared no expense. There were many versions of the ad. The scientist discussing "proof." The daughter telling her mother to "do this for your grandchildren and me." Testimonials about how much younger Juventel "had *already* made me feel."

That was just one piece of the campaign. Doctors, besieged by their patients, received documents outlining the successful trials, the metrics, and the promise, all signed by a past surgeon general who had made an endorsement deal for a huge but undisclosed fee.

But it was the ads that did the real work. These ads spoke to older Americans in a way that no product had ever spoken before. It was not about curing cancer, feeding starving children, or finding a better laxative. It was about their own condition—aging—a condition that robbed their minds, their bodies, and their spirits as well. The incurable "disease" that was transporting them to their graves far too soon.

Inside these seniors, their own genes were orchestrating their demise. But other genes, equally shaped by the firm hand of evolution, spoke to their hearts and minds. Those genes spoke to the most ancient, primal, and primary instinct of humankind. These genes spoke a single, compelling word.

Survive.

CHAPTER
Thirty-Five

"Office of Congressman Nicholas Gonzalez," the receptionist chirped in her happiest voice. "Why of course we know about the Juventel bill." She proceeded to explain that Congressman Nicholas Gonzalez, chair of the powerful Energy and Commerce Committee, was looking closely at the legislation but, no, he had not yet taken a position.

Constituents from all across his Texas district were calling. It was only 10:30 in the morning and the number had already reached 267. Too many to answer, most calls became messages in the rapidly filling inbox holding voicemails. Congressman Gonzalez was not alone.

Congresswoman Jill Weinstein from New York had received three hundred calls this same morning. Congressman Terry Svensen from Minnesota had gotten 212. Across the House, Democratic and Republican, the numbers were the same.

Busy receptionists and mounting voicemails were not the only evidence that the Juventel bill was gaining support. Now renamed the "Life Bill," now being featured in tens of millions of letters and emails launched by Seniors United, now touted in the most massive advertising campaign ever to promote a single product, this legislation was driving piles, large piles, of postcards bearing signatures of voters in their districts. People wanted to know. Why was Congress blocking access to this wonder drug?

Then there were the letters, real ones, actually written by the constituents themselves. Thousands and thousands of letters, the kind of letters staffers might actually bring the congressman to read.

Dear Congressman Gonzalez,

I have a granddaughter who has serious dyslexia. Her school would not provide tutors and learning to read was very hard. She still does not spell so well but she is a fighter and now she is in high school making As. The day she was accepted at the University of Notre Dame was the second proudest day of my life. The proudest will be her graduation four years from now. The problem is that I may not make it that long. I struggle to remember things. I walk with a cane. I get sick so much more often than before. Maybe this Juventel can give me another four years. I have the right to try.

Olivia O'Mara
Age 86
Batesville, Texas

At town hall meetings, the questions were no longer about the budget, Medicare premiums, immigration, or bad service at the local pharmacy. The questions were about the Life Bill, when was it going to pass, and whether Juventel would be covered by Medicare.

Most members said they were still studying the matter. They asked for time. But those meetings were filled with impatience. These seniors were approaching the end. They could feel it every day. How much time was left? You could not know your time but you knew it grew shorter every day.

CHAPTER
Thirty-Six

Colleen Keegan opened her Mention page. She loved this tracking service. All she had to do was give it a word or phrase and it tracked everything—news articles, Facebook posts, tweets, and a lot more. She looked at the list it generated for her today. At the top of the page was Juventel. Colleen stared at the number in disbelief.

In one day, on all mediums, Juventel was mentioned 700,075 times. A week earlier, when she last checked, the number had been 200,000.

Twitter posts everywhere. She clicked on one. "I have been taking Juventel four days and feel twenty years younger. Ponce de Leon, eat your heart out." There was a video attached. She clicked.

Across the screen flashed images from history. Genghis Khan. Joan of Arc. Leonardo da Vinci. Peter the Great. George Washington.

> "Since the dawn of history, humankind has struggled against infection, epidemic, and disease. But even the miracles of modern medicine have been helpless against the inevitability of aging and death. Now science has unlocked the mysteries of aging and delivered a drug that sends our cells the messages of youth. By instructing our cells to repair and replenish just as they do in our younger years, Juventel can extend life by ten years and perhaps even more. Ask your doctor about Juventel. Then you can thank him for another ten years."

There was another video by a scientist who explained how Juventel reprograms our genes to keep us young. A third video showed a woman in her sixties, holding a framed picture of her mom. "I miss my mom more than anyone can imagine." Then she explains that while her mom died too soon for Juventel, it was not too late for your mom.

Other videos attached links to the ads.

None of these videos came directly from Miradol. This was Casey. She looked at the computer screen underneath video.

157,000 likes.

CHAPTER
Thirty-Seven

The Republican caucus gathered in room HC-5 in the basement of the Capitol Building. The room was plain with dark gray carpet and populated with plastic and aluminum chairs. Two large TV screens and wooden paneling adorned the back wall. Unlike the rest of the Capitol it was a room lacking the slightest touch of history or artistic grace, so inexpensively adorned it was a rare tribute government parsimony and thrift.

Joe Hazeldine stood at the podium as the members ambled into the room. When the doorway was empty he gaveled the meeting to order. There was but one subject to discuss, the so-called "Life Bill" that was dominating the news and citizen conversations all across the nation. It was time for Republicans to take a position.

Embry Jones, the respected representative from southern Iowa, was the first to speak. He rose slowly with a pensive expression, as if he were still considering what he might say. For a brief moment he looked at his colleagues, reflecting on the decisions these men and women were required to make. But when he spoke, his own decision was clear.

"We have before us a new issue that lies beyond the imagination of our forefathers, or even ourselves just a few short years ago. We have the power to alter the cycle of life and death. To what extent that power reaches we cannot know. No trials have been conducted to tell us the truth of the claims of this drug. We are faced with a painful dilemma. We must choose blindly, not knowing the consequences of the decision we make.

"What we cannot know is the number. How many years, on the average, will this drug extend life? But let's consider the possibilities. What if this drug gave everyone who takes it five additional years and what if it were covered by Medicare? We can assume that the great majority of seniors would take it because who would refuse its gift? The cost of those five years would be an amount, measured over the next three years, that our nation can ill afford.

"And what if the gift were ten years? What might that number be? That number would be so great that it could no longer be described as a burden. It would be a catastrophe. The word 'bankruptcy' has been used recently with some cleverness by our esteemed speaker. Let us describe the situation otherwise. Ten years of the cost of this drug would leave our nation destitute, besieged by angry creditors, and begging our one-time friends and allies for the comfort of their generosity. We would be a pathetic shadow of the nation we are today.

"The voters cry out for this drug. Let them have it but not paid for by a government already overburdened with spending and debt. But even if it is not covered by Medicare, the consequences of seniors living longer will raise Medicare expenses and deliver a terrible financial cost." Congressman Embry looked pained, shook his head and sat.

While representatives whispered to one another, a second speaker rose. Augustus Rhodes from upstate New York was more animated but no less dire as he began to speak. "We face a decision with serious risks, and the financial condition of the nation is just one of them. The public hunger for this drug— the almost desperation for it—is a trap. What will happen to our majority if the president endorses this measure as he surely will? He will be the savior of older Americans, our strongest voters. We will be like the Grinches who stole Christmas, only worse for we will be stealing not boxes filled with new shoes or ill-chosen ties but years from the lives of the voters who have given us their trust. Maybe this drug does more than give us additional years. Maybe it improves health as well and reduces what we pay for care. What if it cures dementia? Those savings would be more than $100 billion a year.

"As my esteemed colleague acknowledges, we cannot know the costs. We will learn the costs over time. There will be opportunities to adjust. But in my mind, there is one cost more likely than the others. That cost will be the loss of our majority in this House. If we lose this House and the Democrats have the power of the White House, House, and Senate, who will stop their unrestrained urge to solve every problem and fund every program? What will the invoice for those excesses read? Those of you in the Freedom Caucus, I ask what are the consequences—social, financial, and political—of unrestrained Democratic rule? I urge the caucus to support the bill."

Hazeldine searched the large room for Earl Ackerman, and when he met his eye Ackerman rose. He spoke firmly, even defiantly, when he said, "I came to Congress to achieve one goal above all others. I came here to reduce the size of government and to expand the freedoms it restrains. If we support this bill it will mean larger government, higher taxes, and, in the end, less freedom in the nation."

But the Life Bill was not uniformly opposed within the Freedom Caucus. Some believed that the miracles of free enterprise had blessed the nation with a gift that ought to be properly rewarded. If it is a drug that worked, it ought to be covered as well. The pressure of these rising costs might be an opportunity to scale back Medicare in a larger sense and to move it out of the government entirely and into private hands.

Joe Hazeldine listened to these arguments with admiration. How eloquent these leaders could be when not distracted by television cameras and the need for the "sound bites" that reduced complex and life-shaping issues to advertising slogans and empty accusation. There was nothing simple about this issue. His own position was uncertain. Embry Jones was right. The costs could cripple the nation. But Rhodes was right as well. Opposing the bill could cost Republicans their majority and, of course, cost him his job. But whatever course they chose, it was possible that this one drug could transform human society in expected and unexpected ways.

While his members took their turns, Hazeldine counted votes on the Life Bill. Those numbers were not in doubt. A clear majority opposed the bill. His caucus would do the right thing regardless of political consequences. That made him proud.

He had wanted to provide ample time for debate. The meeting was already two hours long. Someone moved for a vote. But before the roll call could begin a messenger knocked at the door. A staffer had been posted to prevent entry. The door cracked open and she leaned into the gap. A note was passed into her hand. She hurried to the podium where the speaker stood.

Hazeldine took the note, unfolded it, and paused to consider its unexpected content. "Ladies and gentlemen. I have an announcement," he said. "The president has announced his opposition to this bill."

CHAPTER
Thirty-Eight

"Well, these things can change mighty fast."

With those words, delivered by Congressman Sam Kelley, the strategy meeting of the Kelley re-election campaign—attended by Sam, his wife Pearl, campaign staff, and a growing cadre of consultants—got underway.

Ann Bell began the meeting. There was no hesitation in her voice. She still did not understand this campaign business but there was thunder in the air and ill winds were rising. She was the leader and she laid the bad news on the table. "We are going to get a poll report in a minute, but first I assume everyone read the report in *Politico*. Jim Villers has signed on to run the Lund campaign."

Villers was the most famous campaign manager in America. He did Senate races and governors' races. He advised presidential candidates around the world. There was only one reason he would stoop to run a lowly congressional race in Middle Tennessee. And that reason was a signal to one and all that Sidney Lund would spare no expense to win this race.

It also signaled something else. Jim Villers, the most accomplished campaign manager in America, versus Ann Bell. The unspoken sentence ringing in every ear.

"We've got a challenge on our hands," she continued. "Let's talk about what to do about it. At the end of this meeting, we can hopefully have some decisions that will move us forward. Sarah, you kick things off."

Sarah Whiteridge rose from her chair and stiffened her back. Her chin tilted slightly upward. "We have a new poll and the news is not good. I won't take long. Research has found a great hit on Lund and we need to discuss it. We may finally have the opening we need."

She ran through the numbers. The same numbers the local newspaper, the *Nashville Tennessean*, had published a week ago. Kelley forty-two percent. Lund forty percent. A margin of error of four points. She had retested the attacks on Kelley. They continued to work. She retested blaming Kelley for higher drug prices. That really worked. Voters did not know Kelley chaired the subcommittee where legislation on drug prices was handled. Lund would have the same polling. That meant more negative ads. These would be more effective than the last.

New to the poll was the Life Bill. Practically every voter over fifty-five had heard about it. It had eighty-six percent support. Whiteridge tested arguments against the drug. It has not been tested for effectiveness. It was not approved by the FDA for aging. Congress should not have been making decisions on the safety of drugs. Big drug companies were supporting the bill to make huge profits on a product they are unwilling to test. It would cost more than America could afford. These arguments reduced support for the bill but just barely. After hearing these objections, seventy-three percent still supported the bill.

"As I have said repeatedly, most campaigns are won with negative ads. In this case, where Sam's age is an issue, I think disqualifying Lund is even more important," Whiteridge said, repeating her mantra.

"There are a lot of seniors in my district," Sam pointed out.

"Sam, the seniors *are* the problem. They are growing old. They feel they aren't what they used to be. They wonder why you are still there. I have seen this problem in other races. It isn't the young people who object to your age. Your age is a far bigger problem with seniors than any other group," the pollster replied, modulating her tone slightly. She turned from Sam, almost dismissively, and smiled at their new guru of research.

"So let me turn it over to our outstanding research firm, Opp Slayer, who have turned up something very interesting about Mr. Lund."

Jessica Munoz rose, teeth on wide display, as she prepared to deliver her bombshell. "I'll begin by quoting from that great classic, *All the Kings Men*, where Willie Stark turns to Jack Burden and says, 'Jack, man is conceived in sin and born in corruption. There is something on everybody.'" Whiteridge snickered.

She had heard this intro before—but still enjoyed it. Jessica continued, "I report to you today that Sidney Lund is no exception."

Click. A PowerPoint appeared on the screen. A headshot of a young, handsome man with dark hair, a little long, and a white silk shirt unbuttoned to the middle of his chest. "Meet Jeremy Willard. Jeremy is certainly a name new to most of you. He was new to us. He is an architect, a midlevel employee at the firm of Cassidy and Branch. He is not wealthy, at least not that we can tell. When we first came across his name in the matter I will soon discuss, we had to ask: What is his relationship with Lund? There is no easy way to put this so let me just lay it all out on the table. He is Sidney Lund's lover."

Eyes widened all around the table and a couple of people actually woke up.

"Yes!" said Sarah Whiteridge, pumping a fist with a tight motion. Salvation had arrived.

"Wait a second," said Sam, patting down the air with his one hand. "We aren't going to talk about that."

"Now, Sam," Pearl said, patting him on the shoulder. "Let them finish."

"Thank you, Mrs. Kelley," Jessica replied. "There is a lot more to this story."

"As you know, Pfinder.com is a publicly traded company. Eleven months ago, Pfinder closed a deal with the CIA. A big contract. The CIA can't have cell phones floating around. They pass documents on tiny microchips. They use an array of physical objects to transmit information, intercept communications, and eavesdrop on conversations, in person and on the phone. They contracted with Pfinder to imbed all of these objects with technology that would identify their location and also allow the CIA, in some cases, to destroy them as well."

"How big?" Mike Barbier asked.

"How big? The contract? CIA budgets aren't public but analysts on the street estimated about $150 million. The day after the deal, Pfinder stock jumped twenty-nine percent." Jessica paused, still smiling. "Three days before the contract was signed, Jeremy Willard bought $1.1 million worth of stock in Pfinder."

"So we are saying that this guy bought on inside information?" Sam asked, his voice tight and clearly annoyed.

"I don't know any other conclusion you could draw," Jessica replied.

"But we don't *know*," Sam answered.

"Well, we don't have a recording of Lund telling him to buy."

"Well, why not send this information to the SEC? They handle these things."

Sarah Whiteridge broke in. "Sam, we looked into all that. The SEC staff has been cut way back. It might take them four years to investigate and issue a report. That is not an option for this campaign, and this gay stuff—that's the juicy part. That's what the media will cover."

Pearl leaned over to Sam and began whispering into his ear. Sam's empty sleeve began to twitch.

"Sam." Whiteridge looked straight at him, her expression stern. "Sam, we can leak it to the news media but that is not what we are talking about. We are talking about putting this on the air. TV ads. Your numbers are falling. This guy can spend anything and will. The attacks on you have barely started."

Sam just stared back, silently, still with the twitch.

Mike Barbier moved in to smooth things over. "I know Sam wants to think about all this. We don't have to make this decision today. But we need a positive message as well. Ann Bell, thank you for distributing Sam's list of accomplishments. Sam, you chair the subcommittee that deals with prescription drugs. I know we discussed this but the Life Bill is a big opportunity. Have you had a chance to think more about it?"

"I'm against it."

His staff exchanged concerned glances. Sam launched into his rationale. "You think Congress should get in the middle of these decisions? Decisions about life and death. Decisions that could cripple our health care systems with huge charges for prescriptions that barely work at all. I have been in Congress for thirty-six years. Congress is the worst place to make these decisions."

Sarah Whiteridge's face fell. In her mind the campaign was lost. The researcher stood silently in disbelief. She had placed the killer bullet in Sam Kelley's hand

and he had no interest at all. When did that happen? Most campaigns weren't this lucky.

But Mike Barbier had a different view. He had worked for politicians for thirty years. Each new generation of candidates was more self-centered, more shallow, than the last. He remembered the old days when high-minded men and women actually cared as much about their principles as the numbers in their polls. Not all of them. Not even most of them. But more of them.

It was no wonder that fewer people of talent and wisdom sought public office. Who wanted to spend three hours a day on the phone grubbing for money? Who wanted to endure social media and ideological news that twisted their viewpoints beyond recognition and made policy positions a question not of judgment and reason but of deep moral turpitude? Who wanted to engage in a war of TV ads riddled with hyperbole and accusations distant from the truth?

Sam Kelley was old. He was an innocent. His campaign was in deep trouble. He was doing nothing that he needed to do to actually win this election. But Sam Kelley cared about what was right.

As a young man, Michael Barbier did not care about the money or the accolades or the power. He just wanted to help the good guys win. But politics had become more disgusting with each passing year. That is why he left the business. Now he was back.

And to his great surprise, he was working for a good guy again.

CHAPTER
Thirty-Nine

"This is Buck Lasker reporting for CSBN, America's leading twenty-four-hour-a-day cable news channel.

"For months we have watched the brutal warfare between the White House and the Republican House over how we tax and spend America's money. That conflict shut down the government and brought our nation to the edge of bankruptcy. Now, a new battle is looming.

"Barely two months ago, no one in Congress had even heard of the Life Bill. Now it is part of every conversation in this politics-addicted city. The Life Bill would allow drugs that delay aging to be used by any citizen so long as those drugs were approved for safety by the FDA. If passed the bill would extend Medicare coverage to these prescriptions.

"Yesterday, urging caution and predicting a budgetary disaster, President Marino came out against the measure.

"Within the hour, the House Republican caucus endorsed it.

"Let's start with the president." The president's face appeared on the screen, dark-haired with olive skin and thick eyebrows that lowered to offer an expression of deep concern.

> "All Americans should be excited at the prospect of a new wave of drugs that enable all of us to live healthier and longer lives. But these drugs remain untested. The FDA is the appropriate agency to make these decisions. Congress can't even pass a

budget, its own most fundamental task. Do you trust Congress to make life and death decision for all Americans?"

"But Congress wants to make those decisions and House Republicans are supporting the plan. Here's what Joe Hazeldine, Republican speaker of the House, had to say:"

> "When in our history has an American president stood in the way of an important medical advance? What if a president had decided to block the polio vaccine or heart transplants or penicillin? We stand at the dawn of a new era where the effects of aging can be delayed and its consequences diminished. The gift of extended life is available to every American. I applaud Miradol for bringing forth this miracle drug. I urge the president to stand aside in his effort to block science and deny the gift of longer and healthier life to every Americans."

"Harsh words indeed and in a battle about life—and death. There will be surely more to come. This is Buck Lasker reporting for CSBN twenty-four-hour news."

CHAPTER
Forty

The ship of state was headed for an iceberg. The Republican caucus had made a political decision. The president opposed the Life Bill. He handed them an opportunity. More seats in the House. A Republican Senate. And President Marino, the guy they all hated? He could be gone as well.

Joe Hazeldine knew the rewards but he also knew the costs.

The numbers. He poured through the numbers. There were so many assumptions. Life extension. How many years? Could it be twenty? That is what the Juventel ads suggested. But those Big Pharma people were liars. That much he knew.

Then there was health. If it improved health, would it drop doctor bills? What if Juventel prevented or reduced dementia. That was $100 billion a year. Perhaps better health might cushion against some of the costs. These were only some of the questions. But no matter what assumptions you made, at the end of the question stood an answer. The answer was repugnant but undeniably true. The longer you lived the more it would cost Medicare. Healthier or not healthier? Two years or twenty years. Even a two-year extension of life bore the possibility of frightening costs to a program that was already bleeding cash.

Every calculation, even the most modest estimates of the drug's life-extending powers, ended in a budgetary nightmare. Only one assumption saved the budget. If the drug did not work at all, no one would live even a day longer. That saved money. But even in that case, Medicare was still picking up the tab.

A larger truth hovered above these numbers. The truth was that the Republican caucus's endorsement of the Life Bill was an act of gluttony. These men and women had entered politics to gain power for their most cherished purposes—smaller government and fiscal restraint. But the temptations of power are seductive. These members had discarded those purposes that brought them to the House. They had done so pursuing power itself.

Someone had to fix this problem. That someone was Joe Hazeldine.

What were his options? One option was dropping Medicare coverage from the bill. The callers, the letter writers, the seniors besieging town hall meetings across the nation, they knew about Medicare coverage and they expected it. It was too late for that. Anything less than full coverage would detract from their victory and eviscerate the rewards they imagined. No, there would have to be another solution.

A tax increase. Forget it. This was the Republican caucus.

But there was one more strategy. In 2003, Congress passed legislation providing for prescription drug coverage under Medicare. Under intense pressure from the pharmaceutical lobby, Congress added a provision that prohibited the US government from negotiating volume discounts on the price of drugs purchased under the Medicare program.

Kill the prohibition and big savings would follow. They might demand a twenty-five percent cut. But what if they asked the drug companies to charge what they charge elsewhere in the world? Prices Americans paid for the seven top-selling drugs were almost *four times* what they paid in the UK, where the government buys all of the drugs in bulk. There was a critical cancer drug that in the US cost six hundred times its price overseas. Juventel? It sold in America for seven times the price they paid in the UK.

Lower the price Medicare pays for all drugs. That is how you pay for Juventel.

Changing the Medicare negotiation ban meant taking on Big Pharma. Big Pharma through its PACs alone contributed $50 million to political candidates—both Republicans and Democrats. That money did not even count individual donations from pharma executives, vendors, employees, and industry friends just wanting to please.

Big Pharma had given Joe Hazeldine $250,000, half of it since he became speaker.

He turned and looked at the photo at the side of his desk, the photo of his young daughter who had died because he could no longer pay $80,000 a year for the drug that kept her alive. He thought of his last moments at her side. She knew she was dying. She was so brave that her last words were to comfort her daddy, to tell him that even death could not remove her from his life. His tears began to flow.

He knew who was responsible for his daughter's death. It was not just greedy companies who charged unreasonable prices that left some to die. They were in business. No, the bigger problem was the politicians. Politicians just like Joe Hazeldine.

Of course, he never liked those drug companies. In fact, he HATED them. But had he done nothing to challenge their privilege, their right to charge anything they pleased? He had not spoken a word against that backroom deal that left Medicare under the dark shadow of financial ruin. No. He took their money and never did a thing.

He was suddenly filled with shame.

He knew the risks. He knew the power of Big Pharma, so much power that they could crush even the second most powerful leader in the land.

He looked at his daughter's picture again. Her smile seemed somehow to have changed. It was brighter, more hopeful, prouder. He felt her presence in the room.

Suddenly he knew something else as well. He understood exactly why fate had handed him this job.

CHAPTER
Forty-One

It was spring now in Middle Tennessee. The dogwoods were bursting with sweet-smelling flowers, and the blossoms glistened like snowflakes that never reached the ground. The redbuds had erupted as well, providing a backdrop of deep lavender. The combination was a sight to see.

Sam's house sat on a broad lawn, wide open but for one superb old oak in the center clearly meant for climbing. The rambling old colonial was large but modest. Its sides were wooden and hand hewn, not that artificial siding everyone used nowadays, and in places the white paint was beginning to crack. The old-fashioned sash windows stood five on either side of a big, red oak door.

Across the lawn, gathering slowly as carloads arrived one or two at a time, were four generations of family—Sam Kelley's family. They were all there for Sam—all six of his children, all sixteen of their children, and even a few great-grandchildren in tow.

Michael Brazier, his camera crew at his side, surveyed the scene. Twenty-nine people in all. Politicians used to make ads about family all the time, so much so that the whole idea had become a cliché. These days not so much.

Most of the ads today were negative, attacking opponents for some misdeed explained in exaggerated and twisted forms. The positive ads were harder. Politicians seldom made the news for the good things they achieved. Government disappointed. Positive was hard because voters no longer believed the good things.

Brazier knew something else. The power of an ad was in the pictures. Many voters may care about the budget, the environment, or the sanctity of the unborn. But some still assessed candidates personally, measured their character and their ability to do the job. Sometimes, they just voted for the people they liked. And Mike Brazier was about to capture a picture that would make voters love Sam Kelley.

Sam and Pearl appeared at the front door and walked into the yard. They were casually dressed, pants and shirt sleeves, Sam with his empty sleeve rolled up almost to his shoulder. As they walked across the lawn, the children, especially the younger ones, rushed to greet them. One or two hugged Pearl around the leg but their target was mostly Sam.

"Get the shot! Get the shot!" Brazier shouted and his cameraman pointed at Sam.

When the children reached Sam, they tackled him, physically bringing him to the ground, smiling and laughing the whole way down. He roared in a loud and mighty voice like a monster or terrible bear and the children squealed in delight. With his one good arm, he pushed them into the air one at a time while others tickled him and pulled his hair. There was no alarm among the parents. They watched and smiled. They had witnessed all this before.

Pearl fussed and tried to intervene. "Sam, we are going to have to get you a new shirt. Children, stop!" But it was five minutes more before Sam rose to his feet, not because he couldn't but because the fun was too great to bring to an end.

After Sam put on a new shirt, unstained by grass, dirt, and red Popsicle juice, and combed his hair, the family gathered for a photo. All twenty-nine of them were elaborately arranged in three rows, carefully positioned so that every smile could say to the voter that this was Sam Kelley and we are his family and he is a good man.

Sam's family was mostly successful. He had one son who was a doctor and a daughter who practiced law. Another daughter came in uniform, a retired colonel in the US Army. His youngest daughter drank too much and had trouble caring for her kids, but every family had someone like that—especially in the South.

Three of the grandchildren were adopted, one a six-year-old from China who was missing her front teeth. There was a fourteen-year-old boy with curly blond hair who came from Russia, and another girl, eleven, had been adopted after too many years in an abusive foster home. Among the great-grandchildren was a baby a few days old.

They were an American family. And they all stood there together, surrounding the man they loved. That love, though not present in a physical form, was as visible as their tousled hair or their sometimes-mismatched clothes.

It was a photo that required not a single word.

When Brazier had his shot, he began interviewing the family one by one. With the camera rolling he asked each person, each who could manage a sentence, to speak about Sam.

"My dad was always a busy man, but he always found time for us kids. Saturday mornings he would pile us into a car and take us on some adventure. Sometimes all six of us squeezed so tight in that car we could barely breathe."

A four-year-old boy said, "Paw Paw is a great grizzly bear. Roooaaaar!"

"My grandfather cares about people. He helped pass the Medicare Prescription Drug Program and he got us the research hospital in Murfreesboro."

A daughter, unprompted, spoke the words Brazier hoped he would find. "You know, politics has gotten pretty nasty and here is what I want to say about my dad. My whole life I can hardly remember him saying a bad word about anyone."

Who could see this shot of this family, with Sam and Pearl, and not believe it was a picture of a man who belonged to a better time?

Brazier wondered if it would be enough. Maybe people believed they needed someone tough and hard enough to succeed in the world Washington had become. He hoped his ad would inoculate Sam. That it would shield him against the unkind words and vicious attacks that had already started. But would it make them want to vote for him again?

All this good feeling had to be translated into a reason to keep Sam Kelley in Congress. An idea came to Brazier as he watched Sam's family mill about, catching up with one another, the genuine affection and respect for which they had for one another evident even from a distance. He would talk about

Washington gone bad. He would ask voters to remember a better time. Instead of reading from a poll, he would tell them the truth he knew.

"They don't make them like Sam Kelley anymore."

CHAPTER
Forty-Two

Big Pharma had won its great battles in Congress. They had enacted a provision to prevent Medicare from negotiating lower drug prices. They had beaten back all efforts to lower drug prices, despite the fact that Americans paid prices many times what they charged other customers around the world. In fact, Joe Hazeldine could not remember a single time they had ever lost. To bring his current proposal to the floor, he needed a majority inside his own Republican caucus. He needed 112 votes, most of them from members who for years had been generously funded with drug company money.

He had invited Lindsey Jenkins, his majority leader, to his office to float his plan. "Joe, what's up?" she greeted the speaker without the usual pleasantries.

"Lindsey, I have been worrying about your caucus. I think our endorsing the Life Bill is going to be harder on our conservatives than the rest of us. I'd like to talk about solutions."

"What do you have in mind?"

"Don't tell any of the other leadership just yet," he said casually, with a hint of the conspiratorial in his tone. "We need a meeting tomorrow. But I have an idea that could make this whole thing pretty close to budget neutral."

"How's that?" Lindsey cocked her head, thinking she hadn't heard him correctly.

"We repeal the prohibition on negotiating Medicare prices," Hazeldine announced, trying to keep from smiling. "As you know, despite the fact that Medicare was about to become the biggest customer on the planet, it was banned from negotiating lower prices with the companies. It was Big Pharma's price for letting the legislation pass. It's really unacceptable that an industry like that has Congress by the ba—ahem, over a barrel."

"You can't do that," Lindsey Jenkins shot back.

"We have to fix this problem, and if we don't fix it I will resign," Hazeldine stated, leaving no room for discussion.

The majority leader paused to consider the implications of Hazeldine's pledge. If the speaker resigned she was next in line. If she opposed his idea, he might do something more sensible and he might succeed. Resignation meant that the Freedom Caucus would finally get their speaker. Hazeldine knew all these thoughts before she thought them herself. She would support the idea because she knew it would fail.

"Well, Joe, I guess you make a good point," she finally said. "It will be a tough one but I won't stand in your way."

.   .   .

Joe Hazeldine picked up the phone and called Dan Westinger, lobbyist for the Health Insurers Association.

"Mr. Speaker, what an honor to get this call."

"Danny, it is my honor to call on one of Washington's great lobbyists. I have a question for you. What if I could cut what you pay for prescription drugs in half? You guys would make some dough, right?"

"Damned right. But how the hell is that going to happen?" he added suspiciously.

"I am getting ready to put the Medicare negotiation ban on the table. I think I can kill it."

"In your caucus?"

"Right."

"I'm sorry, Joe, but I have to be skeptical," replied Westinger, trying to be polite.

"Danny, you are a very smart player in this town. If you weren't skeptical you would not be worth this call."

"Thank you."

"But there's an opening here. Our caucus endorsed this Life Bill and there is no way to pay for it. Those Tea Party guys are getting scared and there is rumbling in their ranks. I need to keep them happy. The only way to pay for the bill is to kill that ban."

"But you know every one of them is taking pharma money."

"Ninety-three percent of senators and congressmen have pharma money. I looked it up. But these guys have religion and that religion is a government cut down so small that you'd need a microscope to find it. If I can get to the floor, the Democrats will do the rest."

"I don't know, Joe," Westinger said, obviously still skeptical.

"This is billions of dollars for your insurers. What if I fail? You pissed off pharma. They aren't doing you any favors now.

"Let's say the odds are just twenty percent. If you lose, your people are going to say, 'Way to go, Danny. You are thinking big and you didn't lose us a thing.' But if you win, you are going to be the biggest fucking hero they ever knew. You could triple your fees, and you know what they would say?"

"What?"

"Thank you, Mr. Westinger."

"Mr. Speaker, I just want to say, you have a rare gift of persuasion."

"Don't 'Mr. Speaker' me."

"Fair enough. I still think the odds are really long, but you're right—the payoff is big. I think I can bring our guys on board. Send me a list. The votes you need. Let me get to work."

"I am not finished."

"What else?"

"I need some money. Big money. I need to tell you how much and how you are going to spend it."

"Careful, Joe, there are laws about all this."

"Do you want this?"

"Of course, I want it."

"I also need $100,000 donated to a Super PAC, the Center for Progress in Richmond, Virginia. I'll explain the rest. Be in my office at two tomorrow."

Next Hazeldine had Fred Baines, the majority whip, on the line. "Fred, I've been going through the numbers. They are a fucking disaster. I talked to Miradol. They think this drug is going to add ten years to the life of everyone who takes it. Ten years, minimum. We jumped too fast and we have to fix it."

"Yeah, a lot of the caucus is having second thoughts," Baines sighed.

"So there's just one way to fix this. We are going to take on the negotiation ban."

"Joe, those drug guys are tough. I took a lot of their money."

"So has everyone else."

"You can't just stick it to your friends. You can't win this. They will kill you."

"There is no other way and here is the thing," Hazeldine said, his voice more emphatic the longer he talked about his idea. "If we don't fix it, it will blow up on all of us. We will be remembered as the leaders who bankrupted America."

"It's great to be a hero," Baines replied, "but a dead hero does no one any good."

"So what would you do?"

"We could not get thirty-five votes right now."

"Fred, if we don't get this done I am finished as speaker. Guess who gets the job?"

"Do you think they would really make that tight-assed Lindsey Jenkins speaker?"

"Freedom Caucus will expect it, demand it. There are only so many times you can say 'no.'"

"Shit! Goddammit, Joe, you are one hard-bargaining sonofabitch."

CHAPTER
Forty-Three

The Russian invasion had begun.

The attack force never set foot on American soil. Isolated in tiny cubicles in suburban Moscow, one thousand hired trolls launched an all-out offensive to promote the benefits of Juventel—and now, the advancement of the Life Bill as well.

Many consider the internet a great democratizing force. But in Russia, China, and other despot nations, social media has become a weapon. The campaign to promote Juventel, launched from Russia, was as elaborately planned and executed as any exercise of war.

Congressmen who tweeted were greeted with an avalanche of replies.

"Are you supporting the Life Bill?"

"What is happening with the Life Bill?"

"Why is Congress blocking the Life Bill?"

"I am taking Juventel. It is a miracle drug."

"I have been prescribing Juventel to my patients. Amazing results. Why are you blocking the bill!"

Each tweet signed by a name so American it must have been listed on the *Mayflower* registry. Each address squarely inside the district.

Party officials, Democratic and Republican, were deluged with similar questions, similar messages.

Doctors were asked if they were prescribing Juventel, and if the answer was "no," they met an avalanche of angry replies and justifying information.

Nonprofits in health and aging got emails asking about their position on the Life Bill.

Trolls spread stories, real and manufactured, via Facebook, Instagram, and other platforms. Altered photos appeared—before Juventel and after—in addition to personal testimonials, doctor testimonials, excerpts from academic articles, and more angry messages about corrupt politicians shortening people's lives.

Behind the bloggers came the bots, the automated responses that searched for the Life Bill, or Juventel or Miradol, and in each instance issued a response, again and again, in varied forms under varied identities. Whatever real sentiment existed in support of this legislation, and indeed it did exist and was growing, that sentiment was magnified from an uprising to riot.

The money was invisible. The voices were false. Truth was the first casualty of war. The internet, the world where individuals were empowered and voices heard, had become a predator, a tool of deception, an instrument of power, and an enemy of democracy itself.

CHAPTER
Forty-Four

Colleen Keegan opened her Mention account. 1,287,165 entries. She began to read, now with some trepidation.

The White House had tweeted that morning. The subject was vaccinations, to which a thousand replies followed decrying the president's opposition to the Life Bill. These were harsh replies, vicious in tone. The facts were distorted and sometimes false.

She typed "Juventel." The fourth entry was an article by a scientist, undoubtedly a fake one, claiming that academicians had modeled life expectancy based upon how Juventel reversed senescence and lengthened telomeres. The projection? An additional twenty years.

Another so-called scientist claimed Juventel doubled the size of the thymus, greatly increasing immunity against any disease. Keegan gulped. Juventel did not affect the thymus at all.

But the worst were the attacks. Vicious attacks simply for opposing the bill.

"Why do you hate old people?"

"Hoping your mom will die sooner to get your inheritance?"

"What gives you the right to send old people to their graves?"

"I bet you opposed the polio vaccine."

Colleen was ashamed of what she saw. She had told Casey to keep this campaign clean. She wanted to stop it but it was all too late. To call Casey Jenkins was too dangerous. No one could know that Miradol was connected to this campaign. No one could know that she was responsible for these lies. She had not understood the agent she hired. Now, she must remain far, far away.

She clicked on Sam Kelley. He was the villain. He was blocking the bill. One after another these Russians eviscerated him. She knew him. She liked him. He was a gentle, kind man.

As she read deeper down the list, each epitaph worse than the last, a little pit of hot anxiety started to burn in her chest. Sam deserved none of this. Colleen was nauseated.

Then she saw it. The label. It was a name so wrong, so cruel that she wondered at how the internet had turned against decency itself, this turbulent, untamed, chaotic space where there were no rules, no honor, no penalty for cruelty of the most reprehensible kind.

Anonymity is a license. Drivers, hidden in their cars, conduct themselves rudely, selfishly, and in a way they would never consider confronting someone face-to-face. But on the internet, behind fictitious names, people could do any wrong and do it for money. Miradol's money, Colleen Keegan's money, was funding this onslaught.

She looked at Sam Kelley's label. In the months ahead it would define him, twist him from who he was into some monster that bore no resemblance to the truth, the person she knew him to be. In politics there were distortions. There were lies. But seldom had an accusation so described one human being in a way so without basis, so completely opposite, and so beyond the realm of decency itself. Two words. Two words to describe Sam Kelley.

"Killer Kelley."

She had made mistakes. Russia was a bad idea. A terrible idea. This whole screw-up with the legislation and that goddamned preacher in Houston. Now, the FDA was after her ass and one way or another Wellstone was going to make her pay. For a moment, her hands began to shake. Her mind went blank and fear radiated from her pores. She gripped the table and feared someone might walk into her office and see her condition.

"Deep breaths. Deep breaths," she whispered to herself. She repeated Siskoff's words of advice. Some measure of calm returned. She knew there was no reason for panic. Last week, sales were $600 million. Six hundred million a week over fifty-two weeks was more than $30 billion. Against that number anything Marvin Wellstone could do would be a pinprick.

She told herself that success had a price. The stock price was up seventy-two percent since the start of the year. Tomorrow, the next day, and the day after it would climb higher again, unless some chickenshit big investor got nervous and cashed out because it all seemed too good to be true. But even that would be a blip.

It was all true. Juventel lengthened lives. Who did not want more years, healthier years?

She thought back to the Board meeting only last week and the memory helped restore her calm. She had entered the boardroom armed with new numbers. She laid them out slowly, deliciously, and watched their eyes grow. Pfister was silent. Casey's bonus? It was not even mentioned. Wellstone and the FDA? Well, there was some discussion, but who the hell cared about him anymore?

She was making all those sonofabitches richer than they could have ever imagined.

Her raise? Ten sweet million dollars a year.

CHAPTER
Forty-Five

The sun had just fallen below the horizon and the sky glowed with the color of a dark pink rose. It was spring, the weather was warming, and the wind gently nudged the trees. An SUV, crammed with campaign and office staff, headed for the Hillsboro-Leiper's Fork Recreation Center about thirty minutes south of Nashville in Franklin, Tennessee, where the congressional office had booked another town hall meeting.

This time, Mike Brazier was on the trip. Working with Ann Bell he had prepared a list of questions Kelley might encounter along with some suggested responses. That afternoon they had practiced. Sam could still be a little long-winded but he was getting the hang of it. He was like a rookie, Brazier thought, a seventy-eight-year-old rookie.

They had booked a classroom big enough to hold fifty people. After all, the last event drew only seventeen, and that included the tracker who filmed the Lund TV spot portraying Sam's age. There was talk in the House about the Life Bill and how it had taken over these meetings. That wasn't good, but how many people would show anyway?

As they pulled into the parking lot it was already full and a large crowd of people, some holding signs, were waiting outside. Many wore lavender T-shirts. "Must be some other event," Brazier thought. Then he read the signs, some printed but most homemade. All of them were about the Life Bill.

"Stop blocking the Life Bill"

"My Life. My Choice."

"Life Bill Saves Lives"

The lavender T-shirts said, "My Life Bill. My Life."

"An ambush," thought Brazier, not wanting to rattle Sam by saying the words out loud.

Kelley's congressional office had made a serious tactical error. Proud that their congressman was visiting voters again, they had published a three-month schedule of town hall meetings across the district. They had signaled their location and the enemy was waiting.

Back in Washington at Seniors United, the money was pouring in. But they did not have to spend that money to rally seniors to Sam's meeting or any of the hundreds of other town hall meetings all across America. They had received a huge check from Miradol for the express purpose of confronting key senators and representatives in their districts with a mob demanding passage of the Life Bill.

Assembling the crowd was easy. They had voter lists with age and a record of how many times each one voted. Their targets were expansive—anyone sixty or older who had voted in at least one election in the last four years. They sent not one mailing but two.

The first mailing showed a woman, somewhere in her seventies, saying, "I could live a longer, healthier life. But Sam Kelley is standing in the way." Sam was accused of ignoring science, turning his back on seniors, and, because he still had his high-paying job with generous health care, not understanding the lives they lived. They were summoned to voice their anger at the one man blocking this drug.

The second mailing was about liberty—about the importance of government allowing human beings to make what could become the most important decision of their lives. That decision was, of course, to buy Juventel. But it was couched not in the language of commercial sales but in the deeper prose of dignity, freedom, and their own quality of life.

The Russians had the schedule as well. Their calls to action were crude and misspoken. They may not have understood what a town hall meeting was but they pointed to Sam Kelley, "Killer Kelley," and rallied the reader to go to the meeting and put a stop to Sam Kelley and the evil deeds he performed.

As Kelley's vehicle swung into the parking lot, many of those gathered recognized the congressman. Most only glared in disgust but some approached the SUV and beat their hands against the windows, shouting accusations that blamed him alone for bringing their lives to an untimely end.

Brazier turned to Ann Bell. "Call the police. We need security here, now!"

As they drove through the parking lot, all of the spaces were filled and they were forced to park far from the entrance. As they exited the car, the crowd moved toward them.

"Make a ring around Sam," Brazier shouted, and the staff held hands in a circle to protect their boss. Sam managed to nod and smile throughout. Progress was slow. People waved their signs and shouted blame. Brazier looked back. The lot was full and a line of cars stretched far from the entrance.

"You don't care whether I live or die!" one protester shouted.

Slowly, they made their way to the doorway, down a long, crowded hallway, and finally to the classroom where the meeting would take place. The room was tightly packed and people spilled into the hallway. Behind those crowding the hall, more people were still arriving. Brazier tried to estimate their number. Three hundred at least. He could not see outside. It might be five hundred. It was hard to tell.

As Sam entered the room a murmur of boos arose, low at first but progressively louder. Sam scanned the angry faces, confused and wondering what he had possibly done to earn this enmity. Nothing had prepared him for this moment. In his entire career he had spoken ill of no one and hardly anyone had spoken ill of him.

He positioned himself behind the "podium," a simple wooden box that sat on the teacher's desk. No one had thought to bring a mic or speakers. His voice was broken with age, not the clear, strong sound he once made, but he lifted that voice strongly to be heard above the din. "Can we have some order in this room? Please?"

The congressman waited patiently as the volume of protests dropped slowly, and when it was low enough to allow him to be heard, he began to speak. "I realize a lot of people are angry here, but I also hope that all of us have come here to learn. I am here to learn from you. I hope that you can also learn about my beliefs and, even if they are not your own, that they are reasonable ones based upon my concern for health care in this country."

He was met with angry muttering. The first question came from an overweight, blue-haired woman who glared at Sam Kelley as if he had stolen her grand-daughter's lunch. "Congressman, there is a drug out there that scientists are telling us can extend our lives by ten years, maybe more. Why are you blocking my access to this drug?"

"I am not blocking access," Sam Kelley replied slowly and patiently. "I simply oppose letting the Congress of the United States make medical decisions they are unqualified to make."

Boos. Sam pointed at a questioner in the back row, who practically shouted, "The FDA takes too long to approve these drugs. They are killing people who could be saved!"

"You need to understand that this is a difficult process," Sam replied, his voice slow and calm. "It takes time to know whether a drug works and whether it is safe. Not every problem is immediately apparent. If they put something out there that is not ready or not thoroughly tested, that can kill people too. The question is who makes these decisions? The FDA has scientists and doc-tors who study these issues all the time. If you had cancer, would you go to Congress to get it fixed?"

There were some chuckles in the crowd, but a lot more angry rumblings. A tall man with bushy white hair rose to speak. "Mr. Kelley, I don't know about science or testing or the FDA, but I know this. I have great-grandchildren on the way, but I am eighty-two years old—older than you. I want to be part of their lives. If this drug doesn't work, what have I lost? I don't have much time left anyway. But if it does work that is my chance to know these children. I don't even care if this drug is unsafe. I have one foot in the grave already. Give me a chance. Give me a chance!"

The crowd erupted in support of this plea with intelligible shouts and the stomping of feet. When the voices finally calmed, Sam answered, "Well, first I want to thank my constituent for letting everyone know that I am not the oldest person in the room."

Sam smiled and it was infectious. There were some chuckles. Brazier was amazed. Sam was charming them.

"Seriously," Sam continued, "drugs are about hope, and almost every drug brought to the FDA offers hope for someone. Hope for a healthier and longer life. But you need more than hope to approve these drugs. We have to protect people's safety too."

The old man, unsatisfied, continued, "Mr. Congressman, I don't need your protection. I'm voting against you, Sam Kelley. I am going to knock on doors and tell my friends to vote against you. And I'm not quitting until you are gone from Congress," he said emphatically, pointing at Sam.

And with that outburst the crowd raised another angry cheer. Outside the room and waiting in the hallway, the crowd, furious at being excluded, sounded a chant. "This is not democracy."

The volume rose and Sam, without a microphone of any kind, became hard to hear. At the door, three police officers appeared. Brazier sliced a finger across his throat, signaling Sam to bring it to an end. The police approached the podium and formed a wedge that parted the crowd and led Sam Kelley from the room. Those inside the room were fuming that the meeting was so short. In the hall, they were angry that their questions were not heard. A chant rose and spread through the room and out the door. "Fire Sam Kelley. Fire Sam Kelley. Fire Sam Kelley."

Sam had been thoughtful. He had been honest. He treated this crowd with a respect they did not deserve. Michael Brazier watched as Sam, protected by police, waded through a sea of loud voices, pointing fingers, and angry signs. He was witnessing the future, a bleak world where the skills of politics were more about inciting anger than in finding common ground. On this night in Franklin, Tennessee, the future had met a more honorable and more decent past. Honor and decency had lost.

After what seemed like an eternity, Kelley and his staff finally arrived at the SUV. A man stood in front of the vehicle, blocking their way. He was thin with gaunt features, his lips a small, tight line and a face so intense that you wondered if it had ever worn a smile. He was holding a sign that displayed two handwritten words.

"Killer Kelley."

CHAPTER

Forty-Six

The ad began in a simple way. A middle-aged man wearing a white coat stood in front of a table with test tubes, beakers, tubing, and scales. Not really the modern laboratory but the ones we still imagine from high school science or old TV shows. Perfect for TV. He began to speak in heavily accented English.

"My name is Andrei Misikoff. Eight years ago I won a Nobel Prize in science, and I am here to tell you about the greatest advance in the history of medicine. It is a drug called Juventel and it can extend the human life by five, ten, or even twenty years. But Congress is blocking your access to this lifesaving miracle. Contact your senators and congressman. Tell them all of us deserve access to a longer and better life."

Sitting at home, in front of her eighty-eight-inch-screen home theater, Colleen Keegan rewound the ad and ran it again. She had two words. "Home run."

It had not been easy getting this ad on the air. Trying to find a Nobel Prize winner to endorse the product was tough. In the first place, there are not many of them. In the second place, they all want to do a study. Here is the research, she would say. They wanted to know who paid for it. Didn't they know how all this worked?

But they had found their spokesperson. He wasn't perfect, not by a long shot. He was Russian and still spoke with an accent. Instead of Andrei Misikoff she would have loved to have found a scientist named Andy Johnson or Suzie Simpson or even Wilson Pendergrast. An American name! But she found Andrei Misikoff, who pronounced every word with a *nnyyyuunnff*, the telltale Russian slurring of the beautiful English language.

She would have liked a better name but there were two words that were even more important. "Nobel Prize." Americans may not have been so impressed when all those Nobel Laureates told them global warming was real. But that was different. Americans did not want to believe in something that required them to sell their SUVs. But they sure as hell wanted to believe they could live another twenty years.

So her staff had found Andrei Misikoff. His Nobel Prize actually had nothing to do with biology, or medicine. He was a physicist. He studied neutrinos. But after he got a big chair at Princeton his girlfriend died and he started to drink. And it wasn't only nighttime drinking. He showed up for meetings sloshed. He slurred his words in class. For a long time the university looked the other way. He looked great on the website where you could not smell his breath. But the episodes grew more and more embarrassing until there was that ugly incident at a Christmas party where he actually groped the dean's wife. So they let him go.

Miradol found him alone in an efficiency apartment in Trenton, New Jersey. A half-million dollars later he was pitching their drug. Two weeks after the ad first aired, Juventel sales jumped another ten percent.

CHAPTER

Forty-Seven

"Earl, thank you for making time to see me," offered Joe Hazeldine as he entered the office of Freedom Caucus Chair Earl Ackerman. "Also, I want to thank you for giving me this job," the speaker said, smiling broadly, without a touch of insincerity. "It's even worse than I thought."

Earl Ackerman laughed. "I thought we had been pretty nice to you. At least until you pulled that bankruptcy incident."

"Well, I am here to redeem myself." Ackerman looked cautiously at the speaker, waiting for the punch line.

"We all know we have a problem and I think it is going to be a lot worse for you guys if we don't get this fixed," Hazeldine said. "I sent you the numbers. They are terrible. Miradol thinks their drug will add ten years to a person's life. Do you know what that will cost the government?"

"Are you suggesting that they are better off dead?" Ackerman asked, his brow furrowed accusingly.

"They are a lot cheaper, that's for sure," the speaker responded, glaring back.

Ackerman pursed his lips and nodded. He knew where this was going.

"You know what makes you different?" Hazeldine's tone was less friendly now. "You and the rest of your group? You are about principle. You have beliefs. You helped get rid of those earmarks and all the corruption that went with them. You guys refused to join those sham caucuses or spend time voting for Boy Scout Day. You've made the House a more serious and principled place."

"Joe, our caucus will not endorse ending the negotiation ban," Ackerman said, trying to stop the speaker before he could continue the platitudes.

"I am going to say this because you won't lie to me," Hazeldine continued anyway. "You know corruption when you see it. When we added prescription drug coverage to Medicare, Big Pharma bought that clause. They paid for it congressman by congressman, vote by vote. It did not serve the government. It grew spending by billions and billions of dollars. It did not serve the people who now pay higher premiums for those drugs."

"I opposed that bill," Ackerman shot back.

"I know you did. But look at me and tell me that Congress did not sell out your principles. Yours! Whether you are for big government or small government, what happened is a perfect example of why you want to get government out of people's lives."

"As I said, I was not for the bill. I was not for that provision. The whole deal, in my view, was corrupt from top to bottom."

"Well, you can't fix all of it but you can do something about that ban. We are in a tough situation. We are supporting something we can't pay for. You are the guys for smaller government. You are the guys for cutting spending. Think of the ads. Earl Ackerman told us he would cut spending, then bankrupted our government."

"I know we are in a fix but your plan is not realistic," Ackerman said, his tone defensive now. "All of our members have their money. Heritage will call it an anti-business vote. They'll score it. You know what that means. Town meeting where our Tea Party voters ask them why they are opposing the conservative line. Nobody wants that. You'll be lucky to get a handful of votes."

"Principle, Earl. Everybody around here grubs for money but you guys have principles. You work for something bigger than paying those money-grubbing consultants for ads in the next election." The speaker continued. "We got so excited to endorse this Life Bill and rub it in the president's face. This was our chance to expand our majority and send Marino home to New Jersey. Our opportunity is real, but only if we can pay for it.

"I don't need a recorded vote. I just need to get it approved by our caucus so we can bring it to the floor. In the caucus we have a secret ballot. Your guys can tell pharma anything they want. They can call up Heritage and engage in deep, tearful dialogue about the tragedy that occurred inside our caucus. But inside that caucus, in a secret ballot, I need those votes."

Ackerman remained silent, his fingers steepled in front of him as he contemplated what Hazeldine was saying.

The speaker went on. "When it goes to the floor they can vote against it—every single one—because the Democrats won't stand with the president on this one. They have been after this negotiation ban for almost two decades. I just need a few Republicans."

"Joe, how will we look if we get to the floor and a majority of Republicans vote the other way?"

"That's my problem and I'll solve it."

"I'll talk to my members," Ackerman said and shrugged. "I can't make the commitment you want on my own."

"I know that. Call me with an answer." The speaker stood and extended his hand.

Joe Hazeldine had come to see Ackerman. His visit to Ackerman's own office was homage to the importance of Ackerman and his caucus in putting together the majority he needed. Ackerman had not budged. He said his caucus would talk about it. It was a promise, to borrow the infamous words of Cactus Jack Garner, former House speaker and vice president, that was not worth a bucket of warm spit.

CHAPTER
Forty-Eight

Sam Kelley walked out of the Rayburn House Office Building and crossed the street. The air was heavy and the thermometer flirted with one hundred degrees. Washington was no place to spend the summer.

The Capitol loomed before him. After thirty-eight years, the sight of this building still awakened feelings. He sometimes imagined the great orators of a century before, Daniel Webster speaking to a full Senate floor, hushed, even enraptured, as he leaned into the podium to deliver a request, perhaps understated but which echoed through history. "I speak today for the preservation of the union. Hear me for my cause."

He wondered what happened to those speeches, now replaced by sound bites. The eloquence of today's politics were two-word phrases like "death tax" or "exporting jobs." He shook his head in disgust.

Sam was not in Congress for the passage of Medicare or the civil rights bill. But he had seen Ronald Reagan and the tax cut debates. He had watched America rein in the excesses of Wall Street and strengthen homeland security. Today, while approaching the entrance of the Capitol he wondered if this Life Bill, for all the hyperbole and even mistruth weaponized by both sides, might be remembered as something larger than it appeared today. That was the problem. You could never know.

Beneath a lofty ceiling decorated with trumpeting angels and crystal chandeliers, he turned to the corridor that led to the speaker's office. Sam knew well what Joe Hazeldine wanted. He wanted Sam's vote and Sam wished he could give it.

Sam admired Joe Hazeldine. He had heard the complaints. The speaker was heavy-handed, even ruthless. But Sam did not blame him. It was hard to get anything done these days and Big Pharma would stop at nothing to get its way. To end the Medicare negotiation ban would be a huge achievement but it came at a price. That price was substituting the judgment of Congress for the decisions of the FDA in certifying the safety and the efficacy of prescription drugs.

It was a price Sam Kelley would never pay.

The receptionist sprung to her feet as Sam entered the door and immediately escorted him to Joe's office. Their handshake had barely separated when Sam spoke his position in a calm and determined way.

"Joe, it's a matter of principle. I cannot vote to allow Congress to usurp the duties of the FDA."

"Sam, talk to me. Tell me what you want out of this bill."

"I want Congress to stay out of the FDA's business."

Hazeldine smiled respectfully and spoke is easy tones. "What about the prices?"

"I support that piece," Sam said. "I never liked that we had to add that negotiation ban. These drug companies are bullies. They throw their money around and get their way. But it was the only way to pass the bill."

"If we pass this Life Bill, can you imagine the benefits? What if Medicare says to Merck you charge $41 a month for that pill in the UK and $120 in America? Can you imagine what we could save those families you represent in Tennessee?"

"I have imagined it for a long time. It would be a great thing."

"So why would it not be worth it, in just this one instance, to bypass FDA on these aging drugs just to help all these families that you and I know are getting fleeced every single day?"

"You can't remove these decisions from FDA," Sam said, his voice even and unwavering.

The speaker looked back at Sam with unblinking eyes. "We can do anything we decide to do."

"Mr. Speaker, you can decide whatever you choose. I will never vote to allow Congress to usurp decisions that belong to an independent body. I will not vote to put politics into a decision that belongs elsewhere, an elsewhere that I have worked to protect my entire career."

The speaker took a deep breath and continued. "I don't think you understand. We have an opportunity to undo a great wrong. These drug companies are swindling us. Juventel. Maybe it works. Maybe it doesn't. But look at the big picture. I have congressmen ready to undo that vote. If we win in the caucus we can save this government and your families billions and billions of dollars every single year. And, Sam, those prices are not just wrong. They are a wrong bought with special interest money, covered with the fingerprints of greed. You know it and I know it. It is corruption. It is wrecking our health care system and fleecing American families. Juventel. One drug. It passed the safety trial. No one is going to die. These seniors are already dying anyway, for Chrissakes! This bill is not about a single drug. It is about an avenue to the greater good. A simple trade-off. We approve a drug already certified safe. What we get in return will pay us back for generations to come."

Sam had expected this lecture, or something like it. He shifted uneasily in his chair and looked at Joe Hazeldine. He could always see the best in everyone. Joe Hazeldine was battling a giant. He was courageous. He was resourceful. But he was wrong. "Joe, I cannot support your bill."

"Sam, I think there is something you don't understand. We are caretakers of this nation. We have been given power and that power can be used to do good. Our actions can put food on the table, cure terrible disease, fuel the engine of capitalism, and lift children from poverty to the pinnacle of success. These things are not easy. We do not always get them right. But we have been granted those powers because we might get it right. We might succeed, and over time this government has succeeded. Don't quote me in front of those Freedom Caucus assholes but government has helped transform this nation from a herd of ass-poor dirt farmers to the most successful nation on the face of the earth."

Sam had expected a long meeting but was losing patience.

"Joe, don't lecture me."

"Hear me out," Joe said, reaching his hand to touch Sam's shoulder. He paused to collect his words.

"Principle is what lies at the center of politics, but, Sam, you and I both know that principle is never enough. Great principles, the loftiest you can imagine, took stained hands to shape into law. Remember Abe Lincoln? Honest Abe? Remember slavery? Well, if there was ever a right and wrong in this world it would be passing the Thirteenth Amendment and ending the curse that placed millions of human beings in chains. That is principle. A beautiful principle. But it was not enough. Honest Abe had to give out jobs and promise projects and lend his support for unsavory matters he would have otherwise never considered at all. He did all that because people are not pure, because people are corrupt or they are afraid or they are sometimes contaminated with prejudice and hate. In a Democracy you need a majority and those majorities include many voices—the pure, the stained, and even the contemptable few.

"Remember the civil rights bill? To pass it Lyndon Baines Johnson bribed Charles Halleck, the Republican leader in the House, with a huge NASA research project for his district, and Halleck made it okay for Republicans to support that bill. That is how LBJ got enough votes to break the filibuster and end a hundred years of second-class citizenship for African Americans. Hell, half our caucus may still oppose that bill, but it was right and it was not passed on principle alone.

"And what about Reagan's tax cut? Would you like a list of the things he had to do to make it the law?"

But before Joe Hazeldine could continue, Sam cut him short. "You are wasting your time. I have made my decision."

For a short moment, Hazeldine grimaced. He was losing and he knew it. He moved to the edge of his chair and tilted forward, as if to enlist gravity itself in support of his argument. His face tightened and his eyes glowed with a determination that defied hope itself.

"You have to understand. Power is a gift. But its successful exercise is a tawdry, humbling, demeaning exercise in sin."

Droplets of sweat appeared on the speaker's forehead. He watched this vote, a vote he desperately needed, stand steadfast beyond his reach. Sam Kelley had been in Congress thirty-eight years but had not learned a thing. His desperate words spoke the unspeakable truth.

"Sam, you are giving me religion, a principle that to you is inviolate and unbending. I respect that. But these choices are never so simple. No one is immune. For centuries, the popes in Rome sold indulgences, money paid for God's personal absolution of individual sin. They did so to finance an empire. Even today do you think that great saint, Pope Francis, is above what his power, marshaled in pursuit of the good, requires of him every single day? Does he not have to placate his enemies with appointments they don't deserve? Do you think he does not have to adopt positions untrue to his own deeply held beliefs just to achieve agreement on other fronts? Do you think he does not sit there, just like me, look at the dream, and ask what distasteful transaction, what compromise, what offense against the rules he must perform to make that dream real for millions of people?

"Don't kid yourself, Sam. You are seventy-eight years old and one day soon you will know. There are no popes in heaven."

CHAPTER
Forty-Nine

"Welcome to *Washington–Believe It or Not!*. I'm Damon Rodriquez, your host of the show that brings you insight and commentary on this week in our nation's capital city. And what is our topic this week?"

The camera cut to three smiling commentators.

"Big Pharma!!!" the three shouted in unison.

"That's right. What happens when the unstoppable force meets the immovable object? Well, we are about to find out. In a stunning announcement House Speaker Joe Hazeldine has shaped a plan to pay for the Life Bill, legislation so expensive some say it will bankrupt the nation. And who is getting the bill?

"Big Pharma, that alliance of the richest and most powerful companies in America. Hazeldine wants them to pay for that wonder drug Juventel, which slows aging, by ending the ban on negotiating lower drug prices with Medicare. And he's not stopping with Juventel. He wants to lower the prices on all other drugs too.

"Our guests today are Robby Santino, former campaign manager for President Marino; Rebecca Wilson, who covers Congress for Politico; and Spud Stevens, founder of Superspin, a hot new political blog.

"So here is my first question: Has Joe Hazeldine lost his mind? Robby?"

"Well, those House Republicans have stepped in it big-time. First, after years of sanctimonious lectures about lower spending and balanced budgets, they voted for a drug plan that could double Medicare spending."

"Double?" Rodriquez asked with a twinkle in his eye.

"Well, nobody knows for sure. There are lots of estimates out there so this is unknown territory. Let's face it. Hazeldine is stuck. To use his own word, he doesn't want to 'bankrupt' the nation. So he is going where the money is. He is sticking it to Big Pharma. He is a brave man, I'll give him that."

"Big Pharma? HUUUUUUGE Pharma!" Spud interjected.

Rebecca chimed in. "To put this plan on the floor he needs a majority of his own caucus. He is not even halfway there. There are only 222 Republicans; 210 are walking around with pharma money in their pockets."

Spud rose in his chair, too excited to sit. "Those Brinks armored cars are going to make a two-mile caravan hauling all that money to Washington just to kill that bill. They'll be blocking traffic for miles. New Jersey, stay off the roads!"

"Thank you, Spud," Rodriquez interrupted. "So, let's have a poll. Can Joe Hazeldine bring his caucus along? Robby?"

"Damon, that Joe Hazeldine is quite a speaker. An amazing talent. But he has no chance. Nobody, I repeat nobody, beats Big Pharma."

"Spud, what's your take?"

"Caesar and Brutus. The long knife. When they unload those Brinksmobiles, they'll have fifty Brutuses begging for the job. Sorry, Joe, you're dead."

"Rebecca, what are his chances? Give me a percentage."

"Gosh, Damon, it's not looking good. I agree with Robby. Joe Hazeldine pulled off an amazing vote with that budget bill. But he can't make this happen."

"Give me a number. A percent."

"Three!" Rebecca answered excitedly.

"Three percent!"

"Well, if you are going to press me, maybe two."

CHAPTER
Fifty

"They are calling it the 'Miradol Miracle.' The number three pharmaceutical company fast on its way to becoming number one in the world. I'm Greta Miska, with Business Today, your six times a day, every day, spotlight on the business world. Today, we are thrilled to have as our guest the remarkable, amazing, inspirational Colleen Keegan, chief executive officer of Miradol and architect of the business success story of the decade. Ms. Keegan—"

"Call me Colleen, please."

"Colleen, we have all heard so much about this miracle drug, Juventel. Tell us about it."

"Well, Greta, the first thing you have to understand is that aging does not have to happen. Not all species age. The whale, the tortoise, even the naked mole rat, they do not age at all."

"Yes, those naked mole rats are probably having too much fun."

Keegan flashed a mischievous smile. "Well, you are probably right about that one. But the reason we age is rooted in evolution. In the early days of our species, when times were good and food was plentiful, our population could expand too rapidly and cause extinction events. In those events, all members of a family group or tribe could run out of food and die. So in times of plenty our genes tell our cells to start dying and keep the population level. In times of hardship, they direct our cells to regenerate and death is postponed."

"Fascinating." Greta leaned in, her chin on her hand.

"Juventel alters the signals received by our cells. It tells them to rejuvenate and repair. In doing so we feel younger. We become healthier. Death is postponed. We live longer, healthier lives."

"How much longer?"

"We obviously won't know for certain until people have been taking Juventel for several years but there are indices of aging we can measure. We can use those measurements to estimate life expectancy. Our models, and these are only scientifically constructed estimates, say Juventel can increase a person's life span by about ten percent."

"So, Colleen, what you are telling us is that if the average person lives to be seventy-eight they get eight years more just by taking Juventel?"

"Our estimate is higher actually. The seventy-eight-year life span is artificially low because people die earlier in accidents and from childhood diseases. If you look at an adult who has already lived to be sixty, we think the extension could be at least ten years."

"Colleen, do you have a bottle on you? I would like to take some home."

Greta laughed. The audience laughed. Colleen laughed.

"Okay, Colleen, here's the real question. How much money is Miradol going to make this year? You have revised earnings estimates four times this year. Your stock price is up 123 percent and still climbing. What is your personal projection for year-end?"

"I have to stick with the numbers my company has released," Colleen said, a sly smile playing at the corners of her mouth.

"Come on, Colleen. It's just you and me talking. Your last number was $53 billion. You know you are going to revise again. These sales are climbing like a rocket ship. Come on, give us your gut. Are you going to end the year as the number one pharmaceutical company in the world?"

Keegan smiled sheepishly. "Well, Greta, all I can say is that is our vision."

"Colleen, can I say something?"

"Of course."

"You are such a rock star. I hope every woman in America watching today can look at you and be inspired. You are such a role model for us all."

"Thank you, Greta. I am just a simple businesswoman trying to shape a better world."

CHAPTER
Fifty-One

Sam was at a fundraiser in Nashville but Ann Bell knew to interrupt. When she got his voicemail she texted, "Call me. NOW!" Five minutes later Sam was on the line.

"Sam, somebody is running ads attacking Lund."

Sam blinked, trying to absorb this information.

"They are attacking him for insider trading," Ann Bell continued.

"How can they do that?" he asked. "This is my campaign."

But that is exactly what they had done. "They" were the Citizens for American Success. The "citizens" they referred to were mostly drug companies. "Success" was their own bottom line.

Lund had endorsed the Life Bill and wanted to end the negotiation ban. Kelley was standing tall against the Life Bill. It was time to show Sidney Lund and everyone else running for Congress the price of messing with pharma.

The ad was dark. Music from Halloween III. A voice so ominous it might have been Satan himself.

> "Sidney Lund, candidate for Congress. New information reveals
> he made a small fortune trading on insider information."

A picture of Jeremy Willard—handsome, sensual—came into view. New music now. Jaws music, right before the teeth sink in.

> "Jeremy Willard, Lund's longtime companion, invested a
> million dollars on Lund's behalf knowing that a contract
> announcement would make Lund a fortune. Illegal. Corrupt.
> Unfair. Can you trust Sidney Lund in Congress?"

. . .

Mike Brazier was viewing the spot when a call came in. It was Sarah
Whiteridge. "Well, Sarah," he said with a smile. "We've finally gone negative."

"It took long enough. This race was over," she said, still cynical about their chances.

"Over? We were even last time I looked."

"Look, I think we call a press conference and demand that the SEC conduct a
criminal investigation. I think we demand that Lund make Willard available
to the press. And if he doesn't, we accuse him of hiding. I think we may have
this guy by the short hairs. He's new. People don't know him. Those are the
guys you can really hurt. Cross your fingers. If we can keep up the pressure
this could finish him off."

Mike nodded even though Sarah couldn't see him and said, "I'll call Sam now."
He hung up and looked at his watch. It was four o'clock in LA; that meant the
six o'clock news in Nashville was coming on. He booted up his laptop to watch.

The anchor kicked off the local news with their race and Brazier girded himself. "Good evening, Nashville, this is Rachel Simpson with WCSB News. We
have new developments in the Fourth District congressional race. Here, with
our report, is Logan Ladner."

The reporter stood before the Lund campaign headquarters, and Mike
Brazier smiled.

> "Thank you, Rachel. This morning a Super PAC called Citizens
> for American Success began running television ads accusing
> Democratic candidate Sidney Lund of engaging in illegal
> insider trading in his own company stock. The PAC is funded
> primarily by pharmaceutical companies.

> "The trading was allegedly handled by a Jeremy Willard,
> described by those close to the campaign as a longtime

companion of Mr. Lund. KCSB had attempted to locate Mr. Willard, who is apparently out of the country at this time. The Lund campaign denies any wrongdoing. But in a surprise development we have a statement from Congressman Sam Kelley, whose campaign was not responsible for these ads. Here is the congressman himself."

Sam Kelley stood on a Nashville sidewalk, surrounded by jostling reporters, their microphones shoved unceremoniously in his face. His lips pursed, his jaw defiant, he stared right into the camera and spoke firmly and with a hint of anger. "I think this ad is disgusting. I call on Citizens for American Success to remove it from the air as soon as possible."

The camera panned back to the reporter. "You don't see many statements like that, Rachel."

"Indeed you don't, Logan. There's something you have to like about Sam Kelley."

CHAPTER
Fifty-Two

It was late at night and Joe Hazeldine was alone in his office. From the large picture window spanning half of one wall, he looked out over the National Mall. The Washington Monument, lit brightly from every side, glistened against the sky. But Hazeldine's mood was dark.

His meeting with Ackerman had been an abject failure. Ackerman led the zealots—the monks. They wanted the liturgy, chapter and verse. They called you a heretic if you changed a word. But they also had a lot less principle than he thought. They were hanging the country out to dry.

Spending. That was the original sin. It was right there in their scriptures. That serpent offered Eve a government pension and the next thing she knew, she and Adam were out on the street. Obviously, they had not read their Bibles at all.

Then there was Sam Kelley. Sam not only lost his fucking arm in Vietnam but he had also lost his way as a leader. One drug, safety tested, slipped through the fingers of FDA and we could cut those Medicare prices in half. We could save the country and all Sam Kelley wanted to do was protect those eggheads at FDA.

The speaker had forty-five votes. He needed 112. And he was not gaining ground.

He thought about Amos Tedford and his advice. "Joe, you can't bribe them anymore because you've got nothing to give. Fear is all you've got. So my advice is to pull out all the stops."

Those were big words. "Pull out all the stops." Scare them. But Republican members of the House weren't scared of Joe Hazeldine. They weren't scared at all.

He looked at the picture on his desk. His three-year-old daughter smiling, glowing at the sight of her daddy. He still thought about her every morning as he rose from his bed. She was the best thing that had ever entered his life.

If the cards were stacked against him, he would need a new hand. He needed control of the things that were out of his reach. The rules? Those rules were for rich lobbyists. They were for companies that could write a $10 million check and dump it on some poor candidate who might never know who was attacking him at all.

The companies and the lobbyists had moved power out of his hands. But he was the one accountable to voters. And who got that power? The predators— the wealthy, the secret, the ruthless, none of whom answered to any voter at all. It was all so disgusting. All so wrong.

He made a decision that night. He would undertake the most important mission of his life. Rules? He would bend them. He would break them if he needed to. But one thing was not going to happen. He was not going to lose.

He looked at his daughter's photo again. "Babushka, we are going to win," he said, then added with a smile, "but watch out for those enemies."

Joe Hazeldine knew what had to be done. He knew the next step and he had the skills and the contacts to make it happen. He had run the committee that investigated Democrats. No one is perfect. No one is clean—at least not as far as those pompous media types define it these days. He needed his hands on the levers. He needed to control the money that flowed to these districts.

He needed an Appropriations chair who would play ball to achieve the greater good.

The current chair was Sean Dwyer, from Queens. He could not control Dwyer. Dwyer had to go. It should not be hard. They weren't so clean up there in Queens.

He picked up the phone and dialed. "Felix?"

"Why, Mr. Speaker, I thought you were finished with people like me."

When Hazeldine had chaired the Oversight Committee, Felix Durand was his secret weapon. Felix was no detective. He had not worked for the FBI or the CIA. He had far more impressive credentials. He had learned his craft with the KGB. He became disillusioned and turned. But before the Soviets could sniff him out, he caught a plane to America. Sergov Koslov, his name at the time, became Felix Durand and he got enough plastic surgery to lose ten years and never be recognized again. He loved his new face and his new French name.

"Not quite. I've got a job for you, Felix. But you can't mention to anyone that I know what you are doing or that we ever talked. Understand?"

"I like this already. Which of those dirtbag Democrats are we after?"

"None of them. We are taking out a Republican this time."

CHAPTER
Fifty-Three

"You are not going to believe this!" Sarah Whiteridge practically screamed into the phone in her excitement. Michael Brazier held the phone away from his ear, waiting for her to continue. "We are up ten points."

A lot had happened since the last time they polled. Sam's new spots had aired, for one thing. There he was, in raucous play with his grandchildren, not looking so old at all. There he was with his beautiful family of twenty-nine, not lecturing anyone about family values but living the reality, the picture worth so many words.

From that spot spun three others. People talking about how Sam had helped them. His work bringing prescription drug coverage to Medicare and, of course, his daughter telling the world that her father never said an unkind thing about anyone in his whole life.

Perhaps that was too much to believe but when Sam called on that secret committee to stop running ads on his opponent, voters began to believe that maybe he was different. They began to understand that, well, maybe they didn't make 'em like Sam Kelley anymore.

"All we needed was a good Lund smacking," Whiteridge practically sang. "Another half million dollars in negative TV ads and we can put this race away." She was secretly pleased that Citizens for American Success had ignored Sam and did not pull their ads.

"Well, send me the poll," Brazier responded. "Then I can get a handle on what's going on."

"Lund's negatives are up. It was the attack ads."

But when Brazier looked at the poll, he read it differently. The poll asked voters to state their opinion, favorable or unfavorable, for both candidates. Lund's favorable rating had fallen a few points. His unfavorable was up from twenty points to twenty-nine points. Twenty-nine percent unfavorable was nothing in politics today. It was an outright badge of honor.

But Sam's numbers were way up. His favorables grew from 46 to 59 percent—a sterling number for any incumbent. But there was also trouble in Sam's numbers. Those voters who did not like Sam REALLY disliked him. Only thirty percent viewed him unfavorable but twenty-six percent viewed him *very* unfavorable.

Then there were Sam's personal measurements.

EFFECTIVE: 53%. Not great.

STRONG LEADER: 43%. Worse.

HONEST AND TRUSTWORTHY: 68%. Off the charts.

Brazier opened the cross-tabs where voters are sliced and diced into scores of categories and you can view any question through the lens of any demographic. Among voters sixty-five and older, Sam's unfavorable was fifty-five percent, almost three-quarters of those "very unfavorable."

The seniors were sure to vote. Politics was not about the majority. It was about the majority that showed up. The seniors always voted. It was also about intensity. If voters have intensity they talked. Nobody really believed those TV ads anymore. The best advertising was word of mouth. Right now, Sam was ahead. But the intensity was on the wrong side.

CHAPTER
Fifty-Four

Congressman Sean Dwyer's district was in Queens, a tough district for a Republican but he had held it for twenty-two years. It had taken Dwyer six years to get a seat on the Appropriations Committee. Those southern and western Republicans were suspicious of a guy from New York City, but Sean Dwyer was patient. He was loyal to the leadership, and they had finally given him the committee he wanted. Today he was Mr. Chairman, head of one of the most powerful committees in Congress.

Even so, the committee wasn't what it used to be. In the old days they came to the chairman for earmarks and he was a dealmaker who knew how to get something in return. Now, there was not so much to give. Still, he was tough and thorough. He took care of business on the Hill and in his district at home.

But he also loved the good life.

His home in Forest Hill Gardens was six thousand square feet of white marble and walnut floors. He was a single man now, his wife having died in a car accident when they were in their twenties. He took lavish vacations, sometimes with gorgeous companions, to Mexico, Italy, and the Grecian Isles. For years, some people wondered where he got all that money.

Joe Hazeldine had wondered himself, but now he was more than curious. He had a job to do and that job was to collect 113 votes. Fear would not be enough. He needed to deliver the love, as Amos Tedford had called it. Love required control of the Appropriations Committee. Love meant having his guy as chairman, someone who would play ball. Someone who would not waver if he bent the rules. Dwyer had to go.

Ten days earlier, he had called Felix Durand, the former KGB operative. America was a new place for Durand. A beautiful place. But he had had to learn it. It took him time to do so. But the trails that a man follows in pursuit of his prey are the same all over the world. Money. Love. Fame.

Felix Durand had a nose for all three.

"Well, Mr. Speaker, this one was so easy I might have to cut my fee." Durand had lost his Russian accent and now spoke with an inflection that was faintly French.

"I'll believe that when I get a bill. What did you find?"

"So what is the only money Congressman Dwyer touches? Remember, he sold those dry cleaner businesses that never made money anyway."

"Well, he is chairman of Appropriations."

"I'm sure there are opportunities but that money is tougher. Federal accounting. Reporters. Not so easy to lift."

"So it must be his campaign money," Hazeldine said, drumming his fingers impatiently on his desk.

"Right."

"Okay, don't keep me waiting."

"Well, some expenditures come in groups," Durand began.

"What do you mean?" Hazeldine interrupted.

"Take the TV budget. If you are buying ads, you are also paying production costs."

"But he's in Queens. Who can afford TV ads in Queens? Cable maybe but he has to use mail."

"And if you spend money on mail you need printing and postage."

"Right." Hazeldine nodded.

"Well, in his last campaign, which wasn't really a campaign, our guy Congressman Dwyer spent $350,000 on printing but spent nothing on postage. Does not smell good to me." Durand shook his head with a comically disapproving smile. "I looked at the address of the printer and go for a visit. I was going to give them a job, you know, get to know their people a little. But I go to this address and the door is locked and there is no sign on the outside. I look through the window and there is no printing equipment at all."

"Okay," the speaker said slowly, liking what he is hearing.

"So then I check out the company. It is owned by an Elmore Dillard. Ever heard of him?"

"Never."

"Well, neither has anyone in Queens. But there is a registry. You can go to court and change your name. And so I look to see if anyone has changed their name to that of Mr. Dillard."

"You found someone."

"Grimaldi. Alfonso Grimaldi. He is the mentally disabled son of Franco Grimaldi, nephew of the crime boss of the Bonacoursi crime family. He lives at home, never leaves the house, but owns the Remsen Brothers Print and Mail Company. Now, Elmore Dillard, he has a nice non-Italian name." Felix smiled. "I bet he did not get a penny of that money."

"So you think Dwyer is paying a sham company, owned by the mob, who takes a piece and hands him the rest?"

"That was the last campaign. Over the last eight years he has paid Mr. Dillard's company six times for printing and not a penny for postage."

"Holy shit," Hazeldine said, using his handkerchief to wipe his brow, which had broken out in sweat at the thought of Durand's news.

"Exactly, except I don't have Dwyer's bank records. For all I know he could have taken cash. So we don't have the money in his hands."

"Felix, this is politics, not the DA's office. The rules are different. I have every number I need."

"One more thing, Mr. Speaker. Who do I bill?"

"Bill the Center for Progress, Post Office Box 2145, Richmond, Virginia, 23221."

CHAPTER
Fifty-Five

The sign said "Layla's Bluegrass Inn," a music bar that offered a taste of "Nashville's Hillbilly Music." Jaden Owens stepped inside.

Owens was a troublemaker, at least in some eyes. He was a blogger, and his blog "Ole Betsy" took shots at politicians, mostly at Republicans, but he did not mind hitting both sides of the aisle. But tonight it was not some grizzled local alderman in his sights. Single, with no plans, he was cruising and Layla's was a great place to score. Who needed a great pickup line when you could just ask a woman to dance?

Inside, the bar was narrow and long with worn brick walls on either side. Those walls were adorned with American flags and a collection of old, tattered license plates nailed into place, maybe from all fifty states but then who had time to count?

The band was playing one of Jaden's favorites, "Guitars, Cadillacs and Hillbilly Music" by Dwight Yoakam, when he strode in. It was all Jaden could do not to belt out the chorus.

> *Now it's guitars, Cadillacs, hillbilly music*
> *Lonely, lonely streets that I call home*
> *Yeah my guitars, Cadillacs, hillbilly music*
> *Is the only thing that keeps me hanging on*

He scanned the bar and spotted a bright-eyed young redhead talking to her girlfriend. He moved quickly to take the empty seat at her side.

Jaden was not a bad-looking guy. He wasn't tall but was at least a little sculpted with straw brown hair and tiny dark eyes that suggested he was full of all kinds of serious thoughts. He sat down and waited for the girl to turn his way. But she was talking to her friend in an animated way and did not look back at all. After fifteen minutes, she rose and headed for the ladies' room. Her friend looked at Jaden and reached out her hand.

"Hi, I'm Susan Weidman," she said with an accent more from the lower counties than Nashville itself.

She wasn't quite as attractive as her redheaded friend but the skin on her round face was clear, her dirty blond hair was stylishly cut, and her smile was warm and inviting.

"Jaden Miska," he answered, taking her hand. "You from around here?" You had to ask, despite the accent. The bars on Broadway drew a lot of tourist traffic. Not always a bad thing.

"Yep, East Nashville." She had a twinkle in her eye. Jaden leaned forward, his alert meter rising. "So, tell me what you love besides hillbilly music?" she asked

"A lot of things," he replied, returning her smile. He did like a lot of things, but he was searching for which of all those things might connect with this girl and win him the night. It probably wasn't politics.

"Well, do I get to hear even one? What do you do for a living?"

Now he had no choice.

"I'm a blogger. I write about politics," he said slowly, half expecting this answer to put his big chance out to pasture.

"Well, I don't know much about politics, but I once got run off the road by Sam Kelley's nephew."

"Were you okay?" he answered, not really curious but trying to keep the conversation alive.

"I broke my leg."

"Ouch."

"And he was driving Sam Kelley's campaign car."

"Oh my," said Jaden with an emerging smile. "Can I buy you a drink?"

CHAPTER
Fifty-Six

At the Mandarin Oriental Hotel in New York City, limousines were a common sight. But today, a caravan of them stretched all the way around the block. At the entrance to the luxury hotel, the doormen scampered to the doors, holding them open, even bowing slightly as passengers stepped out. It was a grand show for a grand assembly, and every employee had been briefed on the arrival of these august guests.

Big Pharma was gathering. Invited to this meeting were the top twenty pharmaceutical companies in the world. Genovo, Cinegon, Provosten, Rist, and more. They were represented not by vice presidents or political directors or keepers of the money. They were represented by the chief executive officers and the chairs, no more than two from each company. Many brought staff for questions and support, but when they gathered no staff were admitted to the room. Most waited in the lounge, where they drank coffee and ate pastries at $48 a pop.

Among the pharma giants only Miradol, now the number one pharmaceutical company in the world, was not present. Colleen Keegan had been crossed from the list.

They were meeting with an urgent purpose. They were gathering to muster their resources for the biggest political fight in more than fifteen years. They were preparing for battle, an all-out brawl, that would extend from the beaches of Hawaii to the thick, woolen carpets of the Oval Office itself. They had gathered to defend their largesse, and every single company in the room understood the cost of losing was many multiples of any price they might be asked to pay.

There was one more purpose they had in mind. In addition to saving the Medicare negotiation ban, they were going to discipline Miradol and, in particular, that money-grubbing bitch, Colleen Keegan, who had sold them out, risked their very livelihood, all to push herself and her company to number one in the world. And what hurt, what really hurt, was that she had already succeeded.

The meeting was on the thirty-sixth floor in the Grand Salon Room, a stunning space with windows overlooking midtown Manhattan. As the participants gathered there were handshakes and smiles, friendly smiles but not too friendly because they were not only colleagues, they were competitors as well.

At the head of an imposing oval conference table stood Sampson Kraft, CEO of Genovo, the number one pharma in the world, at least until Colleen Keegan began her dirty deeds. He was tall, six-foot-four, and slender. Though in his sixties, he still ran five miles most days. His physical presence was impressive enough to dominate most rooms, but it was his eyes, blue and penetrating, that commanded the attention of friend and foe alike. He cleared his throat and called the meeting to order.

"Good morning and welcome. Thank you all for taking the time from your busy schedules to attend this meeting. I think we all know why we're here, but I want to start with a number. That number is $60 billion in revenues." He paused to let that sink in before continuing. "Last year Medicare spent $120 billion on prescription drugs. If they get the right to negotiate—and remember, we have a Democratic administration—they will show us our own prices from all over the world. They will point out, correctly, that we are charging Medicare four, five, and six times what we charge for the same drugs elsewhere in the world. You know where this conversation will end. They could cut Medicare prices in half.

"Losing that negotiation would have spillover effects. If grandmother pays half of what mom has to pay, do you think there won't be complaints? Do you think there won't be anger? It won't stop with Medicare. There will be calls for price controls. Those health insurers will move in for the kill." He paused again, his brow furrowed with consternation, a look of pain in his overall expression. "A terrible calamity lies before us.

"We have a price structure that places on the American consumer the heavy cost of researching and developing these drugs. Without that money, many of the miracles we produce would never have happened at all. But if the speaker of the House, Joe Hazeldine, wins and this negotiation ban ends, that price structure will fundamentally change. It is the first in a series of steps that will change this industry forever. So I ask you, what price is worth paying to stop this maneuver?"

One by one the pharma execs rose to share their own stories of how attention to this issue had already angered their customers and tarred their industry. They rose to offer extravagant numbers for funding they would commit to this battle.

Then Sampson Kraft called into the room Kevin Blake. Blake, a political consultant and veteran of several presidential campaigns, was joined by lobbyist Steven Garrett, who had worked for a number of companies in the room. Their presentation covered three topics—donations, independent expenditures, and lobbying.

Donations were a problem. Why? Because there were 435 members of the House and 400 had already gotten drug money. Ninety-seven senators had taken their money as well. A PAC can only give $5,000 to a candidate. That was nothing. If they wanted to give more money to all these candidates, they needed more PACs.

A Washington attorney explained to the assembled group how that could be done.

Independent expenditures were more complicated. The money had become easier. There was now the Super PAC. A Super PAC could spend unlimited amounts of money against any candidate. A Super PAC could take a check written directly from Genovo, Cinegon, or any other Pharma and drop that money right into their campaigns. But this strategy was tricky.

If the candidate under attack could say all these ads against him were paid for by Big Pharma because he was working to lower drug prices, that made him a hero. But only if he could tie the money to the drug companies themselves. Big Pharma had a Super PAC, Citizens for American Success. But everyone knew it was funded by Pharma. Their fingerprints were on all the ads. To solve this problem, Blake offered a new strategy. They would use the "Russian Doll" loophole, so called because each contribution was hidden inside another contribution until the money spent on the ads could no longer be traced. It was all legal.

The attorney continued his explanation. "So here is the plan. We set up a Super PAC, the 'Fund for Struggling Families'—a name that has nothing to do with pharmaceuticals. Each company in this room contributes to a group that you set up and name exactly as our lawyers suggest. These groups don't spend campaign money but contribute to another group. That group contributes to another group. Finally, the last group gives its money to our Super PAC. Each of your contributions is concealed behind three money transfers that do not have to be disclosed."

Rex Baldrige, chair at Rist, a Swiss pharma, rose to speak. "Guys, I know we have a big problem here and we have to be smart. There is something sleazy about all this. Frankly, I am uncomfortable. Can't we be a little more straightforward?"

Kevin Blake responded. "There is a different way. That different way is to fight this bill on its merits. Currently, voters oppose this negotiation ban in numbers exceeding eighty percent. Any message we deliver, as an industry, will be treated with distrust and disdain. We cannot allow these campaigns to become a referendum on the ban. We cannot make this a referendum on our industry either."

Baldridge continued. "We don't have to talk about the ban. We can talk about other issues. We just don't have to hide under the table, slithering around in the darkness to avoid the public eye."

"If the public knows these are our ads, they will know why we are running them," Blake answered. "How do I know this? The other side will tell them. It is a fact of life."

"Well, who is the other side?" Baldridge asked. "Who has the money to compete with the companies in this room? Good government? Low prices? There is no money behind those causes."

Sampson Kraft stepped into the debate. "I'll tell you who has the money. And don't think they won't spend it, because if this Life Bill passes they are going to lift tens of billions of dollars right out of your pockets and into their own."

Baldridge knew the answer and so did every person in the room.

"Miradol."

There was much grumbling in the room. Stealth. Dark money. Ads for Big Pharma profits disguised as pleas for struggling families. Maybe they felt like taking a shower. But they also knew the numbers and their fiduciary duty to their own stockholders. They saw their losses. And they saw Colleen Keegan smiling as she took their money, truckloads of it, straight to the bank.

Blake took his seat. No one questioned the strategy again.

Steven Garrett, the lobbyist, took the floor. It was not that Big Pharma was not lobbying. The previous year, they had spent almost $4 billion to lobby Congress and legislators across the nation. Was that enough? Of course not. Now their strategy required something new.

Tens of millions of Americans wanted the "miracle drug." They wanted Juventel and the ten precious years it might add to their lives. They wanted better health that could come simply by lengthening those little telomeres that capped their DNA. They had read about DNA and evolution and how this wonder drug tricked their bodies into sparing their memories, growing their muscles, making them into the people they once knew—not the haggard, crumbling version they barely recognized today.

Juventel was a fascinating story, a miracle of hope, a Bronx cheer to the Grim Reaper waiting at their door. This story, unchallenged, had swept the nation, raising anger against the slow machinations of Congress that were blocking their dreams. Without a challenge to the drug itself, the legislation was sure to pass.

In front of these titans, Steven Garrett described the challenge he had in store. A new research entity had been launched three weeks earlier with money from Genovo. They were assembling a team of top scientists whose job it would be to examine the Juventel trials, to expose methodological error, to identify new side effects, and to publicize new dangers that might occur with its use.

Garrett continued, "This new research institute was created for the purpose of advancing aging science and correcting public misconceptions about products in the field. It is called The Institute for Standards in the Science of Aging. The first action of the institute will be to file a lawsuit, tomorrow, to obtain the detailed trial data that Miradol is using to promote off-label sales. If Miradol refuses to release that data we will launch a campaign they will never forget. When we get the data, we will use it to discredit Juventel.

"Gentlemen," Garrett concluded, for without the presence of Colleen Keegan there were only two women in the room, "as long as Juventel remains a miracle drug we will struggle to win. Miradol has gotten a free ride but that ride is over. We have to raise questions, doubts, and fears. We must convince the public that this drug is a sham. The Institute is our means to achieve that goal."

Now there was excitement in the room. These chieftains looked gleefully to one another, their approval clear without the utterance of a single word.

Sampson Kraft distributed envelopes addressed to each company represented around the table. Inside the envelopes were three figures—their new PAC contribution amount (and the number of new PACs that would be required), money they would put into that chain of Russian Dolls, and their share of the costs to run this new institute.

The total tab was $6 billion, in addition to the money they were spending already. It was big money—bigger than what the presidential campaigns had spent in the last two elections. But that amount was a mere ten percent of the $60 billion risk that Sampson Kraft had outlined before them as the meeting began. A $60 billion liability that would grow with inflation and continue year after year until a time no one could know.

And it was not just money lost. That money would go straight into the pocket of Miradol and Colleen Keegan. The thought was unbearable.

There was not a protest in the room.

CHAPTER
Fifty-Seven

Sidney Lund was not a tall man, and on this day piles of one-dollar bills, stacked one neatly on top of the other, soared above his head on three sides. In front of all this money, he was a midget lost in a tower of unimaginable cash.

Before him stood the Nashville press corps, gathered tightly against the platform on which he stood. Behind them were the cameras, standing on platforms carefully positioned by the campaign to capture the image, their candidate, and the piles of money rising from the stage. Sidney Lund, his forehead glistening and his eyes unsteady, darting about the scene before him, began to read his statement.

"To the people of middle Tennessee," he said, his speech halting and slow. "I have come here to expose a fraud, a lie, and a betrayal so outrageous as to shock every voter in the Fourth Congressional District. The incumbent, Sam Kelley, has alleged that he was an architect of legislation that brought about prescription drug coverage under Medicare. And it is true that he helped author this legislation.

"But what he has not disclosed is that he handed the big drug companies a gift worth hundreds of billions of dollars—a prohibition on Medicare, the largest purchaser of prescription drugs in the world, against negotiating—even asking or even suggesting—lower prices for these drugs. And as a result, Tennessee seniors, through their premiums, and taxpayers with their hard-earned tax dollars, have paid an enormous price.

"I stand here today in front of $337,266 in cash—the amount that the average family of four will pay, over their lifetimes, for Sam Kelley's sell-out to Big Pharma. Some call it a deal. Some call it business as usual and surely it is.

But I call it robbery. Sam Kelley robbing taxpayers and families to reward his largest contributor, the prescription drug industry in America."

This was Jim Villers, Lund's new campaign manager, at work.

The money was 337,266 one-dollar bills. The bills, which could not stand so high in a single stack, were affixed to plywood backdrops so that they would appear that the wall of bills might be several layers deep. Between each bill was a smaller piece of paper, cut too small to show but which pushed the stack even higher.

The numbers were questionable. The Lund campaign calculated the average prescription drug costs per year per American and multiplied it by four. Then they multiplied that by a lifetime estimate of eighty-two years because surely young families of today would live longer than the seventy-eight-year life span of today. Then they assumed that mere negotiation could reduce current prices by seventy-five percent, and not just Medicare prices but all prescription drugs, their theory being that if Medicare prices fall the others will follow. They were numbers pulled from the air. But no journalists questioned their figures. And all that really mattered was the size of those three green walls of George Washingtons and how they towered above Sidney Lund.

Voters may never remember a number, but the picture was one they would never forget.

Lund continued his attack.

"Now, Sam Kelley is standing in the way of the Life Bill, which would not only grant extra years and greater health to millions of seniors, it would also repeal this ban, which is costing Americans $75 billion per year."

While Lund was holding forth before the media, Sam was in Lebanon, Tennessee, shaking hands. One of the TV stations had dispatched a reporter to get Sam's response.

"Congressman Kelley, Sidney Lund says you swindled Americans out of $400,000 per family by supporting a law that bans Medicare from negotiating lower prices with the big drug companies. What is your response?"

"I don't know about that number, but I never liked that negotiation ban. It seemed wrong to me. I spoke out against it in committee."

"But did you vote for it?"

"It was the only way to get that bill passed."

"Did you vote for it?

"Yes, I voted for it."

"Thank you, Congressman."

Sam's last line was all that made the evening news.

CHAPTER
Fifty-Eight

"Mr. Speaker, Earl Ackerman is on the line."

"Shit," Hazeldine muttered to himself. Nothing about this call could be good. "Earl, so great to hear from you."

"Thank you, Mr. Speaker. I wanted to report that I talked to our caucus."

Hazeldine braced for the worst.

"We are not endorsing your plan. That would be a little too tough for some of our members. But we are not opposing it either. We have decided to let members make their own decisions."

Hazeldine sat up in his chair. This was better than he expected. "Well, that's great news. But let me ask you, did you get any indication of who is likely to come our way?"

"I think you'll get several votes. Maybe even ten."

There were thirty members of that caucus. Ackerman ran through a list of names, supporters and undecideds, but there was one of those names Hazeldine had not expected. "Rich Fletcher. He was on board?"

"I think he's a safe vote. He's a little shocked that we are going to spend this money. You know, he's got a pretty tough race on his hands. He could use some help."

"Thank you, Earl. You don't know how helpful you have been."

Joe was excited. Fletcher was from Chicago. Rogers Park. He had been an alderman in Chicago, where politics is played a little loose. He was also a member of the Appropriations Committee. He was still looking for a new chair of that committee and had someone in mind. But Fletcher would be better. Fletcher was also Tea Party. That was something he could undoubtedly use. He would be easier to get through the Steering Committee. The speaker always had a big say in these appointments but there were thirty-nine members of the committee. Thirty-nine! *Who made these rules?* he wondered.

Some Steering Committee members would say that Fletcher was too new. He would respond that he owed the Freedom Caucus the appointment. With the speaker's support, and Earl throwing a tantrum, no one would put up a fight.

He buzzed his assistant. "Can you tell Rich Fletcher to get to my office ASAP?"

"Yes, Mr. Speaker."

. . .

Ten minutes later, Fletcher was seated in the chair on the other side of Hazeldine's desk. Joe liked his promptness.

Fletcher was a young man, not yet forty and already in his fourth term. He was a lawyer, a graduate of Northwestern, but after two years at one of those big, fancy law firms he left for a more interesting career. He was elected to the Board of Aldermen at twenty-eight. As one of the few Republicans he should have had no influence at all. But the Democrats were in a cat fight and he adroitly exploited those divisions to become a dealmaker for this district. He was a comer, a guy on the rise. But youngsters never got a prize like Appropriations.

"Rich, I understand you have a tough race."

"There are not many Republicans left in Chicago, even where I live."

"I think I can help you. Bring me a list of projects you want funded and let's see what I can do."

Fletcher looked at the speaker, surprised. "I thought that stuff was over."

"Well, there are still ways to do it. Imagine you are secretary of HUD. You have been begging for money for internet infrastructure and ending the digital divide. You want money for homelessness. What happens?"

"We nuke them."

"Right," Hazeldine answered. "But what if we gave them some of that and what if, to show their appreciation, they gave us some projects. We give them the list. You're from Chicago, right?"

Fletcher smiled. "That would be hard to do in Appropriations," Fletcher answered.

Hazeldine paused for effect. "You would need the right chair."

"That's for sure."

"How would you like to chair the House Appropriations Committee?"

Fletcher looked at the speaker, at first shocked by the offer, but then his face transformed to a look of sly admiration. Under ordinary circumstances, he might have waited twenty years for this post, assuming he could get re-elected in a district that was growing more liberal every year. But if he heard the speaker right, here it was, right in front of him, his for the taking. In this job he would have power, power to trim the government, power to move his agenda. And if he understood the speaker, there were going to be projects again and some of those projects would be in his district and help save his seat.

He understood the unspoken words. In the short term, he would need to do the speaker's bidding. He would have to play ball. But that would not be for long. The speaker was taking on pharma. There would be a new speaker next year.

"And Rich, if we work together and make these things happen, guess whose district gets the most projects of all."

The answer was unnecessary. Rich Fletcher already knew.

CHAPTER
Fifty-Nine

It was Colleen Keegan's favorite day of the week. Friday. Friday was numbers day.

She got sales figures every day and she loved them. But on Friday she got the charts, the demographics, and the research. The dailies were great. Toplines. But on Friday she got to wallow in the numbers, one slide at a time, a gorgeous chance to more thoroughly appreciate all of her beautiful, unbelievable success.

She did not even feel snubbed by all those guys who had disinvited her to their Big Pharma powwow. She laughed at them. Their meeting was about jealousy, envy, and being righteously pissed off that a woman, she, Colleen Keegan of the female species, had whipped their butts from top to bottom.

She smiled and imagined all of them, crowded into that room, scared and not sure what to do. She wasn't finished. There was more fucking on the way.

Three staff members burst into her office. They were excited. They loved Fridays too.

"How about some numbers, Ms. Keegan?" asked Walter Schmidt, Miradol's new marketing boss, with a twinkle in his eye and a playful bow. He opened his laptop, found his PowerPoint presentation, and directed it onto Colleen's whiteboard.

POWERPOINT SLIDE ONE: Weekl y sales approach billion-dollar mark. $728 million.

POWERPOINT SLIDE TWO: Growth in sales. Beautiful stair step graph. Still climbing.

POWERPOINT SLIDE THREE: Worldwide Sales Distribution.

The map showed sales all over the globe. France—$32 million. China—$50 million. Russia—$27 million.

POWERPOINT SLIDE FOUR: Customer Demographics American Market—Income.

In America, the more money you have the more likely you are to buy. No surprise. Two hundred a month is a big chunk of a Social Security check.

POWERPOINT SLIDE FIVE: Customer Demographics American Market—Age.

Keegan had been looking at this graph for weeks. At first the market was almost all sixty-five-plus. Then the fifty-year-olds started to buy. Today, the average age moved downward again. There were twenty-somethings taking Juventel.

"Who told these people to buy Juventel?" she blurted out. "They have all our stuff in their blood already." It should have been great news. If everybody buys the drug the market has no limit. Maybe the almost eight billion human beings who inhabit the planet minus the starving poor and those without access to a doctor to prescribe it. But something about this information made her nervous.

After more PowerPoint slides, more graphs, more good news, and more revenues, they moved to the market research.

FIRST QUESTION: Have you heard of Juventel? Three percent "no." Keegan chuckled. Cave-dwellers.

SECOND QUESTION: Do you have a positive or negative opinion of Juventel? Negative—seven percent. Positive—eighty-eight percent.

THIRD QUESTION: Do you believe that most people who take Juventel will experience at least five years of longer life? Seventy-two percent "yes."

Now for the big question. If the Life Bill passed and Medicare picked up the tab, what would that do to sales?

Among Americans over the age of sixty-five, who were not currently taking Juventel, 81 percent said they would take Juventel if Medicare picked up the tab.

Keegan leaned back in her chair and stared at the screen. This drug was a freight train traveling at runaway speed. No one was standing in her way. They were going to pass that law. She knew politics and she had the money to play.

She had no words. Nothing she could add to the accumulation of evidence that her product, her drug, was going to be bought and consumed by half the planet.

Then she was afraid. She put her hands under her desk so no one would see them shake.

This is all too easy, she thought. *Way too easy.*

CHAPTER
Sixty

"This is Meredith O'Leary with *Inside Congress*, a weekly report about news and information on Capitol Hill.

"The big news this week is the announcement that Sean Dwyer will be stepping down from his chairmanship of the House Appropriations Committee to take a position leading the newly formed "Task Force for Tomorrow's Republican Agenda." Here is House Speaker Joe Hazeldine explaining the move.

> "In the House, we become so engaged in the day-to-day business of the American people that we too often lose sight of challenges just over the horizon. Sean Dwyer has always been one of our party's visionaries. That is why I have asked him to step down as Appropriations chair and take on an even bigger and more important task. Charting our destiny in the future."

"I have with me today *Politico* correspondent Rachel Evans. Rachel, do you believe it?"

"Not for a second. Who would leave one of the most powerful posts in Congress to chair a task force that at the moment has no budget, no offices, and, for that matter, no other members?"

"Well, that does say a lot about this move. So why would Sean Dwyer give up his post?"

"Meredith, Sean Dwyer was forced out and the move has Tea Party fingerprints all over it. First, look at his replacement, Rich Fletcher. Tea Party. Freedom Caucus. Earl Ackerman never got over the way Hazeldine ate his lunch on the budget deal. They've been making trouble and I think Hazeldine finally caved."

"Well, Rachel, does this mean Hazeldine is losing control?"

"It is certainly a sign of weakness."

"What do we know about this new chair, Rich Fletcher?"

"Well, first of all he is young with little seniority. So why would Hazeldine give him the job without a gun at his head? I think Hazeldine is trying to endear himself to the conservatives in hopes of getting some votes for his new Life Bill."

"You mean the version that ends the Medicare negotiation ban?"

"That's the one."

"Well, will it work?"

"He'll get Fletcher's vote but, I have to say, that is a very expensive vote. But I don't see much progress." Rachel Evans flashed a knowing smile. "Frankly, I think we are going to see a new speaker next year."

"Tea Party rising. The speaker on his knees. And new leadership next year. Pretty dramatic stuff, Rachel."

"It's always interesting around here."

CHAPTER
Sixty-One

The enormous, oval blue lights glowed from the ceiling high above the ballroom floor, casting a soft glow over the thousand guests assembled below. They had arrived in their Armani suits and I. Magnin dresses to celebrate the success of an organization that had risen to power anew. It was the annual fundraising dinner of Seniors United.

Seniors United had crawled back from shuttered offices to new floors in Washington's most expensive real estate. Mirabelle Jenkins, once counting her layoffs, had hired two hundred new staff. Their current membership? Well over one million. And now the wealthy and well-connected of Washington had come to pay tribute to Seniors United and the stunning success its president had achieved.

Neither love for seniors nor their sympathy for their plight had populated this vast gathering. Seated at the tables, which went for $1,000 per seat, were vendors, printers, ad buyers, real estate companies, and consultants—scores of consultants—whose contributions were extracted each year in exchange for the business they had already received. Then there were the party leaders, the allied associations, lobbyists, and networkers all gathered to be seen and to be familiar to this rising power in case they needed its help.

And, of course, there were the luminaries. The speaker was there, the majority leader of the Senate, and even the vice president himself. All three were given the opportunity to make a short speech, to praise Mirabelle Jenkins, and to express concern for the plight of seniors who now with their retirement protected by automatic tax increases faced a more terrible threat. They might tragically be denied their monthly allotment of Juventel, paid for by Medicare, so they could enjoy those retirement benefits even longer into the future.

One by one the other speakers on the program rose to praise Mirabelle Jenkins and to explain exactly why the Life Bill, the right of every American to a longer life, was essential to America's future. And when the last of these speakers had finished and Seniors United was bathed in the adoration it had surely earned, the moment came that they all had awaited—the reveal of who would be inducted into the Seniors United "List of Luminaries," a list that included Franklin Roosevelt, Lyndon Johnson, Claude Pepper, and other heroes for the seniors' cause.

Senator Eugene Miller from the fine state of Nebraska walked to the podium to bestow this coveted honor. "Ladies and gentlemen, in the course of human history there have been few men or women who have with their own vision reshaped our society as we know it. I speak of leaders who have seen a future, unimagined by the ordinary among us, and who reached for a dream that almost no one thought possible.

"What does it take to change our world? It begins with vision but vision is hardly enough. It takes courage. It takes example. It takes integrity and it takes a persistence shared by only a tiny few.

"Tonight, we honor just such a leader. Tonight, we honor a congressman whose work, while still unfinished, has the potential to grant to people all across America the ability to experience a dream imagined for many millennia but now within our reach, a dream of a longer and healthier life. Ladies and gentlemen, I give you that great visionary, that great lawmaker, that fine moral example for all of us to follow. I give you the man who wrote the Life Bill with his very own hand. It is my great honor to add another great name to the Seniors United List of Luminaries. Tonight we add the name of Congressman Josiah Rush of Texas!"

Reverend Rush rose from his table. Perhaps he had taken $150,000 and double-crossed his donor. Sure, he rewrote the bill to provide Medicare coverage that, in its original form, would have bankrupted the nation. But who cared? Who knew? Josiah Rush had inadvertently provided Seniors United with their ticket to power once again.

So they honored him.

As he approached the podium to accept this award, he glowed in appreciation as a thousand Washingtonians rose to their feet to applaud this new example of heroism in the nation.

CHAPTER

Sixty-Two

The sun was beaming like a dad with his newborn nestled in his arms, and Nashville bathed in its glow. Sam Kelley was walking down Fifth Avenue on his way to a speech at the Bridgestone Arena where the Nashville Kiwanis were holding their weekly Friday morning meeting. He wore a suit, dark blue with a red tie, and, in the summer heat, rivulets of moisture striped his face.

"Good morning, ma'am, I am Congressman Sam Kelley and I'd like your vote," he said pleasantly to a middle-aged woman trying to shepherd three unruly children across the street.

Not many candidates hand-shook the streets anymore. It was inefficient. How many people was it possible to see? When you saw them, did a passing hand-shake change anyone's opinion at all? It was an outdated tactic, but Sam himself was an outdated candidate.

Sam had grown to actually enjoy the handshaking. He liked people. People recognized him, and he liked the conversations he sometimes had.

He had not represented Nashville in the past; redistricting had given him some of its precincts. But there had been television ads, lots of them, running in that media market, and although these ads were often skipped on the DVR or missed by viewers choosing Netflix, Amazon, or Hulu, most people seemed to know him and they seemed to have their opinions already.

There was hostility in some, an anger that was tempered by the gentility of this mostly southern town. Others remembered his big family and that he was against negative ads. They liked that. But this campaign was so unlike that first campaign Sam ran way back in 1978. People were just different now. Everyone had his or her own information and no one's information was the same.

He continued down the sidewalk, smiling, nodding, offering his hand. Out of the corner of his eye he saw a big-screen television and his picture was on the screen. It was in a bar that served lunch with a lot of TVs. Rippy's Bar and Grill. He walked inside and watched.

The photo was grainy, and he looked really old. An ominous voiceover began:

> "Sam Kelley is blocking the Life Bill. Science has given us a chance to live longer, healthier lives, but even though the FDA has approved Juventel, a life-extending drug, Sam Kelley says 'no.'"

An older woman appeared on the screen, angry. A young boy, about four years old, walked into the shot and the woman put her hands on his shoulders and positioned him between her and the camera. She was emotional as she said:

> "Sam Kelley. It's my life. I want to see my grandson graduate from high school.
>
> Stop opposing the Life Bill."

The announcer returns.

> "Dreams. Beautiful dreams. Congressman Sam Kelley is standing in the way. Paid for by Americans for the Life Bill."

Sam could only blink, shocked by the anger and meanness of the ad. That was Miradol. He had heard they were pouring money into these campaigns—assassinating the character of anyone who dared to oppose their bill. As he turned to walk away, a picture of Sidney Lund appeared on the screen, again grainy and a little blurred.

> "Sidney Lund, billionaire businessman, trying to buy a seat in Congress. But did you know that Sidney Lund was delinquent in paying his taxes?"

A picture of Lund entering a long black limousine appeared.

"We all pay our taxes and do it on time. But Sidney Lund, one of the richest men in Tennessee, is a tax delinquent. And not only that, he was arrested for driving drunk."
"Sidney Lund. Can you trust him in Washington?"

A feeling of nausea swept over Sam. Lund had only been late one time and only by a few days. Sam had been late THREE times. And that DUI, it was years ago in college. He looked at the disclaimer. Fund for Struggling Families. Sam was new to these negative campaigns but he knew better than that. Struggling families had no money to fund a PAC. But before he could turn to walk away, another ad appeared.

A picture of a family of four, husband in a work shirt, wife dressed like a teacher or office worker. Two kids, a boy and girl, about six and eight, teasing each other, smiling. Mom speaks.

"Like many families these days, we both work."

Dad speaks.

"And it is still hard to make ends meet."

Back to Mom.

"That's why we were shocked to learn that Sidney Lund, a candidate for Congress, wants to go to Washington and raise our taxes."

Back to Dad.

"His tax plan would raise taxes by an average of $650 per family."

Back to Mom, shocked expression, speaking slowly, enunciating every syllable.

"Six hundred and fifty dollars."

Two kids speaking in unison.

"We can't afford that?"

Announcer.

> "Sidney Lund's tax plan is a disaster Tennessee families can't
> afford."

Another ad from these struggling families. Kelley knew what this was all about.

Lund had proposed raising taxes on the wealthiest two percent of Americans.
Sam was against that bill but he knew that Lund's plan would not have cost
that family a dime. "Average" meant the tax increases divided by all taxpayers
whether they got an increase or not. He stared at the TV screen, wondering
if still another ad would appear. It did.

A picture of a house, a nice house, but with a '50s ranch-style look.

> "1978, the year Sam Kelley entered Congress, the average
> house cost $13,500.

Cut to picture of an old-fashioned gas pump, circa 1948, numbers moving on
a rotating wheel.

> "A gallon of gas cost seventy-eight cents."

Cut to picture of a young Robin Williams in a space suit.

> "At home, families were watching *Mork & Mindy* on TV."

Picture of a shining new car, circa 1978.

> "And the Oldsmobile Cutlass was the number one car in
> America.

> "Sam Kelley may have worked hard for Tennessee, but he is
> from another era. After thirty-eight years, it's time for new
> ideas and new leadership."

Another Miradol ad. In all, four straight ads. Not one of them came from the
candidates.

Sam had not paid much attention to campaigns in all his years in Congress. It
had been thirty-eight years since he had faced a real opponent. But he knew

what these ads meant. They meant that outside groups were making what Brazier would call a "huge buy." They were dumping money into this race and in unprecedented amounts. His own ads would hardly matter. He did not have that kind of money. People would see those ads against Lund and think they were HIS ads.

It was just plain wrong.

CHAPTER
Sixty-Three

"Well, hello, Mr. Speaker. So nice to hear your voice!" Domingo Caldero, secretary of Housing and Urban Development in the Marino Administration, was on the line and he was nervous. A call from the Republican speaker could not mean anything good.

"Domingo, I want to talk to you about your budget request," Joe Hazeldine said, his voice genial.

"Is there anything left of it?"

"Well, that's exactly the purpose of this call. I have been looking as your budget and I know we in the House have not been treating your department well."

"I appreciate your candor," Caldero replied in a cautious tone.

"I am thinking we need to do better by you. You know the pieces we cut last year. Tell me, in this budget request, of the things that we would probably take away, what is really important to you?"

The secretary walked through his list. Internet infrastructure to bridge the digital divide. Programs to end homelessness. *Who is he kidding?* the speaker thought, but he made perfunctory notes anyway. After Caldero finished, Hazeldine asked for a number.

"Seven billion," Caldero said more confidently than he felt.

"Can you make it three?"

"I can but what is the catch?"

"Well, I can do this," Hazeldine began, "but I need some help. I am going to send you a list of projects. I may not need all of them. It's not an expensive list and you can add them to the tab. If I get your commitment, I believe I can get your money."

"Mr. Speaker, it sounds like we are earmarking again," Caldero said hesitantly.

"No, I think you are misunderstanding the rules. You and I are not earmarking. Earmarking is when Congress decides these projects. You and your agency have the complete right to select these projects. Am I not correct?"

Caldero was really nervous. He knew what was going on. Hazeldine was going to buy votes for his Life Bill that repealed the negotiation ban. Democrats, at least the ones who weren't bought, hated that ban. But the speaker was drawing him into something that did not look good. And the president was opposing the bill.

"With all due respect, this conversation is making me uncomfortable."

"That's fine," Hazeldine said, his voice less genial now, "but as HUD secretary you have a lot to think about. Remember, we have this new Appropriations chair. He's a Tea Party guy. If you don't get some help your whole staff might fit in some two-story office in a strip mall in Toledo. These guys are dangerous."

"I understand the situation."

"I can get control of the situation but it won't be easy. You understand that it is you I am trying to help?"

"Yes."

"Look, I don't want to drag you into something messy. It's all your call. If you want my help, call me and tell me where my staff person can meet your staff person to discuss budgets and deliver your list. There is no point in having this conversation at our level."

There was a pause on the line before Caldero finally said, "I think that makes a lot of sense."

"It's entirely your call but don't keep me waiting. We are making decisions over here. We are making them now."

"I understand."

"You do what is comfortable for you."

"I will, Mr. Speaker."

"But if you duck, don't come to me for help when Rich Fletcher says he only has twenty-seven cents to fund HUD next year."

CHAPTER
Sixty-Four

The beautiful young anchor tapped her earpiece to make sure it was functioning again before she said in a clear, articulate voice, "And for our next story, we turn to *ABC World News Tonight* correspondent Ralph Benson in New York."

"Thank you, Angela. Juventel is the biggest blockbuster drug in the history of the pharmaceutical industry. Even though it was only approved for a rare skin disease, evidence that it also delays aging has produced skyrocketing sales and moved its creator, Miradol, from number three to the number one pharmaceutical company in the world.

"But today a new research institute, the Institute for the Advancement of Aging Science, is raising questions about the drug. Here is Dr. Hachiro Sasaki, the president of this new institute, with a different perspective on this so-called miracle drug. Dr. Sasaki, what do you have to tell our viewers about Juventel?"

"Well, Ralph, the first thing I would say is our institute was created to help people understand what is real in terms of aging drugs. There are a lot of scams out there."

"There are indeed, but what about this Juventel?" Benson asked.

"Well, Juventel is produced by Miradol, one of the world's leading pharmaceutical companies. They have a great reputation but there are reasons that all of us should be concerned about this drug. First of all, as you acknowledge, it was never approved to address aging at all. The FDA approved Juventel to address a skin disease called Recipothosis, which affects a very small number of people. So the first thing you should know is that Juventel is not approved for aging at all."

"Interesting, and good to know," Benson said, nodding seriously.

"The second thing you should know is that in our view the sizes of the clinical trials were too small to really assess whether this drug works and whether it is safe. Most importantly, the evidence they use to support their claim is not based on proof that people live longer. It is based upon measurements of complex cellular processes that might be associated with good health or longevity. But the interaction of these factors is complex. We can't know what they ultimately mean. In the end, Juventel may not extend life at all. In fact, it is entirely possible that the drug could shorten your life."

"Amazing!" Benson exclaimed, clearly genuinely interested in this story. "Listening to all those ads you might think that you could live forever."

"Unfortunately, Ralph, nobody gets out of here alive. If you are taking Juventel, the Grim Reaper may visit sooner than you think."

CHAPTER
Sixty-Five

Congressman Alexander May from Connecticut was nervous. He had only been in Congress for four years and here he was in the office of Speaker Joe Hazeldine, the mastermind who had produced the budget deal and was being hailed as the most effective speaker in recent times.

May was green but he wasn't dumb. The speaker wanted his vote for the Life Bill.

Alex May was not going to budge. There was a price to telling the speaker "no." But there was a bigger price for saying "yes." He had taken money from Big Pharma, a lot of it, $127,000 in all. More importantly, he had four pharmaceutical companies located in his district and Miradol was not one of them.

The ad war had started in his district. He was being attacked by Miradol for opposing the Life Bill. That was tough. But a PAC called Fund for Struggling Families was plastering his opponent. A lot of people wanted that Life Bill. But the pharmas were good citizens in his district. Their location gave him cover.

He had thought all this through, what it meant for his re-election and his career. There was no way he could vote against the negotiation ban. No way.

"Alex," the speaker began. "I have been talking to the agencies about some projects and there are some things they are looking at in your district."

"Really?" May responded, a little confused.

"I think that DOD has a couple of initiatives that might be located in your district. There's a $4 million project for Honeywell that helps develop the advanced turbine engine. There's another $6 million for the Bradley airport. You've got some bridges in your district that are in bad shape. Four to be exact. The Department of Transportation is ready to fix them. $33 million."

May was flabbergasted now. He practically stuttered, "I am not complaining. Not at all. But I thought these earmarks were against the rules."

"You should read the rules. They say you can't put specific projects into the legislation. Decisions on projects are left to the agencies themselves. There is no rule against my talking to the agencies to help out members I care most about."

"I really appreciate that. It's tough for a Republican in Connecticut these days."

"I can get all this done but I need some help as well."

"Wait a second, Mr. Speaker," May said, shaking his head. "I can't support the Life Bill. I've got Genovo and three other pharmas in my district."

"Listen, I know this is a tough vote," Hazeldine replied, his voice placating, "but I'm asking you to see the big picture and there are three pieces of that picture. The first piece is our Republican caucus. You saw what it was like to be in the minority. But now we are in a bad spot and you know it. We can't pay for what we endorsed. If we figure it out and give people this aging drug we can win big in these elections. If we don't we're dead. Is that what you want?"

"No," May said, hanging his head.

"Do you care about this country?"

"Of course I do." His head popped back up.

"Well, what happens if we don't fix this problem? What happens if we cut money for schools and highways and defense—all because we seized an opportunity we did not think through? Bankruptcy. Do you remember that word?"

"Yes."

"And what is the third piece of the big picture?"

May was shaking now. "I'm not sure."

"Well, let me educate. The third piece is you," Hazeldine said, pointing at May. "You are a young member. There are going to be a lot of times when I can help you get a bill on the calendar or get you on a committee worthy of your talent and goals. Politics is about partnership. I have been on the phone with all these goddamned bureaucrats trying to stir up some projects that you can carry back to your district and wave in front of the voters. I am making you a hero." Hazeldine was almost shouting now. "But what are you telling me? You are telling me that on the most important piece of legislation you may ever vote on, that you don't give a shit about what I am trying to do for you, that you don't give a shit about the Republican Party, and that for all you care the United States of America can go to hell in a handbasket because you have four fucking pharma offices, some of them not much bigger than a goddamned beauty salon.

"One of these days you are going to need help from me. You are going to need a bill put on the calendar. You are going to want a committee assignment bigger than that half-assed committee you sit on today. Alex, I've got a long memory and you are not going anywhere in this House if the first thing I think when your name comes up is that that bastard screwed me on the most important favor I ever asked."

Hazeldine's voice was calm and smooth again. "So here's your choice. Play ball and move up in the world. Play ball and be a hero back home. Or kiss pharma's ass and kiss your career in this House good fucking bye."

May's eyes were wide and his hands shook.

"Now do you want me to call DOT and DOD and tell them you are not interested in this money?"

"No sir, Mr. Speaker, I don't."

CHAPTER
Sixty-Six

"Killer Kelley.

"Killer Kelley.

"Killer Kelley."

That was how they greeted him, Sam Kelley, their congressman, blocker of the Life Bill and the longer lives it placed within their reach.

He was at a town hall meeting in Murfreesboro, Tennessee. There were at least eight hundred people there, rallied by Seniors United, funded by Miradol, driven by the relentless messages of a thousand Russian trolls who had decided, on their own, to make Sam Kelley the most hated man in America.

They had learned a lesson last time, and today Sam had arrived with two police cars, lights flashing and sirens blaring. He walked slowly as four officers cut a path through the crowd. Some voters just glared. Others unleashed their anger in shouts and epitaphs. He was the enemy; he was blocking the bill. He was the one man standing in the way of their closing dream.

Michael Brazier had warned against more town hall meetings. Ann Bell had urged the congressman to drop them altogether. But while the schedule had been reduced to a handful of events, Sam Kelley insisted on facing the voters. Warned that hostile crowds would make the meeting unwieldy, Sam replied, "I have no apologies to make. If they want to embarrass themselves, that is their own business."

A new poll had been released just that morning by the Nashville Tennessean.

Lund forty-eight percent, Kelley forty-three percent. Sam had fallen fifteen points—a stunning decline.

People had forgotten the family ad. They forgot him defending his opponent, calling on the drug companies to pull their negative ads. Now it all seemed pointless. There were so many ads, so much twisted truth. In this firestorm of accusations and counter-accusations, what voter could know or remember that one candidate actually comported himself in a dignified way?

In the TV ads, he was taking years from their lives. On social media, a thousand Russian trolls backed by ten thousand bots delivered their insults and fake news. One story stated he had not paid taxes in six years. Another said he had bought marijuana from his drug-dealing son. He had become the terrible villain. There was no tempering the charges. There was no slur too appalling to withhold. And on this issue of the Life Bill, it was as if the Fountain of Youth were finally discovered and he had surrounded it with angry dogs and barbed wire.

They had cursed him on the TV screen. They had shouted at him on their computers. Now, he stood before them in the flesh. The signs appeared once more. "It's My Life." "Defeat Kelley." "Support the Life Bill." There was a new sign too, a picture of the Grim Reaper with Congressman Kelley's name scrawled underneath. And, of course, the internet catchphrase, the meme, that Kelley was hearing again and again and again.

"Killer Kelley."

If Sam Kelley was shocked, if these cruel taunts pained him, he did not let it show. Inside the large meeting room, standing at his podium, he raised his hands in supplication and waited, patiently, until the room was quiet enough to allow him to speak. When he did speak, his words, his demeanor, his composure were surreal in the angry room.

"I want to first thank everyone for coming out tonight. You have every right to your opinions and I respect them or I wouldn't be here. We won't agree on everything. Perhaps we will disagree on many things. But I am here to answer your questions, hear your voices, and have a conversation about our future in Tennessee."

It seemed like a hundred hands shot into the air. Sam pointed to a woman in the front row. She was clearly angry and frustrated when she demanded, "The

FDA says Juventel is safe. If it is safe, there is no risk to anyone who takes it. It gives people a chance. Why are you denying us that chance?"

The crowd cheered, and as the applause diminished catcalls rose from the mob. Sam replied in a calm voice. "The safety trial is only the first step. After the first step, there are two more trials to measure the effectiveness of any drug before it enters the market. As to Juventel's effectiveness on aging, there have been no supervised FDA trials at all."

A low, angry murmur overtook the room, punctuated by scattered boos. Sam took a deep breath and pointed to an elderly man in the back row. His voice was frail but steady when he said, "Congressman, I don't care about the FDA. There is a Nobel Prize winner on TV telling us that Juventel works! How many Nobel Prize winners work at the FDA? Do you think they are smarter than him? Are you smarter than him?"

Sam smiled ruefully. "I don't think I am. In fact, I am sure I am not. I am also not as smart as the scientists at the FDA. The question is whether you want Congress deciding what drugs you can take. Last time I looked, there weren't many scientists in the House."

More boos erupted and the next questioner had to shout to be heard. "Look at me, Congressman. I am eighty-two years old. I am dying a little day by day, week by week. I can feel it." He looked around the crowd. "Do you feel it?"

A thunderous "yes" followed and the crowd of septuagenarians started to stamp their feet in unison.

"So look at me," the questioner, an elderly woman in a faded housecoat, continued. "I am dying right now. How could this drug hurt me? I've got nothing to lose. One, two, six years? They let cancer patients, the incurable ones, take drugs that are untested. Well, you know something. Aging kills you too. We are all on our way to the graveyard. Death. That is incurable. We deserve the same rights."

With this speech, the crowd erupted in shouts so loud that it was a long time before Sam could speak. Head held high, calm in his eyes, he waited for his turn before he finally asked, "What is your name?"

"Sandy Butcher."

"Ms. Butcher, do you how old I am?"

"Seventy-eight." They all knew.

"Every day, I share the same experience as you do. The good Lord is nudging me along as well. If we have an answer, if we have a way to spare your memory and restore your body's strength, then I want you to have it. You can buy this Juventel now, if your doctor will prescribe it. I am not blocking this drug. I am saying we cannot approve this drug and pay for it with Medicare without knowing it works. We have a process at the FDA—"

Catcalls. Jeering. The congressman could no longer be heard. He waited, and when the crowd had quieted again he tried to lighten the mood. "Anyone know a good joke?"

For the first time there was laughter in the room, but several people shouted, "You!"

Sam Kelley continued until more than an hour had passed. They asked him about jobs and Social Security and one person asked him about Sidney Lund. "Sidney Lund," he replied, "is a fine man."

Finally, he graciously, without a hint of malice or disrespect, thanked all in attendance, thanked them for coming to his meeting, thanked them for their questions, and thanked them for the viewpoints even if they were not his own.

From the side of the auditorium, Ann Bell watched. In the beginning of his campaign, Sam had been confused. The polling, the ads, the strategies. He understood none of these things any better now. But there was something else he had learned.

He had learned he could campaign with graciousness, dignity, and respect. He chose not to criticize. That was not Sam Kelley's way.

Deep inside, he was baffled by what these elections had become. Democracy was in the throes of a terrible disease. If his campaign accomplished nothing else, he would not be tempted by the darkness. He would shine a light and show voters a better way.

CHAPTER

Sixty-Seven

"Shit!" she mumbled quietly to herself. Winter Brooks, Washington consultant extraordinaire, had not found what she expected.

Her eyes ran down the table, the Excel spreadsheet, she had just prepared. On one side was a list of congressmen supporting the Life Bill. On the other side was a list of those opposing the Life Bill. Down the middle was a list of undecideds. Next to each name was the amount of money spent by the Fund for Struggling Families, the Super PAC that had suddenly appeared in a mammoth way in Congressional districts all across the country.

In districts where the member supported the Life Bill, the PAC had spent $35 million. In districts where the member was undecided, they had spent $32 million. In districts where the member opposed the Life Bill, they had spent $28 million. If Big Pharma was funding the Fund for Struggling Families, why were those numbers almost the same?

She picked up her phone and dialed. "Jim Villers, please. Tell him Winter Brooks is on the line."

"Winter," he said, his smile radiating in her ear. "I bet you're chasing the same thing I am."

Jim Villers, the campaign manager for presidents, was now working for Sidney Lund. Winter had worked for Villers in three campaigns and, with Sam Kelley opposing the Life Bill, they were on the same side again.

"Jim, why is the Fund for Struggling Families spending money whether you are for, against, or undecided on the Life Bill? They have some other agenda."

Villers had approached the problem a different way. He had his media firm analyze their TV ad buys district by district. "You're not going to believe this," he replied. "If you oppose the Life Bill they are running positive ads, whether or not you have a race. You should see those ads. Music from God's own symphony. Candidate walking six inches off the ground through a garden of roses. As he approaches, the rosebuds lift to attention and the stems part to let him pass. They'll be changing water to wine in the next spots."

"And it won't be cheap wine either!" Winter laughed.

"You got that right. And if they are for the Life Bill, they get dirty, nasty ads on anything Big Pharma can find."

"So it is pharma."

"Could not be more clear. They are doing the Russian Dolls. They write a check to a c4. That c4 writes a check to another c4. Nobody has to report because none of the money is spent on campaigns—it just goes to another c4. When it finally hits the Fund for Struggling Families they report the c4 that gave them the money but you can only trace backward one step."

"So how do we prove it's pharma?"

"That's the question that might decide these elections."

"I sent a free intern to Genovo's law firm, the one that does their PAC," Winter explained. "She had a degree from Columbia and she was really, really hot. Could not get in the fucking door."

"What is the world coming to?"

"Maybe we just accuse them. They can't deny it."

"I'm still working on it. Call me in a week."

. . .

Back in Washington, DC, Joe Hazeldine reached into his drawer and pulled out a disposable phone. He had a dozen of them. He dialed up Felix Durand, ex-KGB agent, now Hazeldine's go-to gumshoe.

"Felix, have you ever heard of the Fund for Struggling Families?"

"No."

"Do you own a TV? They have bought half the commercials on TV."

"I read books, Joe."

"Well, this outfit is spending a lot of money and I need to know whose money they are spending. Can you handle that?"

"I'm on it."

CHAPTER
Sixty-Eight

"You are not going to like these, Ms. Keegan," her research assistant warned as he placed a thick stack of papers on her desk.

"I don't have time to read all this. Give me the CliffsNotes."

"Well, Ms. Keegan, this new institute, the Institute to Advance Aging Science, has been pretty busy."

Keegan looked up, her eyes tired.

"These are academic articles, seven of them, each one poking holes in our Juventel trials."

"I suppose they are all the same stuff?" She sighed. She had seen Hachiro Sasaki, the institute's president, doing interviews everywhere. *PBS NewsHour*, NBC, CNN, all of them except FOX. FOX was on their side.

"Well, for the most part. There is one article that disputes the relationship between telomere length and aging."

"Right." Keegan rolled her eyes.

"Then someone says that the FDA should not have approved Juventel for Recipothosis because it helped only twenty percent of the participants in the trials and the statistical significance, because of the small number in the trials, did not meet a respectable standard of proof."

"Yeah, yeah," she said, dismissing all concerns with a wave of her hand. "Listen,

I appreciate this research but I don't give a shit about these academic articles. Who reads them anyway? Just write me a three-paragraph summary."

The assistant apologized for the interruption and scampered from the room.

Next, for Keegan, came the best part of the day. It was Friday. Sales numbers. Market research.

The marketing team entered the office. Walter Schmidt did a lighthearted bow and announced, "Numbers for the queen of pharma." Keegan loved that Walter.

PowerPoint slide one: Weekly sales approach billion-dollar mark. $724 million. Down slightly from the previous week. Keegan frowned.

PowerPoint slide two: Growth in sales. Beautiful stair step graph, except the last bar was a little lower than the previous one.

Keegan looked at Schmidt. "Are we topping out?"

"Not exactly. Let me get to that in a minute."

PowerPoint slide three: Worldwide Sales Distribution. Continued overseas growth. In the US, a pronounced drop in sales.

PowerPoint slide four: Customer Demographics American Market—Income. Falloff was highest among upper-income customers.

PowerPoint slide five: Customer Demographics American Market—Age.

This graph was troubling. Among seniors the falloff in sales was high. Among young people sales continued to expand.

"Okay, so what's happening?" Keegan barked.

"Let's move to the market research," Schmidt said. He had been tracking a list of questions in his weekly polling.

The first question was whether the consumer had ever heard of Juventel. Juventel name recognition was roughly on par with the president of the United States. No change.

Second question: Do you have a positive or negative opinion of Juventel? In past polls, the positives had grown to almost nintey percent. Now they had fallen. Seventy-nine percent. Negative had doubled to fifteen percent.

Third question: Do you believe that most people who take Juventel will experience at least five years of longer life? In the last poll more than seventy percent said "yes." Now the number had fallen to sixty-one percent.

Keegan's eyes narrowed and white knuckles showed on her tightly fisted hand. "Goddamn that Sampson Kraft," she shouted, referring to the Genovo chair. "He can't do this to me."

"Colleen, these are great numbers. Most companies would die to have these numbers."

"Can't you see what's happening? That institute is nuking our product."

"I would not overreact. We need a strategy."

"The strategy should be to explain to the American public that Hachiro Sasaki is making a half-million dollars a year to lie about our product."

"We don't know what he is making."

"Well, find out. This is war and—"

Keegan's assistant cracked the door and looked in at her boss, her face painted in concern. "Ms. Keegan, the speaker of the House is on the line."

Keegan froze for a moment. Then, smiling broadly, she waved the staff from the room.

"Why, Joe Hazeldine. So nice of you to call."

CHAPTER
Sixty-Nine

"WCSB has a new poll today showing movement in the Fourth District congressional race. For that story, let's turn to WCSB News correspondent Logan Ladner."

"Thank you, Dan.

"For some of us who have been around politics for a long time, it is a sad scene. Sam Kelley spiraling downward toward almost certain defeat. A new WCSB poll released today shows Kelley trailing Lund by eleven points. From his previous lead these numbers reflect a drop of more than twenty points for the longtime Tennessee congressman.

"We asked Jim Villers, campaign manager for Sidney Lund, to comment on the numbers."

Villers, tall, without a hair on his head, beady-eyed, and speaking with a thick Louisiana accent, appeared on screen.

"Sam Kelley is dropping faster than a housecat thrown off a ten-story building. Do you know why? Science is giving people a longer life and he's not letting them have it. Who does this guy think he is? Frankly, he could probably use a little bit of that youth medicine himself."

Ladner delivered the closing line. "Dan, we are not reading the eulogy but it looks like we are getting close."

"Sam Kelley no longer in Congress. It's just hard to imagine. Thank you, Logan."

CHAPTER

Seventy

The wind tugged at the brightly colored balloons that bounced against their strings, begging for the sky. Flags and bunting covered the buildings with America's colors, and monster trucks, six of them with wheels as tall as a small elephant, lined the fairway waiting for their grand parade. There were cows and bulls with passive eyes and numbers pinned to their ears. In a giant barn, they waited for the verdicts of judges who might rule them the heaviest and handsomest of all. Between these buildings, across a broad expanse of asphalt, walked five thousand people who had arrived that evening in Fort Wayne, Indiana, for the legendary Allen County Fair.

That night, there would be pig wrestling, where a team of four raced against the clock to stuff a greased pig into a barrel. There was pedal racing for young children, a watermelon race, a demolition derby, rides of all kinds, booths with darts and toy guns, hot dogs, and a pizza-eating contest sponsored by Papa John's.

Also on the schedule was the outhouse race, where teams of four—one located inside and three pushing the box, mounted on wheels, raced against the clock.

While fairgoers of all sorts and sizes filled the grounds, there was also one unexpected visitor. There on the causeway, standing tall and still as a statue, stood Colleen Keegan, chief executive officer of the largest pharmaceutical company in the world.

Keegan had gone to great lengths to keep her visit secret. She had flown into Pittsburgh for an alleged meeting, rented a car, and driven all the way here. She paid cash at her hotel. No one could track her path. She was there for a meeting, and though she stood in plain view, she was beyond recognition to any who walked the fair.

She searched the crowd. "Mr. Speaker," she shouted while seeing Hazeldine approach. "Joe," she added on reconsideration, thinking formal was off-key at the Allen County Fair. "Can I call you, Joe?"

"Sure can," he said with a grin. "Why don't I give you a tour? I bet you've never been to one of these before."

The speaker represented Fort Wayne and a square section of northwest Indiana. This was his district and, in his district, the Allen County Fair was one of the biggest events of the year.

"Well, I went to school in the Midwest," she said, almost shyly.

"Where?"

"Oberlin."

The speaker laughed. "I don't think they have county fairs in Oberlin."

Hazeldine had asked Keegan to wear jeans and a "work shirt." She was wearing jeans, Stella McCartney High-Rise Flared Jeans, and a work shirt her assistant had bought the day before at Elizabeth Charles. It wasn't really a work shirt but it was blue. He thought the brown booties with the towering block heels might be difficult to walk in with the dirt, straw, and even mud, but Hazeldine just smiled and shook his head.

As they walked, one of the monster trucks edged by, pulling a wagon stacked with hay and wide-eyed young children giggling and shouting their excitement. There was a music stage, and a band called Janice Anne & Miss Kitty's Revenge played "Harper Valley PTA."

On the fairway, people recognized their congressman. He was the speaker of the whole United States House of Representatives. He was from northwest Indiana and he had made them really proud.

"Congressman, great to see you."

"Mr. Speaker, you're doing a great job!"

"Joe, you got Washington under control?"

To that one Joe always smiled. "Never."

There was a hot air balloon with fantastic colors of red, blue, and yellow tied to the ground, and it swayed and pulled against its rope.

Colleen Keegan had never been to a county fair, but she kind of liked it. She looked at the speaker as he spoke to his constituents. He was not a handsome man. He was overweight, his hair was disordered, and his skin had that pasty indoor look. But she liked that he was strong. She could feel that. And he was so unlike those California men—pretentious, chatty, and often a little fake.

"This is a piece of America I have never seen," said Keegan.

"It's a beautiful piece, if you see it in the right way," he said, nodding his agreement.

"Well, Joe, you were right about one thing."

"What's that?"

"Nobody will recognize me here."

Joe stopped at a food booth and ordered the grilled cheese crunchy Frito sandwich.

"Ms. Keegan—"

"Colleen, please."

"Here, Colleen, is fine delicacy praised by county fair gourmets everywhere."

She took a bite. "Tastes great," she lied.

"I knew it would," he replied, a twinkle in his eye.

Keegan was actually having fun but, always impatient, she moved to business.

"Joe, where can we talk?"

A fairgoer reached to shake Joe's hand.

"Congressman, ya got a new girlfriend?"

"A guy has to have some fun," he said, winking.

Keegan flashed a warm smile. Hazeldine turned back to Keegan. "I'm not sure where we go. I guess I did not think that part through."

Keegan looked around, searching for an empty space with a place to sit. Then she saw it and her face broke into a mischievous grin.

"There," she said, pointing upward and across the fairground. "No one can listen there." She was pointing at the brightly lit Ferris wheel.

"Colleen, I think you're more fun than people know."

Sitting side by side, Colleen and Joe were lifted into the air high above the Fort Wayne skyline, modest but brightly lit. The speaker began to explain Fort Wayne. It was the site of the first professional baseball game ever played. In Fort Wayne, it is illegal for men to wear mustaches, for anyone to stand at a bar, to drink beer from the bottle, or to buy a round for the house.

"Our law enforcement has not caught up to our rules," he added, smiling.

Keegan laughed and looked at Joe. *He might be more fun than people know*, she thought but did not say.

"So, Joe, how many votes do you have?" Keegan asked, getting back to business.

"Well, I started with thirty-five."

"How many?" Be patient, she told herself.

"Well, I need 112 and I have been picking up a lot. Twelve this week."

"So what does that add up to?"

"It looks like sixty-eight. I've come pretty far."

The Ferris wheel stopped. The attendant opened the door to let them out. Keegan handed him a $50 bill.

"Yes, ma'am!"

"If you keep doing that people will recognize you for sure," Hazeldine whispered, looking around.

She laughed.

"But Joe, you are forty-four votes short and we are running out of time."

"Those pharma folks are pretty tough—no offense."

"None taken."

"I've got probably another twenty calls and meetings this week. And I've got a couple of moves up my sleeve. Basically, I've got to convince these guys to look at a $120,000 donor and tell him 'kiss my ass.'"

"That's not easy."

"It's possible."

"So what are these tricks?"

"They work better if I keep them up my sleeve."

"Well, now I am really worried."

"Listen, I know my business and you know yours. Trust me. But remember, I called this meeting."

"That's right."

"To pass this bill there are things I'm going to need."

"What?"

"You have a Super PAC. I have a Super PAC. Your Super PAC cannot coordinate with a candidate or office holder. That means your Super PAC cannot talk to me. But my Super PAC can coordinate with your Super PAC and my Super PAC is run by Beau Jefferson, my former chief of staff. Your Super PAC needs to talk with Beau every day. If Beau tells you to stop ads on a member of my caucus, I need you to stop them without delay. If he says turn up the heat, turn up the heat."

"What else?" Colleen asked, making a mental note.

"I have a schedule. As long as I make that schedule available to everyone, anyone can get it and use it for any purpose. Since it has never been available to anyone, the press will not know to ask. If they do we will give it to them. But only for the next two months. Only until the vote."

"So what do I do with that?"

"The week before any meeting of mine with any member, unless they are committed to the Life Bill, you are to increase your TV buy and, if there's time, bombard the district with mail. When they walk into my office I want them scared. Really scared."

Keegan smiled. She liked this guy. She nodded. "I can do that."

"Another thing. I've got three members who are not on board and who have Miradol facilities in their districts. How can that be? You need to orchestrate a showdown. You need to explain to them the consequences of their actions. Two of them will require really rough treatment. The third requires a softer touch. But I need all three. My Super PAC will send you the list with notes."

"Done."

"Colleen, this is going to be hard. But I have a personal stake in this bill. It's the biggest thing I will ever do—the biggest thing ever in my entire life."

She was a little taken aback by his intensity. She did not understand the details but she knew it was a good thing. She put her hand on his. "Thank you, Joe."

"You know the other side even better than me. They will be ruthless and their hands are untied. The good guys have rules. To win this we both have to be ruthless. Sometimes the price for doing good is doing things you would rather not do. Do you understand?"

"I can be ruthless."

"Good!"

Keegan and Hazeldine left the fair an hour later and ate dinner at Paula's on Main, a seafood restaurant with a wine list that was pretty good for Fort Wayne. They had completed their business and began telling stories. She told him about the pottery shards she had sifted in India when she thought archeology would be her career. He told her about hiding cash contributions in his first campaign for Congress and a backpack trip he took to Belize before he got married. He talked about books and the histories he'd read and what he learned from each one. It was a step outside the lives they lived. They were two people who lived alone. They were two people without children or spouses or time to build any other life than the one that consumed them every day.

Joe Hazeldine was speaker of the House. He had learned to ask for what he wanted. That evening Colleen Keegan, whose salary that year might reach $50 million, spent, for the first time in her life, a night at a Hampton Inn.

CHAPTER
Seventy-One

"Leonid, this is Sergov, Sergov Koslov. I think you remember me."

Click.

Felix Durand shook his head and dialed again with another phone.

"Who is it?"

"It's Sergov and don't hang up."

"I can't be talking to you," the voice shouted. "They'll rip out my fingernails and throw my daughter off the top floor."

"I am calling from an untraceable phone."

"There is no untraceable phone."

"It is untraceable to me. Listen, Leonid, I have a lot of money and you can have a big piece of it."

"Sergov, there is no way I am going to turn."

"Goddammit, Leonid. I am not asking you to turn. I am not doing that shit anymore. It has nothing to do with your government. I need a hacker. A great fucking hacker. Actually, I don't even need a great hacker. A half-ass hacker will probably do. I need to look at some law firm emails. I can pay a lot of money to break what should be a pathetic cardboard wall."

"Well, Servov, why didn't you say so? Are you sure no one can trace your phone?"

"Leonid, I am not Sergov anymore. I have a new name. A French name. OOOHH LA LA! I got a face job that makes me handsome and ten years younger. If you saw me you'd think I was one of those American middle-aged model schmucks. And, I've got $3 million in my pocket and I am trying to spend it."

"A hacker? That is all you need? They are a dime a dozen over here."

"So pay them peanuts and keep the change, you dumb punk!"

"Well, Mr. Young Richie Frenchman, if you put it that way, let's talk business."

CHAPTER
Seventy-Two

"Good evening, this is Mari Lovelace with the *CBS Evening News*. Our lead story tonight is about the miracle drug, Juventel, which promises to delay aging and extend our lives. But today, FDA Commissioner Marvin Wellstone announced that the agency will be looking into allegations of improper marketing by the drug's owner, Miradol. With the story is CBS News correspondent Max Jennings."

"Thanks, Mari. The FDA's move to investigate Miradol came as a big surprise. Miradol is pushing legislation that would give the drug the equivalent of FDA approval as an aging drug. Because of this legislation, they claim that their TV ads are protected by the First Amendment. But the FDA wants to take a closer look. Here is FDA Commissioner Marvin Wellstone. Marvin Wellstone, tall, distinguished-looking, and standing before the enormous glass and brick façade of his agency in Rockville, Maryland, spoke with what was, to anyone who knew him, barely contained fury.

> "Miradol has the right to run any ads it wants. But the FDA has never approved Juventel as a remedy for aging. We want to take a close look at their data and determine whether or not their claims fairly state what the evidence supports. I want to remind all Americans that anyone taking Juventel to delay aging is doing so without FDA approval and without any FDA trials indicating that this drug is effective at all in prolonging life."

Max Jennings continued, "The FDA has also asked to review those trials to see if representations made by Miradol are consistent with scientific data. There are also reports that Dr. Wellstone, who had submitted his resignation, is staying on for a few more months to pursue the investigation.

"In the meantime, a watchdog group, The Institute for the Advancement of Aging Science, has applauded the FDA's decision. Here is Hachiro Sasaki, president of the institute. Dr. Sasaki, what is your reaction to FDA's announcement that it will investigate Juventel marketing?" The camera panned to a studious-looking Dr. Sasaki, whose furrowed brow and pursed lips spoke silently of impending doom.

> "Max, we think that the FDA should not only investigate the marketing of Juventel; we believe that it should also investigate the safety and effectiveness of Juventel as well. Juventel was approved on the basis of very small trials, too small to protect the American consumer. Some of the claims being made about this drug are outlandish, to say the least."

Again, Max Jennings picked up the thread. "These criticisms come on the heels of a spate of academic papers questioning whether the drug is effective at all. Meanwhile, Juventel has become the best-selling drug in the history of the pharmaceutical industry. A longer life? Some news is just too good to be true. Mari."

"Thanks, Max. I guess it's going to be years before we really know."

"Right, Mari, it could be a lifetime."

. . .

Colleen Keegan snapped her remote and the TV went dark.

"That fucking Sampson Kraft," she screamed to no one at all.

The phone rang and she angrily tore it off its cradle.

"Colleen, this is Jake Siskoff." His voice was firm but calm.

"Do you see what those fuckers are doing to me?" she yelled. "We bring to market the greatest lifesaving drug in the history of humankind and those greedy bastards want to kill it. Kill it!"

"Colleen, calm down."

Keegan's hands began to shake but panic became anger. "Sampson Kraft is going to pay. You watch! You watch!"

Siskoff waited silently until he could feel her anger dissipate. Then he delivered a lesson about the politics of crisis. "Colleen, the first thing you should know is that this investigation is a sham. Wellstone knows that what you're doing is protected by the First Amendment. But announcing this investigation is his chance to shoot at you and raise questions about your product."

"Well, he is succeeding."

"The second thing you should know is the fact that all the other pharmas have come together to fight your drug and fight your legislation is a testimonial. It is a testimonial to the fact that you whipped their asses, moved to number one, have the largest-selling drug in history, and are out there emptying their pockets and filling yours."

He paused a moment, waiting for her response. When it didn't come, he continued, "You had to expect this, Colleen. You would have done exactly the same thing if you were in their shoes."

He was right. But she was still pissed.

"The third thing you need to know is that you are going to lose this vote in Congress. Hazeldine is pretty good but he is probably fifty votes from getting this bill out of the Republican caucus."

"Our count is forty-four," she said sullenly.

"Forty-four…fifty—what does it matter? That is too far to move. We are too late in the game. No one, not even Sam Rayburn, Tip O'Neill, and Amos Tedford combined, could move that many votes in the time we have left."

"But I like Joe Hazeldine," she said, almost softly, and smiled to herself.

"Colleen, I like him too, but he got backed into a corner and there is no way out. Forget about him. He can't deliver. We need a backup plan. Fast."

"Is that all?"

"No, it's not. Colleen, all this institute stuff, how much did they pay these people? I bet they pay Sasaki a million dollars a year. A million dollars to lie through his teeth. God almighty," he said, as he shook his head in disgust. "But, Colleen, you can't get mad about it. You've got to have your own storyline and your storyline is that miracles happen and when they do some people get mad and try to block progress.

"That's true, but they are winning."

"Only if we let them," Siskoff continued. "We need to counterattack. We need an event that will capture the attention of the world and show every fucking asshole who wants to live another year that Miradol stands behind this product and the miracle it delivers.

"I like it. I like it," she said, nodding and finally rousing herself again to the fight. "Tell me what you have in mind."

CHAPTER

Seventy-Three

Her face was scarlet. Her lip curled upward in an unpleasant sneer, her arms extended straight to the conference room table—her hands palms down, planted flat against the top. Sarah Whiteridge, pollster for the Kelley campaign, was taking her stand.

"This is not just about Sam Kelley. Republicans have a five-vote majority, and losing this seat could cost us control of the House. It could put the DEMOCRATS back in power!"

The thirteen people in the meeting grimaced in unison. Sam, his wife, Pearl, Ann Bell, and ten consultants, each lobbying for a bigger piece of the campaign budget, all understood the ramifications of what she was saying. And because Sam had not been making his fundraising calls, that budget was less than they thought they needed to succeed.

There were good reasons behind Sarah's outburst. She had just presented a new campaign poll, and support for Sam continued to fall. Lund had moved past fifty percent. To fifty-two, in fact. Sam's support had fallen to thirty-seven percent. He was losing some Republicans. Among seniors, the single most important group, his support was a tragic twenty-eight percent.

Sarah Whitehead continued, "We have fallen almost twenty-five percentage points in the last two months. Say what you want. If we continue with our so-called strategy…" She spoke the "s" word slowly and sardonically. "…we will lose. It is not a prediction. It is a fact. And I want to start by asking Sam Kelley…" She glared at the congressman. "Can we please stop telling voters what a great man our opponent happens to be?'"

Nods around the table. The consultants knew what to do. When in doubt, attack!

All eyes focused on Sam. But Pearl interjected. "Sam, I think you need to listen to these people. They are smart and they know what they're doing."

But Sam was unruffled. In a quiet voice he said, "I think I would like to hear a few more opinions from around this table."

The direct mail consultant argued for mail tying Lund to Wall Street. Lund had straddled a question about regulation, although he later corrected his answer.

Opp Slayer, the research firm, had some new items on Lund, details of a sex discrimination suit against Lund's company and a statement questioning price supports for the farmers. "Good attack piece in the mail." Lund was also nailed by a reporter for not knowing the price of a half-gallon of milk. "Too rich to understand your problems."

The National Republican Congressional Committee rep, Sally Benjamin, suggested that the NRCC was losing faith in Sam's chances and might cut its spending in his race. She had only heard that "third hand" because the money they were spending was an "independent expenditure" and could not be coordinated with Sam's campaign or even the NRCC.

As they worked their way around the table it was finally Ann Bell's turn to speak. Ann Bell, who had taken her job utterly without political experience. Ann Bell, who in an early meeting did not even know what a research firm was and proved unable to spot Lund's tracker at their first town hall.

But Ann Bell had proven more capable than expected. Despite her age and inexperience, she had put together a first-rate staff. She kept the consultants on schedule. She raised the important questions. She knew what she did not know, and what she did not know she learned fast.

"Look," she said, scanning the table. "This struggling families group is running $300,000 a week in negative ads on Sidney Lund and they have been doing it for two months. Where is he? He has fifty-two percent of the vote. And what about all these positive ads that Miradol is running praising Sam? What has that gotten us? Sam's unfavorables are now fifty-eight percent.

"I am new to all this. But here's what I know. We don't have control over this campaign. We are just spectators. Eighty percent of the money is being spent by these Super PACS. We have a half-million dollars in the bank and it's all chump change compared to what is raining in from the outside. Who wrote these rules anyway?" Ann Bell asked, glaring around the table.

No one answered.

"Sure, Sam is not punching Sidney Lund in the nose. Maybe he should. But other people are hitting him hard and it's not working. I don't think voters believe these ads anymore."

Around the table, mouths dropped, aghast.

"I think there is something wrong with the playbook!" Ann Bell declared. "We need to start thinking out of the box."

The consultants exchanged angry glances. A couple smirked. A few more angrily crossed their arms, pushing back from the table. Who was Ann Bell? She knew nothing.

"Michael," snapped Sarah Whiteridge, before Ann Bell could continue. She was sure that the campaign media consultant would defend his craft. "What do you think?"

"I think Ann Bell is right," he answered simply.

Whiteridge hurled her poll report against the table and a large smack echoed throughout the room. She stared at Brazier with the look of a jaguar who had just lost her cubs. When she regained her composure, she whispered to Sally Benjamin, "We are going to make sure that sonofabitch never gets another fucking campaign from the NRCC ever, ever again."

Being used to anger by now, Sam Kelley rose and spoke, politely as always. "I want to thank everyone for sharing their strongly held opinions, which I know are meant to help me win this race. I need a few days to consider what has been said. I won't linger. I know we are in trouble and I know we need to move fast. Ann Bell, please set up another call on Monday. We will have decisions by then. Changes are on the way."

CHAPTER
Seventy-Four

Joe Hazeldine opened his email and winced at the number of unread messages before something caught his eye. It was a secure email transmission that could only be opened with a password. The password had been provided to him by Felix Duran. He had put Felix on the trail of the pharma money in the form of the Fund for Struggling Families. It was the question that could reshape politics as this election year marched toward a close. Who was funding the Fund for Struggling Families?

Everybody knew it was Big Pharma, but knowledge was not enough. They needed proof. Going after Big Pharma was like shooting a grizzly bear. You could take your shot but you better not miss.

The speaker typed in the passcode and an email appeared. The subject line read: "FW: Plan to Fund Super Pac. Privileged Communication." The sender was Phil Stenson, an election lawyer for Stenson, Milbank & Cooper, the leading advisor to Republican candidates, parties, PACs, 501 c4s, Super PACs, and whatever else someone might think up to dance around the law and poison the political process. The recipient was Sampson Kraft, chair of Genovo.

The message read:

> *"Sampson, so good to talk with you last week and I appreciate the opportunity to advise Genovo on this critically important matter. I have attached a memo describing how we recommend that the companies participating in this partnership might move their money through a series of—"*

"Yes!!!" Hazeldine shouted so loud that his assistant opened his office door to see if he was all right. He waved her away and dialed Felix's number. "Felix, my man. You are one marvelous motherfucker."

"Well, thank you, Mr. Speaker, always happy to be of service to America's cause."

"How did you do it?"

"Don't be stupid, Joe."

"Okay, you're right. I don't want to know."

"There are more of these. I have 487 emails, all transmitting information about the plan, back and forth between Stenson, Milbank & Cooper and Genovo. It covers everything. You know these lawyers. They love emails. It runs up their clock."

"Felix, you know you just saved my ass."

"I am sure of it."

"Let's talk more later. Send me the rest of the emails. I have some calls to make." He buzzed his assistant. "Regina, get me Thomas Hinson with *The New York Times*."

CHAPTER

Seventy-Five

"Casey, this is Colleen. We need to talk."

Casey Jacobs, Miradol's former marketing VP, paused in the middle of reading the latest report on the Russian social media campaign. "Colleen, we aren't supposed to talk. Where are you?"

"I'm in a Texaco station in El Cerrito."

"What?"

"Have you tried finding a pay phone these days?"

"Jesus, Colleen, you could have just bought one of those disposable phones. You know, like those other drug dealers use?"

"Pretty funny. Let me make this short. We are getting fucked by Genovo. Sampson Kraft. He set up this institute to discredit Juventel."

"I read the papers," Casey responded impatiently. He liked Colleen but he found her patronizing at times and he had grown tired of this entire assignment weeks ago—tired of Moscow, tired of the trolls, tired of the viciousness of the campaign. Tired of the gutter.

"I know, sorry. Look, I want to take down his stock price. Just a little shot over the bow. The Russians can do that. Right?"

"I can't go back to the Russians. They are out of control. I did training. I wrote scripts. Did all that make any difference? Not one fucking bit."

"I know that, Casey. I guess that is what they do. I've got a score to settle. This is right up their alley."

"Colleen, this is a bad idea, a really bad idea."

"Do it."

CHAPTER
Seventy-Six

The speaker sat in a wingback leather chair that had been purchased by Nicholas Longworth, the famous speaker from the 1920s who expelled progressive Republicans and championed the economic policies that helped deepen the Depression. For these accomplishments, one of the three House office buildings bore his name.

But Joe Hazeldine was not thinking of Nicholas Longworth or Sam Rayburn or any speaker of the past. He was thinking about the future because in a few short minutes, Cynthia Jarvis, a second-term member from Arizona, a moderate and a recipient of $186,000 in pharmaceutical contributions, would enter his office. Needless to say, she was not supporting the Life Bill.

"Cynthia, thank you for taking the time to come by," he said, rising to greet her.

"Any time, Mr. Speaker. I am honored by the invitation." She was short and heavy and a little old for a newcomer. But there was an intelligence in her eyes. She knew the world and how to get around.

"I want to talk because I am worried about your race," he said solicitously, gesturing for her to sit.

"Well, everything seems under control. I've got a nine-point lead and, really, my opponent is pretty weak."

"Well, you need to know that *The New York Times* has a story that is breaking next week."

"It's not about me?"

"Well, it's about this Fund for Struggling Families."

"Oh." Her face fell.

"The *Times* is going to report that all of the money going into that PAC is coming directly from the twenty largest pharmaceutical companies." He grimaced. "And it gets worse."

Jarvis was dismissive. "Everybody knows that anyway."

"Not the voters. Anyway, you also know that Big Pharma is in a cat fight with Miradol and Miradol is running ads."

"I've seen a lot of those as well."

"Well, I can't really talk to them directly. You know how all that is. But I got a copy of the ad they are ready to run on you. I think I can get this stopped."

The congresswoman fidgeted in her seat. She looked around the room, trying to avoid Hazeldine's direct gaze, and was surprised to see a screen emerge from a credenza. The speaker clicked his remote and an ad started immediately. A room full of money appeared on the screen. An unflattering picture of Congresswoman Jarvis filled the screen.

> "$786,436, almost a million dollars. That is what big drug companies have spent to keep Cynthia Jarvis in Congress."

Picture of a senior couple, wearing old, worn clothes and sitting on a ragged couch. Expression of disbelief clouded their tired faces.

> "Why? Because Jarvis supports a law that allows drug companies to dictate prices to our senior citizens and Medicare. That is why we pay seven times the prices seniors in other countries pay.

> "Cynthia Jarvis. They bought her vote. On Election Day, remember one thing. They did not buy yours."

"Mr. Speaker, I was at three town halls last weekend. People are crazy for this drug. One of 'em accused me of trying to kill her. They were lynch mobs, I swear to God. This issue is gonna kill me."

Hazeldine moved to the couch where she was sitting. "I am so glad I was able to get a copy of this spot before it aired. There is still time to stop it."

"Oh, thank you," she said, actually reaching to grab his hand.

"I just need your vote on the Life Bill."

CHAPTER
Seventy-Seven

"Ann Bell, I'm just not sure what to do." Sam Kelley was torn. He hated this campaign. He generally found something to like about everyone he met, but these consultants were testing that talent. The worst was the hate. The hatred of voters. The hatefulness of those meetings. It was all beyond his ability to understand.

But Sam Kelley also felt he had let people down. He had let down his friends who gave him money. He had let down the volunteers who knocked on their neighbors' doors. He had let down his campaign staff and the Republican Party that he loved.

He just could not run a modern campaign, the kind that all the experts said he had to run if he wanted to win.

Ann Bell, on the other hand, had a different opinion. Her perspectives had been slow to develop but they were strong. "Sam, these people are blind. All these ads running for you and against you, for Lund and against Lund. I don't think they've made much difference at all. Two things have made a difference." She paused and took a deep breath. "People want that drug and you've gotten pretty old."

"Well, I'm not getting any younger and I ain't voting for that drug."

"Right. But there's one other thing that can make a difference. You yourself are different and you are different in a beautiful way."

"I'm beginning to think that doesn't really matter."

"Well, I may not know much about politics, but that just might be a good thing. I look at all these people in Washington. They're disgusting. They can't speak a sentence without reading three polls. They grub for money on the weekends and spend the week returning the favors right there on the House floor."

"Ann Bell, it's not that bad."

"Well, that's what I believe and a lot of voters believe that too."

"So what does that mean?"

"I've been talking with Michael Brazier. He left Washington because he was disgusted. We've got some ideas. Let me explain."

CHAPTER
Seventy-Eight

Colleen Keegan had come to New York. From her podium she looked out on a sea of reporters and behind them stood platforms holding at least thirty cameras. Curiosity seekers gathered at the doorway and spilled over into the hallway, unable to gain entrance to the event.

As she looked out over the packed room, her hands began to shake. *Slowly, breathe slowly,* she told herself. She looked down at her speech and her hands shook once more. The pages were out of order. Eager eyes stared at the podium, waiting for her to start. There was no time to sort. Panic gave way to focus. She cleared her throat and began.

"I have called this press conference today to defend the promise of what I believe to be the most important breakthrough in the history of medical science. At Miradol, we have developed and successfully tested a pharmaceutical that does more than cure or relieve the symptoms of a common disease. We have developed a drug that alleviates aging itself—a process that is the source for cancer, heart disease, and many other fatal conditions; a process that is not merely the cause of many common diseases but a disease itself, an affliction, cruel and unforgiving, that touches every human being on this planet.

"In recent weeks our product has come under attack from the Institute for the Advancement of Aging Science. This institute was formed and funded not to advance science at all. It was formed and funded by other pharmaceutical companies who believe that the Life Bill will lower the prices they charge Medicare and diminish profits they have unfairly taken from our government and the American people. We believe that the cloak of secrecy must be lifted from this institute and its funders. We call on the institute to disclose fully and accurately all the sources of its funding.

"Just as importantly, we call on the institute to reveal the salaries of its top twenty employees, because if these scientists are being paid to distort the facts and unfairly criticize valid scientific advances, the American people have a right to know what those people are being paid.

"Finally, we call on the institute to reveal any and all fees paid to academics who have published articles criticizing Juventel, because if a scientist is paid to argue against scientific progress, you have a right to know how much they were paid."

Colleen Keegan, normally a speaker of average ability, had riveted her audience. There was a silence in the room, the silence of a spellbound crowd leaning toward the podium, eager to capture every word. "But it is not enough to criticize those who would betray science, rigorously and truthfully practiced. When someone says that a new development is 'too good to be true' we must all remember that these things were spoken of the telegraph, the railroad, the automobile, the polio vaccine, and many more milestones in the progress of humankind.

"I will admit that it is hard to believe that aging, a condition as old as the first mammal that appeared more than a hundred million years ago, is within the reach of science to delay. But at Miradol, we believe in Juventel and we believe that it will extend the lives of almost every person who uses this drug.

"So we are making a guarantee and we are putting $1 billion behind it. I repeat. We are making a $1 billion guarantee that Juventel will extend the lives of almost everyone who chooses to take it. Here's how it works.

"We invite every American over the age of sixty-five to submit his or her name to test our product. We will accept the first ten thousand names we receive. We will calculate, based upon their expected life span at their present age, the expected time of their passing and we will provide them with daily doses of Juventel, free of charge. If any of those individuals do not live beyond their natural life span, no matter what the reason, we will pay the surviving family $100,000.

"If our product fails to perform, Miradol will have to pay as much as $1 billion. That is, ladies and gentlemen, how strongly we believe in the effectiveness of this drug."

It was a shrewd and calculated move. It was not a billion-dollar guarantee at all. For if Juventel had no effect, half its users would live beyond their expected date and half would expire early. But even full price was a bonanza. Juventel had already generated $50 billion in sales. The event would boost confidence and restore declining sales. In the most pessimistic estimates, their stratagem would generate far more in new sales than $1 billion they were putting at risk.

Journalists rushed to the headquarters of the institute, where they caught Hachiro Sasaki leaving work. They asked him his salary, his funders, and whether he had paid academics to write articles criticizing the drug. Fleeing to his car, he offered no answers at all. His handlers had taught him how to lie about Juventel. He did not know how to lie about what he was getting paid.

Within the next week, eight million Americans signed up for the test. When the ten thousand were revealed, their names were funneled to newspapers and television stations, where for a day or two they became celebrities of a sort.

Suddenly, Colleen Keegan was an even bigger star, a visionary leader in business who guaranteed her product with $1 billion in cash. Big Red had carried the day.

Miradol did believe in Juventel. They believed in the lengthening telomeres. They believed in lower inflation and the declining incidence of senescence. There was science, real science, behind this drug.

The only thing it had yet to prove was that it actually helped people live longer lives.

CHAPTER
Seventy-Nine

"Welcome to *Washington–Believe It or Not!*. I'm Damon Rodriquez, your host of the show that brings you insight and commentary on this week in our nation's capital city. And what is our topic this week?"

"Juventel!!!" the three commentators shouted in unison.

"That's right, Juventel, the miracle drug that delays aging and adds years to your life, is back! The Institute for the Advancement of Aging Science, which had launched a campaign to discredit the drug, finds itself mired in scandal," Rodriquez continued.

"*The Boston Globe* has reported that the institute was funded entirely by donations from pharmaceutical companies wanting to discredit Juventel and diminish public support for the Life Bill, legislation which would make them charge lower prices for their drugs.

"Meanwhile, the president of the institute, Dr. Hachiro Sasaki, resigned after disclosing that he was being paid $800,000 per year, and three academics came forth and confessed to receiving $100,000 each for publishing articles critical of this wonder drug.

"Then Miradol, the pharma giant that produces Juventel, came forward with a dramatic offer. The president of Miradol, Colleen Keegan, offered Americans a billion-dollar guarantee of the drug's effectiveness."

Four bottles of Juventel appeared on the screen.

"So tonight, I have four bottles of Juventel, purchased from the Canadian

Pharmacy, for a price I shall not reveal. One for me," Rodriquez opened the bottle and popped two pills, "and one for each of our panelists: Suzie Glint, former head of media at the National Republican Congressional Committee; Carlos Baskins, former chief scientist at the FDA; and, of course, Spud Stevens, founder of *Superspin*, a hot new political blog. Rodriquez passed out the bottles and they all took two pills.

"Spud, on second thought, you might be too young for this drug."

"Damon, it's never too early to start living late," Spud said, smiling mischievously.

The audience laughed and applauded loudly.

"Okay, panel, let's get serious. It is amazing how this one drug has taken over politics in America. But Carlos, you're an expert. Were the institute's criticisms valid?"

"Well, Damon, no scientist gets paid $800,000 a year to tell the truth. These academics? Some of them made more for one article than they make in salary for a whole year. In science, you can nitpick almost anything. To me the institute was about Big Pharma killing the Life Bill and giving payback to Miradol for whipping their butts."

"What about this Miradol guarantee?" Rodriquez asked, turning the bottle of Juventel in his hands while he pretended to read the label.

"Oh my God, I hear sales of Juventel are skyrocketing. I mean who makes a billion-dollar guarantee?" the former FDA scientist said. "That is a load of dough!"

Rodriquez turned to Glint, the NRCC veteran. "Suzie, do these developments have political implications as well?"

"You better believe it," she said, smacking the table. "The more people want that drug, the more pressure on House members to support the Life Bill. Right now, the president is opposing it and the Senate is silent. I mean why take on Big Pharma if you can let the House kill the bill? And in the House, the whole battle is in the Republican caucus, where Joe Hazeldine needs a majority to bring it to the floor."

"This news helps him, right?"

"Damon, this is not the Little Sisters of the Poor he's fighting. This is Big Pharma. BIG Pharma. Do you know there are only three senators who have NOT taken their money? Will this help the speaker? Sure it will. But he is a LONG way away from the votes he needs and I don't know anyone who thinks he can get there."

"Spud, what is your take on all this?"

"Damon, I am twenty-six years old and I feel younger already."

CHAPTER
Eighty

"I CANNOT FUCKING BELIEVE THIS IS HAPPENING!" Tim Maris, a congressman representing Chico, California, and nearby agricultural outposts screamed at his cowering assistant.

Tim Maris was no ordinary member of Congress. He had another big job. As chairman of the National Republican Congressional Committee, it was his job to get Republican members of Congress re-elected. It was his job to grow their numbers, expand their majority, and retain power in Republican hands. To achieve that goal, he had to raise money, $100 million in the two-year election cycle, and spend that money on ads that destroyed Democrats and said positive things about Republicans—with the former being his preferred approach.

In order to hold their majority in the House, one seat might make the difference between success and failure. And Tim Maris had just been handed some remarkable news.

Sam Kelley had fired all of his campaign consultants.

And he was not planning to replace them.

"WHO—" he screamed as his executive director rushed to slam the door, his hands pumping up and down, signaling his boss to lower his voice and not panic the staff. Maris was undeterred. "WHO DOES HE THINK HE IS?"

"Tim, I know you're upset. I think Brazier is staying on in some capacity."

"Michael Brazier!" Maris lowered his voice a little. "Brazier is an idiot. But he is not as big an idiot as Sam Kelley. He doesn't have a political bone in his body. And now he's fired his fucking consultants?"

"Well, I hate to be the bearer of bad news but it gets worse."

Maris just looked at him with an air of beaten resignation.

"Take a look at this. This is just the first one." The ED pushed a button and Sam Kelley appeared on the video screen to the left of the congressman's desk. There was no music, no graphics, no background of any kind. Just Sam, plain and simple, speaking into the camera.

> "I'm Sam Kelley, congressman from the Fourth Congressional District. Many politicians read a poll and decide what to believe. Not me. I know most of the voters in my district support the Life Bill that would give to Congress, instead of scientists at the FDA, the right to decide whether a drug is safe and whether it works. I am against that. I will fight for your health and safety even if it costs me my seat in Congress."

The tagline written across the bottom of the screen was "They don't make them like Sam Kelley anymore."

"He's leading with his chin! Oh my God. This is the thanks I get for all I have done for that asshole." Maris' face was beet red.

"Calm down, here is the next one."

The screen lit up. Same face. Same background. The kind of uncreative ad any media consultant would be embarrassed to make.

> "Hi, I'm Sam Kelley, congressman from the Fourth District. Big Super PACS with millions of dollars written directly from the accounts of giant corporations are running ads attacking my opponent, Sidney Lund. I know Sidney Lund. He is a fine, decent man. I call on those PACs to stop these ads, get out of Tennessee, and let me and Mr. Lund have a civil debate about the issues that really matter to you."

The tagline written across the bottom of the screen was the same: "They don't make them like Sam Kelley anymore."

Maris, slumped forward, face in his hands, speechless.

"Tim—?"

"Don't tell me there's another one."

"Sorry."

Same face. Same background.

> "Hi, I'm Sam Kelley, congressman from the Fourth District. Some people say I've been in Congress too long. Well, I've been in Congress long enough to remember when members of Congress treated each other with civility, when differences of opinion were respected, not vilified, and where compromise was a tool of progress and not grounds for pillory and attack. Washington has changed. I haven't. That makes me worth keeping, working for you."

"This is the most ridiculous shit I have ever seen," Maris moaned, stretching out every word.

"They're different," his ED said, shrugging. "Maybe they break through."

Maris glared at his staffer, wondering how this idiot had ever gotten that job. "We are finished with the sonofabitch. He is twenty points down, still falling, and now he is breaking every rule of modern campaigns. Cut off his money. No TV ads. No mailings. No digital. Not one fucking penny."

"Yessir. But remember, no one will be happier about that than Sam Kelley."

CHAPTER
Eighty-One

"Ladies and gentlemen, I'm Pete Hays with FOX News, and tonight we are speaking with that great American, Republican leader, and speaker of the House, Joe Hazeldine. Joe, thank you for all you do for Republicans and for America."

"You're welcome, Pete. Pleasure to be here."

"Speaker Hazeldine, this week *The New York Times* broke a story showing that the Fund for Struggling Families was nothing more than a front for Big Pharma. What's your take on that?"

"Well, Pete, I was just as shocked and surprised as I'm sure you were. As you know, Republicans in the House are fighting for the Life Bill, which would make Juventel available to our seniors and also end the law that allows Big Pharma to dictate the price our seniors pay for prescription drugs."

"But some people say letting government negotiate is a mistake and that the Life Bill is anti-business," Hays interrupted.

"Not at all. Business, free enterprise, is a continuing negotiation between the seller and the customer. That's capitalism as I know it and cherish it. Medicare is the customer. If you let these companies dictate prices, frankly, it takes the 'free' out of 'free enterprise.' Who could say there is anything Republican about that?"

"I guess there isn't," Hays said, furrowing his brow as he thought about it. "But let's get back to the *Times* story. Our information says that you are a long way from picking up the votes you need in the caucus to put the Life Bill on the floor. Do you think this news will help?"

"You may not be aware but we have picked up a lot of new votes. Twenty-nine new commitments, all well before the *Times* ran this story."

"I did not know." Hays looked surprised.

"Yes, twenty-nine votes from Republican members who looked at this issue on the merits and decided to do the right thing for our country and our party," Hazeldine said, flashing a sly smile.

"Twenty-nine? Amazing. But even twenty-nine votes leaves you, at least by our counts, a good twenty votes away. Where are those votes coming from?"

"Pete, if I gave you those names those pharma folks would be like the Knights Templar guarding the Holy Grail. I may be speaker but I could not even get past their office doors."

"Time is running out. You have three, maybe four weeks. Can you really make it happen?"

"You know the president is opposing this bill and it's hard to beat an incumbent president. I think when it comes time to vote, those members will not side with the president. They will side with our Republican Party."

CHAPTER
Eighty-Two

"How are you, ma'am? My name's Sam Kelley. I'm running for Congress and I'm asking for your vote."

There he was. On Main Street in Franklin, Tennessee. Shaking hands. Franklin was a town of seventy thousand people about twenty miles south of Nashville. Across the street was McCreary's Irish Pub, Pony's Restaurant, and, of course, a Starbucks. Franklin was new to the congressional district. Sam needed to do well here.

He had been out shaking hands since the campaign started. At first people barely knew who he was. "Sam who?" "Running for what?" But $2 million of TV ads fixed all that. Then they knew him, and the main thing they knew was that he, Sam Kelley, was keeping Juventel out of their hands for reasons they did not understand.

Some were polite. This was small-town Tennessee after all. But some weren't. "I'm voting for Lund." "Support the Life Bill." "Don't bother me." One voter said, "Nice to meet you, Killer Kelley."

As the campaign entered September it all got worse. At times, Sam was discouraged but he soldiered on. No one was going to say he lost because he didn't do the work.

But today was different. He could feel a change.

"Sam Kelley, so glad to meet you. I've seen your TV ads."

"Sam Kelley, I'm still undecided but I have to say you've got my attention."

"Sam Kelley, I like what I'm hearing."

His cell phone rang. It was Brazier. "I got our internet poll back."

"What's it say?" Sam asked warily.

"Well, it says they're starting to like you again."

"I'm feeling that," Sam replied. "I may not be winning but I think I'm no longer just another phony."

"The voters are liking your ads. They are liking them because those ads are you. Your favorables are way up."

"And the votes?" Sam asked, a little hopeful now.

"Not so much, Sam. You've stopped falling but your vote is only up two points. Remember, sometimes your favorables move before it shows in the votes."

"Well, we've still got eight weeks to go. I'll make the most of it."

"Sam, I think you have a chance. Sometimes you have to do something different."

"Michael, I believe I can really win this thing."

"I may be crazy, but I think we have a chance."

Sam put away his phone and got back to his handshaking. A few minutes later, a man stopped at the sound of his name, stepped back, and looked at him like he was a five-legged rhinoceros. "Mr. Kelley, I never thought I would see it in my lifetime. An honest politician. I guess that means you're gonna lose."

"Not if you get to the polls," Sam replied with a smile.

CHAPTER

Eighty-Three

She lifted her sunglasses so she could peer into the sky. It was bright and hard on her eyes but the blue was amazing. It began at the top of the sky—the soft, rich color of a bluebird's wing—and gradually lightened until it kissed the water almost white.

The air, that tropic air so close to the equator, was cooled by the ocean to a temperature that caressed her skin. Before her lay her own personal pool, one that came with her villa along with a staff waiting for her at the villa door—a butler, a maid, and a personal chef. She was in the Seychelles, four degrees south of the equator, at Fregate Island Private, a resort in the middle of the Indian Ocean, one of the finest and most luxurious in the entire world.

Colleen Keegan had earned a vacation and, by God, she was doing it right.

She had taken the walk, seen two of their seven beaches, touched a giant tortoise on the nose, and looked at tropical birds until she almost collapsed in boredom. The masseuse had paid a visit; the chef was amazing and filled her glass with fine chardonnay again and again, sometimes when the glass was not even empty. But why say no? The wine was great. This was her vacation and she sipped until at six in the evening she staggered to bed. Who cared about the hangover? Good times happen in the now.

It would, however, have been nice to travel with a friend. She thought about Joe and she laughed trying to imagine him here. No, that would not have worked. There were no grilled cheese crunchy Frito sandwiches on the Fregate menu.

But life was good. Juventel sales had recovered. Goddamn that Jake Siskoff.

What a genius! The guarantee was his idea. One billion dollars they would never lose for $5 billion in new sales.

She thought about money. She had a salary: $50 million a year. But there were bonuses. Bonuses based upon sales. Humongous sales. All those numbers were straining her brain. Anyway, why be greedy? What else did you need past $50 million a year?

And the Life Bill. That damned Joe Hazeldine had picked up thirty more votes. They were less than fifteen votes away. When Medicare picked up Juventel there would not be a bank big enough to hold all that money.

What more could she ask for? How good could it all become?

A messenger knocked at her villa door, a cell phone in his hand. All of a sudden, she was nervous.

"Breathe slowly. Breathe slowly."

CHAPTER

Eighty-Four

"Mr. Speaker, if you can hold for a moment, I'd like to put the president on the line."

Joe Hazeldine smiled. He expected this call. He knew it would happen. And it had arrived none too soon. The caucus would vote on the Life Bill in three days. He was nine votes short.

The president was a Democrat. Democrats never liked that negotiation ban. All the new ones campaigned against it. The older ones…well, they started getting pharma money so they spoke with a softer voice. But there was nothing the president shouldn't like about the Life Bill except that until a few weeks earlier it did not have a snowball's chance in Hell.

"Mr. Speaker, so nice to speak with you."

"It is my honor, Mr. President. What can I do for you today?"

"Well, I've been following your work on this Life Bill. Amazing. I know you're still a few votes short and who knows what will happen. But I think you're doing the right thing. If we can pay for this Juventel then I'm for the bill and it looks like you have found a way. I'm calling a press conference tomorrow to endorse the bill."

"Hold on, Mr. President," the speaker replied, feigning panic. "I need you to wait."

"Okay," the president said slowly, clearly not understanding.

"I need you to do two things, sir. I need you to wait and I need you to meet me at the White House tomorrow. If you endorse this bill now, it's dead."

CHAPTER
Eighty-Five

Sam Kelley's campaign staff gathered around the television. The big debate had happened the previous night and everyone wanted to see the coverage on the eleven o'clock news. Dan Berringer, news anchor for WCSB, appeared on the screen.

"Last night, the two candidates for Congress from Tennessee's Fourth Congressional District squared off for their only debate. Here is Marge Rivers with the report."

"Thanks, Dan. Let's look at some highlights. The evening kicked off with the question about jobs, an issue of significant concern to voters in the Fourth District. Here's Sidney Lund."

"Over the last twenty years, America has lost more than a third of our manufacturing jobs. Bad trade deals, tax breaks for companies that move jobs overseas, and runaway deficits. Congress has failed us. We need new leadership in Washington."

"Now, listen to Sam Kelley's reply."

"Mr. Lund, with all due respect, those jobs aren't coming back, not unless we want to pay American workers three dollars an hour. We have good jobs available but manufacturers can't find people with the skills to fill them. If our kids want those jobs, they need to start doing their homework, take math and science in school, and understand that there is no free ride. Government can't give you a good life. Parents and kids have to earn it."

"Another issue that came up was transgender bathrooms," the reporter said. "Here is Lund."

> "I think people should use the restrooms of the gender of their choice."

"And Kelley."

> "The women's restroom has stalls. In the men's bathroom, they also have urinals, but you need the proper equipment to use them. Can we please talk about a real issue?"

"And, of course, there was Juventel and the Life Bill. Here's Lund."

> "Modern science has offered us the gift of a longer and healthier life. Juventel has been tested under FDA supervision and proven safe. We can't spend the next ten years in clinical trials trying to decide whether this drug adds five, ten, or fifteen years to someone's life. People deserve access to this drug now."

"And Kelley."

> "We don't know whether Juventel adds even one year to anyone's life. That is the job of qualified scientists at the FDA. Congress is not qualified to make these decisions. When Congress starts approving drugs, people will die."

"And here are some clips from the closing statements. First, Lund."

> "Sam Kelley is seventy-eight years old. He has been in Congress thirty-six years. He is responsible for the high price of prescription drugs and now is blocking your access to Juventel. Sam Kelley is from another time and he is standing in the way of progress. If you want to fix Congress, if you want new leadership and new ideas, then vote for Sidney Lund for Congress."

"Now, Kelley."

> "Thank you, Mr. Lund, and I agree with one thing you said. I am from another time. When I started in Congress, we didn't have to read a poll to decide what we believed in. Instead of

blaming the other party or tearing down the institution, we reached across the aisle, compromised, and found solutions. And Mr. Lund and I agree on something else. We have lost our way in Washington. We have lost our civility, we have lost our decency, and we have, too often, lost our honesty as well. Mr. Lund is a fine man. I have not criticized him once in this campaign. Who is best able to restore what we have lost in Washington? That's up to the voters to decide, and I know that on Election Day they will make the right choice."

"Dan, I'll say one thing about this race. That Sam Kelley may be seventy-eight years old but he sounds pretty new to me."

CHAPTER

Eighty-Six

They found a private jet in Dubai to retrieve Colleen Keegan from paradise. The plane landed in San Francisco at 3:13 in the morning. A limo picked her up and drove straight to Miradol headquarters, where three members of her staff anxiously waited.

She walked into her office, unshowered, her red hair clumped in unruly strings, bleary-eyed and in a rotten mood. Her staff had never seen her without makeup and completely put together, and they were taken aback by her appearance. Standing before her were Miradol's chief research scientist, Devon Foley; its Public Relations vice president, Naomi Butler; and Henry Quinn, vice president for Regulatory Affairs.

Keegan sat at the small conference table in her office and looked up at the three staffers with trepidation. "Let's start at the beginning. Tell me again what's happening."

Foley spoke first, his voice solemn. "Colleen, some of our Juventel users are getting cancer."

"How many?"

"One hundred thirteen. Not a lot but the numbers are growing."

"We have millions of customers. How can one hundred have the slightest statistical significance? I mean, we need to watch these things but people are going to get cancer. Why is this number so goddamned alarming?" she said, her voice rising despite her dismissive response.

Foley paused, waiting for Keegan to recover from the news. "The incidence is isolated to a particular demographic. Users under forty."

They had never tested young people using Juventel. They had never imagined that young people might buy the drug. Those stupid fucking kids.

"Devon," she answered slowly, "this drug replicates elements contained in the human blood. How in the world can giving someone something that is already a part of our own human biology create a danger to anyone?"

"I have a theory," he said, a little hesitantly before swallowing hard. "It's just a theory."

"Oh my God," Colleen whispered.

"Juventel is based upon elements in a young person's blood. It adds proteins that gradually disappear as a person ages. These elements signal our genes to repair and replenish the cells. In older people, these signals are their salvation. They work because otherwise these genes would be directing their death."

"I know all that," Keegan snapped.

"Well, in young people, who already have these proteins, it's possible that adding more creates too much replenishment and too much cell division. I don't know that. It's just a theory. But if the incidence of these cancers continues to grow, that might explain what's happening."

Dosage. In the pharmaceutical world and elsewhere, dosage is critical.

A bottle of scotch in an hour can kill you. Over a week, it's a good time.

Colleen Keegan was no scientist but she had learned a lot in her career. Devon's idea was plausible. These proteins, these signals directing the master genes to initiate repair, growth, and replenishment, were already present in young people. Why had no one thought of that?

"There are two more things you should know," Devon continued. "The distribution of these cases is younger. The younger you are, the more likely you are to have cancer."

"And what is the other?"

"The incidence is increasing. The first case appeared six weeks ago. We saw fifty in the last week." Devon paused again, waiting for the impact of what he was saying before he continued. "The drug has been on the market barely a year."

Colleen Keegan had entered the room, even after the long flight, energized and ready to fight. Now she was just tired.

Henry Quinn, the regulatory VP, said, "I think we need to give FDA a heads-up."

"No!" Keegan shouted, a little too loudly. "They know that one hundred cases is not an epidemic. They know there is no reason to panic."

"If we don't give them a heads-up this whole thing gets worse down the line," Quinn admonished.

"Henry, the FDA is after our ass. They are pissed. If Marvin Wellstone puts all this together, he will have an orgasm. This is exactly the news they have been waiting for."

"Still, we can't hide."

"The Congress of the United States is voting on the Life Bill in three days," Keegan said tightly, her voice quivering as her hands started to shake uncontrollably. "This legislation is a gift, a financial godsend that will retire everyone in this room in some giant mansion anywhere in the world. If we give this to the FDA, it's over."

"Colleen—"

"One hundred cases! Out of millions."

"Well, not millions. Only a few hundred thousand in the age groups where the cancers occur," Foley corrected.

"I am not saying don't watch it. I am not saying this could not be serious," she said, making a concerted effort now to keep her voice calm.

"This is what we know. There will be a lot of cases that are never reported," Foley said, concern evident in his tone.

"Christ, we can't act on what we don't know. We have one hundred cases. We are not causing a panic at FDA!"

CHAPTER
Eighty-Seven

A crowd of unruly reporters stacked thirty deep blocked the entrance to the White House. The White House, expecting a quiet meeting, had notified no one. But the speaker's office made sure that every reporter for any outlet bigger than a high school newspaper knew about the meeting between the president and the speaker and that the Life Bill negotiations that were going to take place that day.

Joe Hazeldine worked his way through the crowd, microphones shoved into this face, questions shouted from every direction. When he reached the entrance, he stopped and made a short statement.

"The president has invited me to discuss Juventel and the Life Bill. As you know, the Republican caucus and the White House have been at odds on this legislation. I am hopeful that our meeting today can resolve those differences."

Five minutes later he was seated in the Oval Office. Despite the fact that he was speaker of the House he had only been in the Oval Office three times. In some respects, it was ordinary: a desk, a couple of couches, a ground floor window. Nice, but surely nothing compared to where the CEO of Bank of America sat. But in the air was a sense that history was about to be written and you held the pen in your very own hand. Joe collected himself. The time for awe was over.

The president greeted the speaker warmly. Rarely intimidated, Joe Hazeldine felt physically bested for a minute by the man standing before him. The president had a hefty build but somehow managed to be graceful in his Armani suit. At fifty-five, he still had a full head of jet-black hair, and his dark eyes, almost black, could burn a hole in granite. His square jaw added to the image of a tough Italian pol who proved bigger and better than the precinct where he began.

After they'd exchanged the meaningless pleasantries required of such meetings, they seated themselves on separate sofas, looking directly at one another. The president began, "Joe, why exactly do you not want me to endorse this legislation?"

"Mr. President, it's a matter of strategy."

"Educate me, please."

"The Republican caucus votes tomorrow and I'm still nine votes short. It's a miracle I've gotten this close."

"I know what you've done. Pharma's no pushover," the president said, reaching to pour himself a cup of coffee. He gestured with the carafe toward Hazeldine, who politely shook his head and continued.

"They are the meanest, toughest, richest lobby on the Hill. We both know that."

"We do."

"Tomorrow, I need to make this a partisan issue," Hazeldine said, leaning forward to make his point. "I need to say to those who are straddling the fence that this vote is a choice between pharma and the Republican Party. I need to say that this is my party's opportunity to deliver this drug and bring down drug prices. Mr. President, if you endorse the bill, you will get the credit. Knowing that, I have members who will move the other way."

The president smiled. "Sometimes this town just amazes me. Okay, I'll be quiet and let you have your vote."

"No, it's going to be worse than that. In twenty minutes, I'm walking out of this office and am going to stand in front of the White House press corps and attack you on national television. I'm going to accuse you of denying seniors this lifesaving drug and I am going to accuse you of kowtowing to Big Pharma. You are going to be pissed but you can't stop me. I need that moment for my caucus. Sir, I apologize, in advance, for punching you in the nose."

The president stared back at Joe Hazeldine a full minute, his mouth ajar. It is not often that anyone speaks to the president in that way. For a brief moment a narrow smile appeared on his face as he shook his head. This was politics at its best and he had seen all of it before. But he wasn't letting this Indiana hayseed off easy. "Joe, I trusted you," he said quietly, with just a touch of menace in his tone.

"It's too late. Put me on your shit list. I'll just have to take it."

"I called you here for a serious discussion and you are going to respond by lying to the press."

"I am sorry but we both want this legislation. This is the price."

"This meeting is over," the president stated firmly, rising to tower over the still-seated speaker.

"Sorry, Mr. President, but I can't leave now. I need to make it look like we had a long meeting."

The president just blinked.

"So, Mr. President, I understand you are a baseball fan. For the next twenty minutes, let's just forget this disagreement and talk about the Washington Nationals. What's your opinion? Do you think the Nats will choke in the playoffs again?"

CHAPTER
Eighty-Eight

Francine and Ray Powers lived about two miles down Old Hillsboro Road from downtown Leipers Fork, Tennessee, population 650. Ray was seventy-six but had robbed the cradle in earlier years. Francine, his wife, was just sixty-two. Both were retired.

Francine had just retrieved the mail and was sorting through the pieces, which included a lot of political mail on six-by-eleven postcards, a shape that afforded lower postage. These postcards were decorated with bold colors, pictures, and often melodramatic headlines. The great work of the creative geniuses of the political mail industry. But today Francine noticed something different.

"We got a letter, an actual letter, from Sam Kelley," she said, surprised.

"Not one of those slickies?" which is how Ray referred to those fancy political postcards.

"Nope, a letter. I guess he doesn't know how he's supposed to do this," Francine laughed and sat down to read the letter.

Dear Francine and Ray Powers:

First of all, I want to thank you for the opportunity to serve you in Congress. I know many are disappointed with the performance of our government in Washington, as am I. The partisanship, the bickering and the name-calling in our nation's capital are disgraceful. I think you know that I have never participated in such conduct.

There is another important issue, however, that I want to address. Most seniors and, in fact, the large majority of voters in this district, support the Life Bill under which Congress would approve a new drug called Juventel for use by any customer and pay for this drug under Medicare.

We have a time-honored system for reviewing drugs. The scientists at the Food and Drug Administration review these drugs, evaluate the evidence and make decisions about what is safe and effective for Americans. It is not a perfect system. Some good drugs take too long to get to market. Others, once on the market, prove unsafe even if the trials were thorough, and sometimes people die as a result. It is a difficult and delicate balance. The last thing we need is unqualified politicians in Congress making those decisions.

I realize that my position is not supported by many voters. I realize that my position may cause me to lose this election and lose the job I love. As you consider your choice for Congress, may I leave you with one thought?

There is value in courage. There is value in a leader who is willing to say "I disagree" and explain why. There are not enough of these qualities in Washington today.

Thank you for the opportunity to serve. No matter who you choose to support, thank you for voting on Election Day and for making our democracy work.

Yours always,
Sam Kelley

"Ray, you need to read this. Look, I don't agree with him on Juventel. But you have to admire him."

"Francine, he is blocking the drug. Don't you ask me to vote for Sam Kelley."

CHAPTER
Eighty-Nine

The website looked innocent enough. World Pharma News. It was populated with articles, most lifted from other websites and publications covering the industry. Today, a new article was added.

SURGE IN HEART ATTACKS REPORTED BY SEDIBAN USERS

Users of Sediban, a pharmaceutical drug that treats high blood pressure, have been reporting an increased incidence of heart attacks, almost half of which have proven fatal. The FDA is reviewing these reports and is expected to take action soon. Genovo, the company that makes Sediban, has refused to comment on this report.

The article went on to quote a leading cardiovascular specialist, Dr. Abdel Kahn, who held a Harvard medical degree. He raised alarms about the reports and stated that he expected Sediban to be removed from the market in the coming week.

The article was completely false.

Abdel Kahn was a fictitious person, but a LinkedIn profile in his name showed his Harvard degree and a prestigious position at a research hospital.

The article was bait. It sat on the World Pharma News site waiting for a legitimate news outlet to pick it up. A day later, a newspaper reporter, saddled with covering health, science, education, and technology as a result of recent staff cuts, picked up the article on a Google search and put it in *The Jacksonville*

Gazette. It appeared in a collection of news blurbs under the heading "Health News."

The click farm went to work. *The Jacksonville Gazette* article was searched and clicked by a small army of "clickers." Each click drove the article higher and higher on the search engine rankings. Three days later, anyone searching Sediban would see the *Gazette* article at number three. Anyone searching "heart attacks" would find the article at number seven. For anyone searching Genovo? Number one.

The news moved around Wall Street, and other publications picked up the story. The impact was exactly as planned.

Three days later, Genovo stock had fallen by five percent.

CHAPTER
Ninety

It was not a blog with a big following. *Ole Betsy* was a local blog that covered politics in Nashville mostly but also across the state. Its audience? Maybe three hundred visitors a day.

But on this day, October 4, the traffic was brisk. Its story on Sam Kelley appeared.

> Sam Kelley, honest Sam, as some would call him, has some explaining to do. *Ole Betsy* has learned that the Kelley family was using campaign property for personal purposes in direct violation of House ethics rules. The story gets worse.

> Not only was a close relative of Kelley's using the campaign car as his personal means of transportation, but he was also arrested for driving drunk, running another driver off the road, and causing her severe injury.

> Ms. Susan Weidman, the victim in this incident, explained that she suffered a broken leg and incurred serious medical expenses.

> "These politicians think the law does not apply to them at all," Ms. Weidman explained. "I had surgery, physical therapy and my leg still causes me pain. All because Congressman Kelley thinks he is above the law."

> The Kelley campaign has refused comment on our story.

The next morning, *The Nashville Tennessean* ran the story, quoting *Ole Betsy* and running Sam Kelley's reply.

"We deeply regret the injury to Ms. Weidman and I apologize for the harm we have caused her. It was my decision to allow my nephew to drive the car that one time for a personal purpose. I take full responsibility."

Back in Washington, the chair of the Democratic Congressional Campaign Committee seized on the story like a lion spotting a crippled gazelle. He demanded that the House Ethics Committee open full-scale investigation of Congressman Kelley's illegal conduct.

> Sam Kelley has crossed the line. These rules were passed to prevent the use of campaign contributions by candidates who would enrich themselves at their donors' expense. Sam Kelley should be ashamed of breaking trust with those who have generously offered their support. Even more importantly, by placing himself above the rules that apply to all members of the House, he has tarnished this institution."

With Republicans controlling the House, the investigation was unlikely to happen. But the chairman's outcry gave the news story another day and was widely quoted in political ads that followed.

CHAPTER
Ninety-One

There are many defenses that protect us from the perils of the modern world. They include eavesdropping, unmanned drones, diplomacy, sophisticated technologies of all kinds, and even human life itself. But against one peril we rely on an odd defense. One hundred and twenty million Americans use prescription drugs, drugs that all bear risks, some even fatal ones, many undiscovered by even the most careful trials. Our defense?

Statistics.

In the office of the Division of Pharmacovigilance, in the Center for Drug Evaluation and Research, a section of the FDA, computers create statistics. To monitor possible safety issues, the FDA has built a database fed by the FDA Adverse Effects Reporting System. Drugmakers are required to report adverse effects to the FDA. Doctors and patients are encouraged to report as well. The result is a database that receives almost two million reports each and every year.

Going through two million reports is no job for ordinary humans. To review that data and identify possible safety issues, the FDA had built a datamining tool that searches each active drug for incidences of adverse effects and compares those incidences with similar adverse effects associated with other drugs across the database. Adverse effects are analyzed overall, by geography and by demographics as well.

The datamining tool produces a measurement, the MGSP, which estimates the probability that the adverse effect is caused by the drug and not the product of random chance. The higher the score, the more likely the causation is real.

So in mid-October, a young FDA staffer named Lucy Castillo was reviewing a list of scores. Lucy was new to the FDA. She had moved to Washington only eight months earlier. To prepare for this work she took courses in biology and statistics—deep statistics. In fact, she had a master's degree from UCLA in "biostatistics," an emerging discipline where the statistics exhibit a complexity incomprehensible to students in the 101 course.

Lucy was small, only four-foot-eleven, and could not have weighed one hundred pounds. Her dad, a Hispanic medical researcher with a PhD, and her mom, a pretty blond real estate agent, were both at least five-foot-ten. No one quite understood what happened to make Lucy Castillo so small. Sometimes, she had to fight to be noticed, but it was a fight she almost always won.

Her eyes scanned the screen. There were two categories of reported effects. The first was "safety signals," where the number of adverse effects rose to a level that required serious investigation. She had reviewed the list. No new drugs had appeared. Then she moved to the second list, the watch list. The watch list indicated, in order of seriousness, drugs that were reporting adverse effects above the expected level but not enough to launch an investigation. Always interesting. There was a new drug that addressed uncontrolled body movement, a side effect of some neurological drugs. Users of that drug reported joint pain. Another drug, an allergy medicine, was causing headaches. Scanning the screen, she saw an entry that froze her in her chair.

Juventel.

The number one drug in America. A little more than one hundred reported cancers. Highlighted in yellow was a "D code." A D code meant that the occurrence was limited to a particular demographic. She clicked on the code and her mouth dropped.

Juventel was causing cancer among users under 40. *Why would someone under 40 take Juventel?* she wondered.

At first, she was a little scared. But slowly a smile spread across her face. Opportunity arrives in unexpected ways. There was no safety signal and she did not need to report it to her boss. If Juventel crossed the threshold, if it generated the safety signal, there would be a causality investigation. Ordinarily, someone senior would get that job. But she knew the politics as well as the statistics. All eyes would be on the investigation. She knew they would fast-track an investigation that, ordinarily, took weeks. If she did the groundwork, in advance, there would be no time to give the job to someone else.

Lucy Castillo leaned back in her chair. The line of her smile stretched almost across her face. She knew an opportunity when she saw one. She would be getting a lot of notice at FDA.

CHAPTER
Ninety-Two

One by one the Republican members of the United States House of Representatives trickled into the room. Today, the members would decide whether or not to bring the Life Bill to the House floor.

Only three days before, their speaker had stood on the White House lawn and attacked the president. His words were contentious and harsh. "This president is standing in the way of science. This president is standing in the way of lower prices for prescription drugs. This president is standing in the way of a longer life for all Americans.

"The Republican Party stands unafraid. We are unafraid to defy America's most powerful special interest in America to pay for this beautiful gift.

"I am disappointed that the president and I could not come to an agreement. But the Republican Party will move forward. Our caucus will vote on Thursday and we will vote to bring the Life Bill to the floor of the House."

The story led the evening news and appeared on the front page of every paper in America. Two million tweets mentioned the episode. The speaker was defying the president to bring Juventel to American seniors.

No one knew that the president had been doubled-crossed. No one except the president and Joe Hazeldine and a couple of White House staffers who had heard the president cursing Hazeldine's name.

Meanwhile, Big Pharma had been muddied. Their struggling-families tactic had become the object of ridicule and scorn, their institute discredited. But they were still Big Pharma and they were playing for keeps.

Talking heads and TV panels debated the speaker's boast. Did he really have the votes? Of course, he could not beat Big Pharma. That was surely why the president refused to go along.

And while the pundits pontificated, the ads, the mailings, and the social media roared like a hurricane through states and congressional districts across the nation. No expense was too great. At stake were hundreds of billions of dollars—a rearrangement of pricing, regulation, and money that would cascade through coming decades.

For months, Joe Hazeldine had worked, one member at a time, to win this vote. When he had walked into the Oval Office the previous day, he was still nine votes short. But he achieved what he needed. In stinging the president, he had painted the Life Bill with the Republican brand. He had made the president their nemesis. He had given the members a choice. Vote with the Republican Party or vote with the president, the Democrat, you hate.

. . .

The speaker sat on the elevated dais in the front as the meeting room, so ordinary and plain, slowly filled with members. There were no smiles, none of the jovial greetings that marked these gatherings in other times. The pressure on these members had been brutal. Those backing the bill had been smeared on television. Those opposing the bill had been smeared on television, coerced, and even blackmailed, many in the speaker's own office. Now they would cast their votes. No matter how they voted, the consequences would be grave.

Some members decided not to vote at all, leaving Washington for their districts. A few of these absences were at the speaker's request. With attendance diminished, Joe needed only 104 votes. No one knew, not even Joe Hazeldine, if he had them or not.

The speaker gaveled the meeting to order. There was only one item to be discussed.

The first to speak was Augustus Rhodes, the congressman from upstate New York who, along with Earl Ackerman, had made Joe Hazeldine speaker of the House.

"Today, we face a terrible choice. Do we invite the ire of millions of Americans fanned into a rage by the Miradol drug company? Or do we instead throw sand in the face of our longtime ally and abandon what has for decades been a friendship? That partnership has lifted this party and given us this majority in the House.

"In all my years in the House, I struggle to recall a more painful choice. But I say to you that our currency is our word. It is loyalty to those who have been loyal to us. To end the Medicare negotiation ban would be a betrayal—a betrayal that will be punished by the pharmaceutical industry. But more importantly, it will be noticed by other partners who are investing in their relationship with this body. These partnerships are only as valuable as the belief in our word, the expectation of our loyalty in the future.

"If we decide to stand by pharma and keep this bill off the floor, the president will share the blame. Our speaker championed this bill. We can state that it was only the opposition of the president that kept it off the floor."

There was scattered applause in the room. The speaker wondered how much more pharma money Rhodes had recently received.

The next to address the caucus was Tim Maris, who chaired the National Republican Congressional Committee and was responsible for electing Republicans to the House. "Well stated, Gus. Loyalty is important but so is power. Let's be blunt. If we hold our majority will pharma stand on the sidelines and pout? They will have no choice but to come to the table and do business with us. Right now, eighty percent of Americans support this bill. It's our chance to make this cause our own, as our speaker, Joe Hazeldine, has already done. This issue can expand our majority far beyond the measly five-vote majority we now hold. I call on our members to vote 'yes.' If you do, I can add to our majority and we can retake the Senate and, two years from now, recapture the White House."

Again, there was scattered applause. The members traded arguments among themselves, although those arguments were short and fewer than might be expected on a vote of this import. In most minds, the decision was not a moral one or a calculation of right and wrong. It was a question of fear. Which side did the member fear most—the wrath of Big Pharma or the wrath of Americans, especially older Americans, who wanted their dream of a longer life realized?

Then Sam Kelley rose to speak. The room fell quiet. They knew what Sam would say, but among all those assembled in that room on that day there was no other member more beloved.

"Fellow Republicans. As you know, I have dedicated my career in this House to the regulation of drugs. We have heard about the political consequences of supporting this bill or opposing it. Well, I would like to speak to the consequences for the people of this nation, people who depend upon us to protect their health and their lives by bringing safe and effective pharmaceuticals to the market. If Congress, by legislation, decides to bypass the FDA and approve a drug for use, we have crossed a dangerous line. In the future, any group wanting a drug, safe or not, effective or not, can hire a lobbyist, can spend some money, and ask this body to supplant its own judgment for that of scientists and professionals at the FDA. It is a treacherous path. We are not here to serve the pharmaceutical lobby or the Juventel lobby. We are here to serve the people of this nation. I have nothing but respect for this august body. But these decisions do not belong in our own hands."

There was applause for Congressman Kelley, more for who he was than for the words he spoke. For while they respected his message it was still survival that stood foremost in their minds.

When all had spoken, the speaker took his turn. He was brief. He had spoken to everyone in this room at one time or another, one to one, often in harsh and threatening terms.

"Colleagues. I thank those of you whom have spoken. I respect your viewpoints, but we now stand eye to eye with this president. We cannot flinch. Congressman Maris has spoken of our opportunity in this election and it's large. I have made this bill a Republican bill. It is our own to advance. And if the Senate or the president choose to stop this legislation, they will pay a price and we will reap the benefits. Great opportunities are fleeting. They reward those who act. Here's the question. Are you supporting the president? Or are you supporting this Republican Party and our chance to make our party the majority party once again?"

The speaker, having had his say, signaled for the balloting to begin.

CHAPTER
Ninety-Three

"Ms. Keegan, what's going on with Rex Bunton?" Winter Brooks asked her boss.

Bunton was a senator from Montana who lacked stature in the Senate, but his small size allowed him to fit squarely in the pocket of the powerful mining interests, whom he served loyally and, some said, with commensurate rewards.

"Bunton? Nothing I know about. We just started running ads on the senators. He's not up this year. Where is he on the bill?"

"He's not committed. He called me. He wants to meet."

"Good. Do it. But call Siskoff first."

. . .

As she waked into Senator Bunton's office suite, Winter Brooks noticed a Montana state flag. It was mostly blue with a smaller circle inside. The circle contained a picture of mountains, a lake, and a plow. Prominently inscribed underneath were the words "oro y plata"—gold and silver. *Hmmmm,* she thought. *Those robber barons who made all that money mining had written the state motto. But they had put it in Spanish so common people wouldn't know what was going on.*

Senator Bunton was a tall, aging man with a jaw that protruded in a way that underlined his small-eyed, dimwitted face. He extended his big hand to Winter. "Why, Ms. Brooks, such a pleasure to see you."

"It's all mine, Senator," she said, trying not to recoil from the feel of his cold, clammy hand.

The senator stepped out from behind his desk and sat on the couch next to Winter at a polite distance. He turned toward her and looked her in the eye as she said, "This Juventel matter may be headed to the Senate. Over here in the Senate, we can't believe the money being spent on this fight. Ms. Brooks, how much money do you think is at stake for Miradol?"

"Well, I don't work in accounting but I imagine it's a big sum."

The senator's faced tightened. "Let's not talk in platitudes. This bill might be worth hundreds of billions of dollars to Miradol."

"You're right. There's a lot of money at stake."

"I was thinking about all that money Miradol could make, and surely the company will be looking for investments."

Winter suppressed a smile. She knew what was coming. That sonofabitch was going to ask right here in his own Senate office.

"I've got a real estate company that is looking to invest in some fine Montana properties. It's called Finger Steak Investments. Do you know what a finger steak is?"

"I've never had the pleasure of that knowledge."

"Well, it is a small piece of meat that delivers a load of flavor. An investment banker might call that ROI."

Winter smiled and waited.

"But that hardly matters," the senator continued. "A Montana thing. My new company is investing in mining properties. We need to raise about $30 million, and I was thinking Miradol might be interested. It seems to me that, more than any other stockholder I can imagine, Miradol has the potential for a fine return."

"Senator, I don't do the investment side. I do politics."

"This is politics."

"Well, there is a lot of money getting thrown around here but that doesn't mean we aren't careful."

"I have put a fine proposition on the table. If you walk out of here without considering it, you might regret it."

"There are a lot of things, Senator, that I could regret, and making this deal might be one of them."

"So sorry to hear that, Ms. Brooks. So sorry indeed."

CHAPTER
Ninety-Four

Lucy Castillo knew statistics. There were holes in every number. The problem was that statistics come from data and no database was perfect.

In the case of the FDA adverse effects database, there were problems. Young people weren't in the database, at least not so much. Drugs were in their future, not the present. So she emailed Miradol. *How many patients under 40 are using Juventel?*

She giggled as she hit the send button. Miradol would freak! And she wasn't surprised that the answer was slow in coming but she was shocked by their reply. Roughly 300,000 users between twenty to forty. So the percentage of Juventel users, under forty, reporting cancer was small. But reported effects where only a portion of all effects. She ran a rough estimate. Still, the percentage was small. Then she looked at the incidence of cancer among *all* people twenty to forty. Almost no one under forty had cancer. For all young people the figure was smaller, *much* smaller.

Lucy then obtained a chart showing the growth of Juventel use among the twenty to forty age group. The growth was recent. Few users had been taking the drug for as long as a year. That meant that the cancers appeared relatively soon after taking the drug. She made calls and interviewed doctors. *How long had your patient been taking Juventel before the cancer diagnosis?* Most cases were at least six months. Of the five hundred thousand users, almost two-thirds had been taking Juventel for less than three months. Even worse, the younger they were, the higher the likelihood of getting cancer.

She tracked down the biologist, Alfred Stimson, who worked on the Juventel trials.

"Dr. Stimson, this is Lucy Castillo with Pharmacovigilance. We are spotting some issues with Juventel. It is not yet a safety signal, but with all that is going on I want to understand whether there is a biological explanation for what might be happening. May I talk confidentially about the issue?"

"Well, that was some time ago. I may need to dig into my files."

"That's fine. Here is the issue. We are seeing some cancers among users under forty. Any theories about why that might be happening?"

"Well, there were no young people in the trials. Young people don't get Recipothosis."

"Three hundred thousand of them are taking Juventel."

"That's disgusting. I knew looking at this trial something else was going on."

"That's fine but do you have any ideas about why these younger users would get cancer?"

"Let me take a look at the chemistry. None of this is fresh. But this is what I remember. The drug is based upon protein differences in the blood of people who are young and old. There is a protein, only present in younger blood that generates cell repair and replication. If someone already has that protein, in generous amounts, it could cause cancer. How much time do I have to look more closely?"

"Tomorrow. I need your answer tomorrow."

CHAPTER
Ninety-Five

Colleen Keegan looked at the number.

317.

Three hundred and seventeen cases of cancer among Juventel users, all under forty years of age.

Colleen Keegan shook her head in disbelief. Something was going on. No doubt about it. But a lot of other things were happening too.

At this very moment, the House Republican caucus was voting on the Life Bill. The Life Bill provided Medicare coverage for Juventel—a huge stream of money as far as the eye could see—or at least until Medicare ran out of money, which it probably would, but then that was someone else's problem. But the bill also had to pass the Senate and then it had to get the president's signature.

Joe had said he thought the president would sign. Did Joe know? But what about the Senate? They had been bombing senators. Those Senate offices were drowning in phone calls and letters. Armies of seniors were visiting senators this week. You could not get a hotel room within sixty miles of Washington, DC. But would they pass the bill in a hurry? The Senate NEVER acted fast. She would tell her legislative team to turn up the volume. Up. Up. Up.

She was sweating. She was shaking.

She called Jake Siskoff. "Jake, is the House caucus going to put the bill on the floor?"

"My guess is yes."

"I told you Joe Hazeldine is good."

"Let's wait. It's not over."

"But let's say it does pass. When does it go to the floor?"

"Probably right away."

"And how long in the Senate?"

"Normally, the Senate takes forever but this is an election issue. They recess in a week. I think they want to deal with it before they leave town."

"Will it pass?"

"Yes, the Democrats want in."

"And the president? He'll sign?"

"Joe put on a show at the White House. The president is really pissed but he will sign."

"So if we win in the caucus, how long until we have a law?"

"Could be in eight days."

"Oh, thank you, Jake. Thank you, thank you, thank you."

Now, Keegan looked at her calendar. Did she even have a week? The FDA was getting all those new cases today. They look at hundreds of drugs. Would they spot it right away?

But in the next few days even more cases would hit their offices.

She snatched a Kleenex and patted the sweat from her face.

They had a chance. When Juventel hit the safety signal they would do the causality investigation. Sometimes those investigations took weeks. Sometimes a month. But if they fast-tracked everything the legislation would die. Die!

A bill. If they had the law they could work it out. They could stop sales to young people. Maybe, after all was said and done, she could still get that $60 billion-per-year Medicare check.

If. If. If.

Time was so tight. If the Senate dragged its feet, it was all over. If the president delayed, it was over. If the FDA was really on their toes and acted immediately, it was over.

One week was her best shot, the earliest possible date to get a bill out of the House, out of the Senate, and with the president's signature across the bottom.

She popped a Xanax. One week. One week max.

CHAPTER

Ninety-Six

NBC Nightly News with Sandy Wilson begins now.

"In a surprising development, the House Republican caucus voted today to report the Life Bill to the House floor. The vote could take place as early as tomorrow.

"The Life Bill would make available, with a doctor's prescription, a pharmaceutical drug that purports to delay aging, so long as the drug has been determined to be safe by the FDA. The legislation also provides Medicare coverage for these drugs.

"The vote is a big victory for Miradol, the number one pharmaceutical company in the world and maker of Juventel. It's a setback for the rest of the pharmaceutical industry who, if this legislation passes, would be forced to negotiate the prices they charge Medicare. The pharmaceutical lobby is one of the wealthiest and most powerful on Capitol Hill. Many thought the caucus, almost all of whom have accepted industry contributions, would reject the legislation that the pharma lobby opposed. For more on our story, here is NBC Capitol correspondent Charles Alexander."

"Thank you, Sandy. Let's sum it all up in two words. 'Joe Hazeldine.' Hazeldine, who was elected speaker in a desperation compromise last year, has turned out to be one of the most effective legislative leaders of our generation.

"Two months ago, when Hazeldine announced his plan to pay for Juventel coverage by giving Medicare the right to negotiate lower prices, many considered the proposal dead on arrival. But lobbying by the speaker, the pharma scandal over funding to an anonymous Super PAC, and the phony institute dealt Big Pharma big blows. Then it appears a high-profile showdown with the president gradually turned the tide inside the Republican caucus.

"Chief pharma lobbyist Glenn Hansen called the vote a temporary setback."

> "This vote today is just the first step. We are confident that we have the votes in the Senate to stop this bill. Our ability to bring lifesaving drugs to the market depends on fair pricing. This bill is putting a gun to the head of our industry and can only result in fewer scientific breakthroughs and lost lives."

"Our sources indicate that the Senate may well follow the House's lead, and with the election recess approaching is likely to act fast. Advocates for the bill say that, if passed, the legislation could cut Medicare prescription drug prices in half.

"Pretty amazing day, Sandy."

"Thank you, Charles."

CHAPTER
Ninety-Seven

Joe Hazeldine was the hero of the day, but celebration was not in his plans. Instead of dinner with his leadership team, instead of drinks with his colleagues, instead of adoring interviews from smitten reporters, he sat alone in his office late that night. His office was dark except for the light from his window that looked out on the National Mall, the Washington Monument, and the Lincoln Memorial two miles away. That light shined on the photograph of his three-year-old daughter, Amelia Hazeldine, lost to him by outrageous drug prices that as a young dad, who had lost his job, he could no longer afford.

His friends knew he had lost a daughter. They knew that the loss had something to do with ending his marriage. But he never spoke of the story and the true reason for her death.

He gazed at the photograph, that beautiful little girl who, like most three-year-old girls, worshipped her father. He remembered arriving home after a long day at work and how she would leap into his arms and kiss his cheeks. And he remembered her promise to watch over him and protect him from harm.

Her memory was his anchor. He spoke to her every day, providing playful reports of his frustrations or progress. Sometimes he knew she was there. He felt her presence in the room.

But today was no ordinary day. Tonight, not counting the day she was born, was the biggest day in his life. He had done more than challenge a president. He had challenged Washington's most powerful lobby. But it was not the size of his opponents that made this victory special. It was not the accolades that made him glow.

He had exacted an atonement. The power of his daughter's memory had changed the world.

The caucus' action was just one vote, but he knew what would follow. On the floor of the House the Democrats would join in and the bill would pass by a large margin. In the Senate, with the election looming and millions of angry seniors demanding passage, the bill would pass. And the president? He may hate Joe Hazeldine but it would be a fatal mistake to veto that bill.

Two weeks. In two weeks, the Life Bill would be the law of the land.

He looked at the photo again. She knew. His daughter glowed with a smile that said she was proud. He spoke to her. He told her that he had done all of this only for her. He told her that now these companies could be brought under control, that little girls like Amelia Hazeldine would have the drugs they needed. They would live. They would live because of her.

He spoke to her about his struggle. He told her that there was good and bad in every person but that most people just wanted to survive. He told her that doing good sometimes required doing bad but that people would remember the good most of all.

He told her how much he missed her. He thanked her for the courage she helped him find. He told her that she, Amelia Hazeldine, his beloved Babushka, had changed the world, maybe not forever but at least for a very long time.

He talked and he talked until he had talked so much that there were no more words to say.

Then he put his head on his desk and wept for a very long time.

CHAPTER
Ninety-Eight

Back in Los Angeles, Michael Brazier paced the floor of his downtown apartment. He had never felt about a campaign the way he felt about working for Sam Kelley. He was proud of the way Sam Kelley had risen above the ugly, untruthful, and vicious dialogue that dominated American campaigns and found his voice. A beautiful voice. A truthful voice

It was probably a crazy strategy. In the beginning, Brazier had no idea if it would work. And now he had to call Sam Kelley and give him the news. He had a new poll. He picked up the phone and dialed.

"Sam," Brazier began. "What are you doing?"

"I'm home today."

Brazier was surprised. Sam was a worker. He may have wasted time shaking all those hands but he had never let up.

"Is everything all right?" he asked.

"Michael, this campaign is slipping away. That blogger story saying I broke the law, that's what really hurt. People can like me or hate me for things I believe, but no one ever said I was a dishonest man."

Michael Brazier felt Sam's words in the pit of his stomach. Sam had bravely faced anger and hate. He had grace. He had dignity. But he understood the hurt. He had seen it before. Candidates might be attacked for their positions on issues or even their competence. But their honesty was another matter. It could wound them, especially the best ones, in a deep and lasting way. So Michael told Sam something he had not said before.

"I just want to say that whatever happens in this campaign, of all the candidates I have served and there are almost too many to count, no one has inspired me more than you."

"Thanks. I have to say I need some encouragement. Did you see that ad about Pearl?"

Michael had seen the ad. Someone had looked at Pearl's IRA. She held $5,600 in a mutual fund that invested in two pharmas among many other stocks. The ads said that Sam was opposing the Life Bill for his own financial gain. But, sadly, Michael had more bad news to deliver.

"Sam, I am calling about the new poll. The *Nashville Tennessean* says Lund is pulling away. His lead is now fifteen points."

"I was expecting that," Sam replied. "I feel it on the streets. A few weeks ago, I was a fresh, honest voice. Now I am just another lawbreaker and money-grubbing crook."

Brazier paused to collect his words.

"I am going to tell you something and I want you to listen close. Whether you win or lose you have made a statement. You have respected your opponent, stuck to your beliefs at great political cost, and stood courageously and graciously against mistruth, anger, and even hatred.

"Who does that today? Who?!" Brazier was almost shouting. "People in Washington never ask this question. Are there things more important than winning?"

Sam smiled. "Of course, there are."

"Well, you are providing that answer every single day. You have two weeks to go. Finish what you started. Finish the single most beautiful political statement I have ever seen."

CHAPTER
Ninety-Nine

"Mr. Speaker, Colleen Keegan is on the line."

He reached to pick up the phone, surprised at his pleasure at hearing from her. "Colleen," he said warmly, "are you calling to congratulate me?" Hazeldine was beaming.

"Well, yes, Joe," she said in a halting cadence. "You were masterful. No one thought you could do it. Except me, of course." She paused, uncertain for a moment how to proceed. "But I'm not calling to congratulate you, even though you deserve it. I have terrible news."

"You aren't pregnant, are you?"

"That's not funny."

"Okay," he said, still thinking that it was.

"Juventel is causing cancer."

"Can you repeat that?"

"I said Juventel is causing cancer. We will probably have five hundred cases by the end of the week. All among young people. The FDA will pull the drug. I don't know when."

He simply could not believe it, no matter how many times he repeated the news in his mind. Almost a year of begging, bribing, threatening, coercing, smearing, kissing asses on his hands and knees—the Senate would pass the legislation in the next few days. Then onto the White House.

But now.

"Who knows about this?" he said tightly.

"Only we do. When we learn about adverse side effects, at least that ones that are life threatening, we have to report them every day. I am sure FDA is getting the picture as we speak."

"Someone will leak. That's how it works," Hazeldine said, rubbing his forehead, trying to think of next steps.

"No, Joe. Only a few people know. If they leak, they're dead. The FDA never talks with the press."

"Can't you stall your reports? What is the fine? What if you're late?"

"We can't do that." Colleen shook her head.

"I thought the FDA said the drug was safe."

"We only tested on old people. Who thought young people would buy the drug?" Keegan continued, almost pleading now. "We just need to get the president's signature. Then it will be okay. We'll have the law. Get me that signature and Miradol will pull the drug. So much better. Then we'll negotiate a deal with FDA so no one prescribes to anyone under forty. It's all so simple. We just need the law."

"They're not going to do you any favors, Colleen."

"I know that. That's why we need that signature."

"Colleen, we're fucked. We are all fucked."

"Joe, just get that signature."

"I'm working on it."

The Speaker gazed out his window but he saw nothing at all. His mind was racing. A minute earlier his prized victory was in hand. Now, all of it, everything, was slipping away.

CHAPTER

One Hundred

Frieda Sacks, director of the Division of Pharmacovigilance at the US Food and Drug Administration, looked up from her desk. Lucy Castillo, tiny in stature but erect in posture, stood before her bearing a look of absolute determination. Before Sacks could utter a word, Castillo said excitedly, "We have a safety signal on Juventel."

Sacks, thin with dark, hollowed-out eyes, glared back in disbelief. "Are you sure?"

"Triple sure."

Sacks wondered what to think about this young staffer, not even a year in service, who was so sure of a result that would upend Washington.

"Well, we'd better move on the causality investigation right away."

"I've already done it. This drug needs a recall."

"You don't do causality investigations," Sacks snapped. "This is a very big deal and we need someone senior."

"Dr. Sacks, we don't have time. The Life Bill is headed for the president's desk. When I saw Juventel on the watch list I knew we couldn't wait."

Castillo walked her boss through her findings, step by step. It was an impressive presentation. Thorough, thoughtful, and full of issues that might not have occurred to other investigators. When she finished, Sacks sat, her brow furrowed, and thought for a moment. The ramifications just outlined for her were enormous. Finally, she sighed heavily and said, "We need a few more days. I want our deputy to walk through this data. I am not bringing this to Wellstone until we are absolutely certain."

"But Dr. Sacks, a lot more people are going to get cancer. Congress is about to approve this drug and the president may sign it. It seems to me we really can't wait.

"It seems to me we have to get this right," Sacks responded, her impatience with her subordinate showing again.

"Even at the risk that people will die?"

"People always die. A lot more will die if people lose faith in our work. Welcome, Ms. Castillo, to the FDA."

CHAPTER

One Hundred One

Sampson Kraft, chairman of Genovo, was a desperate man. Big Pharma was reeling. If he did not stop the bleeding, if he could not reverse the tide, the price was beyond imagination.

He was drenched with the stench of failure. Big Pharma had lost credibility. First the Institute for the Advancement of Aging Science was exposed as a Big Pharma sham. It wasn't a sham. It raised important questions about a drug that was unfairly bypassing a process that bound every other pharmaceutical company. But the media and that bitch Keegan—who was undeniably smart, he would give her that—had used the media to tar a legitimate effort and turned it into a nationwide scandal.

Then came the struggling-families revelation. The pharma coalition's whole scheme to hide their backing, and their money, to influence the elections had been revealed to God and country. Everyone did that stuff. Everyone used phony names. But the media had made that a scandal too. Well, maybe they had pushed the envelope. But it wasn't his fault. Those lawyers were too clever by a half.

And what about their cyber security? How could they let somebody grab those emails and share them with everyone? He had been toasted, burned, and disgraced on the national stage.

Worst of all, Big Pharma had lost power. There is nothing concrete about power. You cannot touch it. You cannot see it. It is not subject to taste or smell. It is an illusion driven by the expectation that the person who holds it has the ability to punish you or hand you a reward. When you win, your power grows. When you lose, it can evaporate overnight. Big Pharma had not only failed to win, they had been humiliated in the House of Representatives, crushed by a vote of 363 to 37.

Joe Hazeldine had the power now. Compared to him, the president was a fifty-pound eunuch monk.

Sampson Kraft had spent all day with his lobbyists. He had been in these situations before where the momentum pushed against you like a towering wave, where real victory was just not possible. In the Senate, he did not have the votes.

But not having the votes did not mean that the battle was over.

If the Senate failed to act, Congress would adjourn and the bill would die. If they brought it up in a post-election session, one amendment might snarl a conference committee and the bill would die. What they needed was one dramatic event. They needed an event so large and so shocking that all action would stop while senators considered the implications and squandered their time—that precious, priceless time—arguing about what to do next.

The senators would begin recess next week. A third of them would scurry home to campaigns, to greet the voters and perform all of the mundane rituals necessary to keep their jobs. He needed five days, just five paltry days.

And he knew exactly how he was going to get them.

CHAPTER
One Hundred Two

"As we begin debate on this legislation to advance the use and sale of the so-called miracle drug, Juventel, I feel it appropriate to report egregious misconduct by its maker, Miradol, and Miradol's representative, one Winter Brooks," Rex Bunton, senior senator from Montana, said solemnly from the floor of the United States Senate.

Word of his speech had been leaked in advance. Seventy senators, an unusually high number, were seated at their desks. The galleries were packed and press crowded the halls. Bunton was about to bring the Life Bill to a screeching halt.

"On September 2nd of this year, Ms. Brooks entered my office on the pretext of discussing with me the merits of this legislation. After describing some reasons why I should support this bill, she added another.

"She suggested to me that if I, a United States senator, were to use my vote to support passage of this legislation, a matter as to which I remained undecided at the time, Miradol would invest $30 million in a corporation of my creation or choosing. The implication, of course, was that this money would be mine to withdraw from the business to do with as I please."

"Ladies and gentlemen, this sordid and scandalous offer, presented to me, has soiled the honor of this institution. It has broken criminal statutes and will be, I am certain, the subject of a criminal prosecution. And before proceeding further with the consideration of this bill, I propose that the United States Senate appoint a special committee to investigate this episode, determine by whom this offer was authorized, and also identify any other senators to whom similar offers may have been made.

"A dark cloud hangs over this chamber. We are all aware that the passage of this legislation will benefit almost exclusively the company that has conducted itself in this deplorable way.

"I move that we table consideration of this legislation."

CHAPTER

One Hundred Three

Marvin Wellstone paced his office, waiting for Frieda Sacks to arrive. He had skimmed the report. He knew what he needed to know. He also knew time was running out. He had to get word to the president today.

Frieda Sacks, her deputy, and a young staffer he did not know walked purposefully into his office. The FDA's legal counsel, congressional affairs chief, and its information chief were already waiting for the meeting to begin.

Wellstone was not happy. Juventel had passed its safety trial. But those trials were small and included no one under sixty. He wasn't taking the fall for this one. He was going to make sure that the story was Miradol peddling a dangerous drug that it had spent billions to promote in violation of the clear intent of the law.

Sacks began her report but Wellstone interrupted. "Frieda, just tell me what you have done to be absolutely certain we have causation."

Sacks rattled off the statistics, looking at the issue from several data perspectives. Again, Wellstone interrupted. "What about the chemistry? Why would this drug cause cancer?"

"It has to do with cellular replenishment. Young people have elements in their blood that maintain the cells. As you age your genes allow your cells to go unrepaired. The drug encourages replenishment that is already happening with young people. Too much of a good thing, essentially."

Wellstone knitted his brows, trying to absorb this information. Lucy Castillo interjected, "It appears the key agent of causation is a particular protein,

ME113. The protein signals the cell to repair DNA and replicate. As we grow older the protein disappears from the blood. But with young people, who already have plenty of ME113, it appears to stimulate an unhealthy level of replication, which becomes cancer. The effects are almost immediate. With Juventel users, most cancers appear within six months. Since two-thirds of these young users have only been taking Juventel for less than three months, we have, I would estimate, three to five thousand cases in the pipeline."

Sacks and her deputy gave Lucy a sharp look. "Now I get it," Wellstone responded, nodding as Sacks forced a smile. He continued, "Legal, I think a recall is not what we need. That involves returning the drugs and other logistics. It requires cooperation from Miradol, and given all that has happened we cannot be confident in their response. It seems to me we need a shortcut, a ban on the use of Juventel for any condition."

"Even for Reciptinosis?" the attorney asked.

"All of it. Every single pill," Wellstone answered. For the first time in the entire meeting he smiled. As the room emptied, he pulled Sacks aside. "Who is that Lucy Castillo ? Very impressive. Very impressive, indeed."

One Hundred Four

"No way! I'm on it."

Winter Brooks hung up the phone, leaned past her boyfriend as she grabbed the remote off the end table, and asked, "Guess what?" She smiled wickedly as she clicked on YouTube and Senator Rex Bunton appeared. "A US senator is trying to fry my ass."

Her boyfriend just stared at her, confused as to why she would be so happy that the senator was on the attack. On YouTube, Bunton spoke pompously:

> "She suggested to me that if I, as a United States senator, were to use my vote to support passage of this legislation, a matter as to which I remained undecided at the time, Miradol would invest $30 million in a corporation of my creation or choosing."

"Whoo hooo!!! You dumb shit. Don't you fuck with Winter Brooks!"

Her boyfriend was aghast. But Burton rambled on.

> "Ladies and gentlemen, this sordid and scandalous offer, presented to me, has soiled the honor of this institution."

"OOOHHHH!!! You messin' with the wrong gal, Mr. US fucking Senator."

"Winter!" her boyfriend cried. "Have you lost your mind?"

Bunton continued.

"She has broken criminal statutes and will be, I am certain, the subject of a criminal prosecution."

Winter's face was painted with the biggest smile he had ever seen.

"I propose that the United States Senate appoint a special committee to investigate this episode, determine by whom this offer was authorized, and also identify any other senators to whom similar offers may have been made."

She jumped off the couch, pointed at the TV, and screamed in a playful, theatrical way, "Don't you fuck with this nigger, you sorry dumb ass cracker!"

Her boyfriend grabbed Winter by the shoulders and shook her. "Sweetie, a US senator is suggesting you go to jail. Why are you not afraid?"

"Don't you worry, baby. It ain't me going to jail. He was the one asking for a bribe.

"That Jake Siskoff is one smart sonofabitch. Do you know what he told me what to do? When I went into that senator's office I was wearing a wire."

. . .

The next day, Senator Bunton issued a retraction, blaming his mistake on a misreading of his notes. He disappeared from Washington for several days, but when he returned the FBI was waiting to talk. The recording, taken without his knowledge, was inadmissible in court. But they had the testimony of Winter Brooks. Even worse, Genovo had invested $30 million in Finger Steak, Inc. Bunton resigned from the Senate three days later.

Big Pharma had taken a final blow. The day after Bunton's retraction, the Senate voted on the Life Bill.

It passed, eighty-seven to twelve.

CHAPTER

One Hundred Five

Marvin Wellstone placed the call himself. The recipient, Margaret Bonet, secretary of Health and Human Services and the FDA's boss, needed to be made aware of the situation immediately. Like most FDA commissioners, Wellstone had no relationship with the president. And the president needed to know that Juventel was a health risk. The president also needed to know that the FDA was planning to ban Juventel. But protocol demanded that Margaret Bonet make the call.

Bonet's assistant was on the line.

"I need to talk to the secretary right away," Wellstone demanded, a tremor in his voice.

"Ms. Bonet is in a meeting."

"Well, get her out of the meeting. We have a crisis."

The secretary paused. "I don't think that's possible."

"Let me explain. That great drug Juventel is causing cancer. Lots of it. FDA is issuing a complete ban on its sale or use. The president—of the United States – must know. Congress has passed the Life Bill and it is sitting on his desk. If he signs it, it will be a disaster."

"I will reach out to her right away," Bonet's assistant stammered, understanding the urgency but not communicating the difficulty. The difficulty was real. It was Thursday at 3:30 in the afternoon, and the secretary was not in her office.

Her whereabouts? She occupied a room at the Monaco Hotel in downtown Washington. She was not alone.

Her companion this Thursday, and most Thursdays when that awful government business did not intrude, was Luke Lomax, famed lobbyist, political dealmaker, and secret—well, as secret and anything can be in Washington, DC—paramour of the tsar of Washington's largest civilian bureaucracy.

Bonet was not especially attractive. In her early sixties, she had added a few pounds. She had a bulbous nose and an abrupt manner that sometimes served her poorly in her role. But beauty is in the eye of the beholder. And the beholder's intentions were not merely erotic.

Lomax was younger, in his mid-fifties, with a head of perfectly coiffed, and some said perfectly colored, black hair. He was muscular and square, with a jutting chin and soft eyes that both saw and listened at the same time. Most importantly, he represented a long list of cities, counties, and states who needed things from the Department of Health and Human Services.

There are laws that protect leaders like Margaret Bonet from those who might tempt their integrity. She cannot allow a lobbyist to take her to dinner, buy her baseball tickets, fly her to an opera at the Met, load Dragon Ball on her kid's Xbox, or pour her a glass of 1982 Petrus Bordeaux wine. The list of the forbidden is long, covering all sorts of gifts of any kind. These laws guard the public against lowly public officials who might give out a million-dollar contract in return for the lowliest favor. But the authors of this list of forbidden temptations, long and extensive as it is, omitted one important transaction.

Sex.

And after all, what gift is sooner repaid, a baseball ticket or an evening of unbridled passion?

So on this day, one week before the election, as President Marino was reviewing the Life Bill now passed by Congress, Secretary Bonet lay in the arms of Luke Lomax, who was nibbling on her bare shoulders, a bottle of champagne within easy reach of the bed.

The phone rang.

Bonet lifted her head, knowing that only one person knew her location and that person would never call except in the direst emergency.

Lomax pulled her close, his fingers lightly stroking her arm, and he cooed in her ear, "Darling, pretend you didn't hear it. I've been in this town a long time. There is nothing in politics that can't wait till the morning."

CHAPTER
One Hundred Six

The podium was small but with one impressive component. Just beneath the platform where one might stack papers or notes lay a band of blue emblazoned with a small presidential seal. Behind the podium was a powder blue oval showing a picture of the White House emblazoned in white. The president of the United States walked forward to speak.

"Good morning, ladies and gentlemen. I have an important announcement to make. As you know, two days ago, the United States Senate passed the Life Bill by a vote of eighty-seven to twelve, ensuring that older Americans have access to the drug Juventel, which our best evidence shows will delay aging and provide a healthier life. The vote of support was joined by Democrats and Republicans who, in a show of bipartisanship, sent this bill to my desk for consideration.

"As you also know, I have opposed the Life Bill. I have believed that decisions about which drugs should be approved and sold in America belong with the Food and Drug Administration and not the Congress of the United States. I have also believed that the potential costs of this legislation threaten the solvency of Medicare and that spending Medicare money on a drug whose purpose is to delay aging but whose effectiveness remains unproven is a mistake.

"But after careful consideration I have decided to sign this bill and will do so today at twelve noon. Here are the reasons for my decision.

"First, by eliminating the ban on negotiating prescription drug prices through Medicare, we have a chance to dramatically reduce prescription drug prices and offset the costs of this bill.

"Second, despite the absence of extended trials to measure the effectiveness of Juventel in extending lives, my study and the review of White House experts has convinced me that the science is sound and that while we cannot know its effectiveness for several years, Juventel appears to employ an effective, promising, and reliable strategy to lengthen the life span of persons who use it.

"Finally, and most importantly, Miradol, the company which makes Juventel, has conducted safety trials to identify side effects and risks that may arise from the use of this drug. Those trials were reviewed by the FDA, which has vouched for the safety of the drug.

"Given these factors, the potential savings from lower drug prices, the likely effectiveness of the drug, and the confidence we can all have in the safety of its use, I can now wholeheartedly endorse this legislation and will sign it today.

"Questions."

"Mr. President, Thomas Hinson with *The New York Times*. According to a recent *New York Times/CBS News* poll, more than eighty percent of Americans support the Life Bill. Speaker Joe Hazeldine and the Republican House are widely credited with shaping and advancing this legislation. Is this a political move to recover in advance of the upcoming elections?"

"Tom, this has nothing to do with politics. It is about costs and, most importantly, it's about safety. I now have confidence in the safety of this drug. That is the reason for the position I have announced today."

One Hundred Seven

Sam Kelley had arrived early. The event was a candidate forum sponsored by AARP. Brazier had warned Sam against attending. "This is not your audience," he said. But Sam, proud of the results of his only debate, had insisted on going.

He entered the Park Avenue Event Center in Murfreesboro, Tennessee. With Michael Brazier's urgings in his ear, Sam had regrouped and added to his schedule. He spoke to his audiences about a different politics, about the value of truth, the wisdom of respecting an opponent, and the restoration of grace and dignity to an arena where these qualities had been absent too long. These words may not win an election but at least he could show a better way.

There were a couple hundred seniors in attendance, and as he began shaking hands his reception was mixed. The voters had been following the Life Bill and its progress in Congress and, of course, Sam had opposed its passage. In spite of the recent stories about using campaign money for personal use, he still seemed to most like a nice, honest man. So while some in attendance turned at his approach, most were polite and greeted him kindly.

The moderator gaveled the meeting to order and asked the audience to take their seats. He began by announcing, "I'm sorry to say that only one candidate has chosen to attend today, Congressman Sam Kelley." There was scattered applause, but beneath the veneer of politeness was the low sound of a few boos.

"Mr. Lund informed us that he has a scheduling conflict and will be unable to attend." Lund, of course, had no conflict at all. He was leading Sam by fifteen points. Why give his opponent an opportunity to make the news?

Before the moderator could continue a man entered from the back, waving his hand and holding a note in his hand. The moderator took the note, unfolded it, and read. He smiled broadly and announced, "Ladies and gentlemen, I have a major announcement to make. The president has just signed the Life Bill. The Life Bill, now the Life Act, is the law of the land."

The audience erupted in cheers. People jumped up and down with excitement and hugged their neighbors. Some reached for their phones to text their friends with the news. The outpouring was emotional, joyous, and grand. And for the next five minutes the candidate forum was suspended to allow the celebration to run its course.

From the table next to the podium, Sam Kelley's heart sank. He had known the president would not veto the bill. It had passed by more than enough votes to override any veto. But still, America had discarded a process that protected truth and protected lives.

As he looked into the audience, he saw the joy and the hope in their eyes. He knew what aging did to a person, slowly, steadily changing you into a shadow of your younger self. Now they had their reprieve, their strategy to stem the decline and hold death at bay for just a few more precious years.

The principle of independent review of prescription drugs was lost. His lifetime reputation for integrity had been tarnished. In two short weeks, he would lose an election and the job he loved.

As he approached the podium he discarded the notes he had prepared. And when he positioned himself, eye to eye with the crowd, he spoke from the heart.

"Today was a great victory for those of you who supported this legislation, and I offer you my congratulations on your success. As you know, I opposed the Life Bill. I did so because I believe that the health and safety of all Americans depends upon keeping drug decisions out of the hands of politicians and in the hands of qualified scientists at the FDA. To do otherwise, I believe, will place many Americans at risk.

"I now understand the consequences of my belief. I know that on Election Day, I am unlikely to be re-elected and that my service in Congress is coming to an end. All I can say is that I have done what I believe is right, an honest belief not based upon any political calculation at all.

"That said, I have been deeply honored to serve all of you for so many years.

There are many things about which I feel pride. But most of all, I feel pride to have represented the good people of Middle Tennessee, honest people, fair people. And even if, from time to time, some are angry with me, I know the fair-mindedness that lies underneath. I love all of you. Thank you for giving me this chance to be of service to you."

The audience, many of whom had come prepared to vent their anger, looked at the old congressman and began to applaud. But Sam was taking no questions. He stepped from the podium and turned into the aisle, walking toward the door, his head bowed and his gate slow.

Then another messenger entered the room waving a note. And when the moderator read the contents his face went white. In a slow, halting voice he delivered its message. "Ladies and gentlemen, it is indeed an eventful day. The Food and Drug Administration has just announced a full recall of Juventel. Apparently, this drug may be responsible for a growing incidence of cancer among its users."

In the audience mouths dropped open and people turned to one another in disbelief. They did not know that the cancers only affected the young. They worried for their own health. They worried that this gift of longer life would actually rob them instead. A great murmur arose across the room.

Sam Kelley had stopped to hear the news. He looked around at the confused and worried faces. What was there to say? He turned back to the door.

A local AARP leader who sat near the moderator rose and grabbed the microphone. "Sam Kelley, please stop."

Sam stopped again and looked back at the platform.

"We, many in this room, have spoken against this man. Some of us have mocked him in anger. Next time we will know to listen. Wisdom and courage have become a rare quality in our world today."

Among the audience, slowly absorbing these messages, some rose to peer at this man who had lifted himself above the common expectations of his profession. Someone began to clap and, slowly, others followed. There was no cheering. Just hands striking one another, but before long every hand moved, and eventually every person rose to his or her feet. Whether for repentance, embarrassment, or genuine respect, they solemnly paid this unusual man the tribute he deserved.

He waited and listened to their newfound affirmation. Then, with the applause still sounding, he turned, still in a posture of sadness, and walked out the door.

A few reporters waited at the doorway. They had heard the news and rushed to the scene of an event they had deemed not worthy of coverage at all. Suddenly, Sam Kelley was the story of the day. Logan Lasker pressed a microphone in Sam's face and shouted, "Congressman! Congressman! What is your comment on the FDA recall?"

"Logan," he answered, "I just hope all those people are going to be okay."

Epilogue

COLLEEN KEEGAN

Colleen Keegan had launched a lifesaving product. She had taken her company, Miradol, from number three to number one in the world. She had done what her shareholders wanted. She had produced massive profits and lifted the price of Miradol shares threefold.

What she failed to do was to test Miradol with the young. Who would have thought them a market anyway? But blame was placed on the company. Someone had to take the fall and that someone was Colleen Keegan.

Not long after the election, she resigned her position after a stormy Board meeting that had reported collapsing sales and stock prices tumbling to levels below those when Juventel was just an idea. She argued that she could bring the company back. She argued that the recall was temporary and Juventel had no issues with older people and that is where the market was anyway.

But Miradol needed forgiveness from the FDA. They needed an olive branch. And Colleen Keegan's departure was the gesture that was required. She walked out the door with a $30 million golden parachute in her pocket.

She returned to the Seychelles, to the Fregate Island Private, and considered her future. She bought an island nearby and opened a hotel of her own, Le Grand Rouge. She spared no expense. It never made money. She did not care one bit. She just wanted the best hotel in the world. And four years after opening, *Luxury Travel* magazine rated Le Grand Rouge the top luxury travel resort in the world.

Miradol approached the FDA seeking a deal. Marvin Wellstone had left in disgust. For a year the pharmaceutical company negotiated with the agency and, finally, the FDA announced that Juventel could return to the market but could only be sold to individuals fifty-five years of age or older. Sales renewed and slowly, over a period of three years, Miradol once more became the number one pharmaceutical company in the world.

Ten thousand people had signed up for the billion-dollar challenge. Miradol had continued to supply them with Juventel—except for the year of the recall. Fifty-one years later, the last participant died. They calculated the average number of years these users had lived and measured it against the normal expectation for a person of their age.

Juventel had extended the lives of its users by an average of 7.82 years.

JOE HAZELDINE

On Election Day, House Republicans lost thirty-five seats. Their majority gone, their initiatives discredited, Joe Hazeldine resigned his leadership position.

He continued his work in Congress, but when the Democrats took charge they opened an ethics investigation into illegal earmarks. And though Hazeldine had not violated House rules per se, the depositions, the discovery, and the testimony required lawyers. Then a complaint was filed suggesting that he had illegally coordinated campaign money from his Super PAC and, although no staffers testified to support those claims, he needed even more legal support. They questioned the $4 million in research fees given to one Felix Durand, who disappeared and was never located again. By the end of the first year of his new term, he was $2 million in debt.

To pay off the debts, he resigned from Congress and took a job lobbying with a major firm. The debt was gone in a year. He married a thirty-five-year-old staffer from his congressional office. He bought a house in Potomac, Maryland, where many wealthy Washingtonians lived. He found his new life exciting and satisfying. Asked once by a friend why he so enjoyed his time away from Congress, he answered in this way:

"I don't have to twist arms, kiss ass, or spend my time on the phone grubbing for money. My clients come to me because I was the speaker who knew how to make things happen. When I give advice, they hang on every word. When I tell them what to do, they do it because that is what I told them to do. And I make more fucking money than I ever imagined."

For fun, Joe Hazeldine once appeared on *Washington–Believe It or Not!*—still the number one political talk show in America.

On his desk sits the picture of his beloved Babushka, with whom he still speaks every day.

SAM KELLEY

Courage is a funny thing. In war, in the face of great physical risk, courage is the simple act of looking death in the eye and failing to flinch. Political courage is another matter.

Most political courage is never remembered at all. It is discarded as stupidity, miscalculation, or idealism in its most dreadful form. But occasionally, either through genius or, more often, luck, it is labeled as a great act of daring by one driven by insight or principle uncompromised. Sam Kelley's courage, which in most cases would have sent him to retirement, was rewarded by luck.

But it was rewarded immensely.

He became adored as the lone voice who spoke out for principle and for the wisdom of the FDA. He had warned America about keeping politicians out of the drug-approval process and events had proven him right. It did not matter that the FDA had certified the safety of Juventel. Those details were too small to topple this new legend, mighty and large.

On Election Day, he was re-elected with sixty-two percent of the vote. Two years later, he ran unopposed.

He appeared on the Sunday morning talk shows and in long magazine profiles. The *Times* called him the great political hero of our times. There was even a movie, *Single-Armed Sam*, that brought his story to the silver screen. But Sam was not long for the world. Three years after his re-election he died of a heart attack.

He was survived by his wife, Pearl, and thirty-two children, grandchildren, and great-grandchildren.

Few remembered Sam's statement on the day Joe Hazeldine retired from the House. A reporter asked Sam for a comment.

"Joe and I did not always agree. But he changed our world. He lowered drug prices, improved health care, and lifted the lives of our older Americans. I love Joe Hazeldine. He is as fine a man as I ever knew."